WITHDRAWN

Further Praise for
Vicki Lewis Thompson and Her Novels

"Count on Vicki Lewis Thompson for a sharp, sassy, sexy read. Stranded on a desert island? I hope you've got this book in your beach bag." —Jayne Ann Krentz

"Wildly sexy ... a full complement of oddball characters and sparkles with sassy humor." —*Library Journal*

"A riotous cast of colorful characters ... fills the pages with hilarious situations and hot, creative sex."
—*Booklist*

"Smart, spunky, and delightfully over-the-top."
—*Publishers Weekly*

"[A] lighthearted and frisky tale of discovery between two engaging people." —*The Oakland Press* (MI)

"A funny and thrilling ride!" —Romance Reviews Today

"Extremely sexy ... over-the-top ... sparkling."
—*Rendezvous*

"A whole new dimension in laughter. A big ... BRAVO!" —A Romance Review

D0035551

Also by Vicki Lewis Thompson

Werewolf in Denver

A WILD ABOUT YOU NOVEL

Vicki Lewis Thompson

A SIGNET ECLIPSE BOOK

SIGNET ECLIPSE
Published by New American Library, a division of
Penguin Group (USA) Inc., 375 Hudson Street,
New York, New York 10014, USA
Penguin Group (Canada), 90 Eglinton Avenue East, Suite 700, Toronto,
Ontario M4P 2Y3, Canada (a division of Pearson Penguin Canada Inc.)
Penguin Books Ltd., 80 Strand, London WC2R 0RL, England
Penguin Ireland, 25 St. Stephen's Green, Dublin 2,
Ireland (a division of Penguin Books Ltd.)
Penguin Group (Australia), 250 Camberwell Road, Camberwell, Victoria 3124,
Australia (a division of Pearson Australia Group Pty. Ltd.)
Penguin Books India Pvt. Ltd., 11 Community Centre, Panchsheel Park,
New Delhi - 110 017, India
Penguin Group (NZ), 67 Apollo Drive, Rosedale, Auckland 0632,
New Zealand (a division of Pearson New Zealand Ltd.)
Penguin Books (South Africa) (Pty.) Ltd., 24 Sturdee Avenue,
Rosebank, Johannesburg 2196, South Africa

Penguin Books Ltd., Registered Offices:
80 Strand, London WC2R 0RL, England

First published by Signet Eclipse, an imprint of New American Library,
a division of Penguin Group (USA) Inc.

First Printing, October 2012
10 9 8 7 6 5 4 3 2 1

Printed in the United States of America

PUBLISHER'S NOTE
This is a work of fiction. Names, characters, places, and incidents either are the product of the author's imagination or are used fictitiously, and any resemblance to actual persons, living or dead, business establishments, events, or locales is entirely coincidental.

   The publisher does not have any control over and does not assume any responsibility for author or third-party Web sites or their content.

ALWAYS LEARNING   **PEARSON**

*To the Sisterhood of the Traveling Pens—Andrea
Laurence, Rhonda Nelson, and Kira Sinclair—who
insisted that yes, even werewolves should be hooked up
to social media!*

ACKNOWLEDGMENTS

I've discovered that rich and powerful werewolves require the white-glove treatment. Fortunately, I know several individuals who can provide it, including my assistant, Audrey Sharpe; my editor, Claire Zion; and my agent, Robert Gottlieb. Thanks to all those at Trident Media who work on my behalf, especially Adrienne Lombardo and Mark Gottlieb. You've made my werewolves (and me) very happy.

Chapter 1

**WERECON2012:
HOWLERS CHALLENGE WOOFERS**

**Exclusive *Wereworld Celebrity Watch* report
by Angela Sapworthy**

DENVER—Excitement mounts on the eve of this landmark conference, the first of its kind in werewolf history. A star-studded list of attendees from the far reaches of the globe has been invited by pack leader Elizabeth Stillman to gather at the elegant Stillman Lodge in Estes Park near Denver to debate the conference theme, "Our Future in a Changing Environment."

As readers of *WCW* know, opinion is sharply divided on the topic. Weres have rebounded after being hunted nearly to extinction, but their presence as a significant economic force in all the major cities in the world remains unknown to the human community.

Honored conference guest and eligible bachelor and Scotsman Duncan MacDowell, younger brother of MacDowell pack leader, Colin MacDowell, wants that to change. In May, he founded Werewolves Optimizing Our Future (WOOF), and his wildly popular blog, *Wolf Whistles*, champions his belief that wolves should stop hiding their shape-shifting abilities, openly partner with humans in business, and even consider interspecies mating. Obviously human females would rally to that cause if every male Were looked like Duncan MacDowell in a kilt!

But not all Weres are ready to climb on board Duncan's tartan-clad bandwagon. This summer the Were blogosphere heated up as Denver-based Kate Stillman, granddaughter of Elizabeth Stillman, launched Honoring Our Werewolf Legacy (HOWL). Her well-known dating Web site, Furthebest.com, celebrates Were-Were mating as the only way to go. Kate, who claims she's never dated a human, advocates the beauty of tradition and the safety of keeping our secret secure.

But is the tide turning in Duncan's favor? This reporter recently spoke to the Wallace brothers of New York, both of whom shocked the Were community last year by taking human mates. From all indications, their human brides are blissfully happy. And why not, if they share an address with sexy wolves like Aidan and Roarke Wallace?

Despite the apparent success of what's being called The Wallace Experiment, Kate Stillman predicts that such unions spell disaster. Although Emma and Abby Wallace have proved trustworthy, Kate insists the Wallace brothers' behavior may still adversely impact the Were community. Predictably, Duncan MacDowell considers the Wallaces heroes for bucking tradition.

For months Kate and Duncan have traded barbed comments on their blogs and via our online instant messaging system, affectionately named *Sniffer*. Adding fuel to the controversy, they've each published best-selling books, available only through Were distribution channels, of course, defending their respective positions.

Duncan's followers (Woofers) are poised to confront Kate's supporters (Howlers) at the conference and will no doubt fill the room during the final session when Duncan and Kate face off in what promises to be a heated debate—and great fun for this reporter! Duncan's last *Sniff* before he left Scotland was a succinct call to arms— *Woofers, it's on. #primedforaction*

And so am I, my friends! For on-the-spot conference updates and celebrity sightings, be sure to follow me on Sniffer @newshound or #were con2012. I'll be your eyes, ears, and nose!

Standing at Denver airport's baggage claim with her cell phone to her ear on Friday afternoon, Kate Stillman listened to her assistant Heidi Jenson rant about an apparent server hack that had temporarily taken down their Were-Were dating site, Furthebest.com.

"I wouldn't be surprised if those Woofers are behind it," Heidi said. "When you see Duncan MacDowell, you tell him that hacking into our dating site is the most despicable, underhanded—"

"I doubt my grandmother would want me to start our first conversation that way." Kate checked the arrivals board and noted that Duncan's plane was on the ground. "Her exact words were, 'Warm hospitality will disarm him, my dear. You'll catch more flies with honey than vinegar.'"

"Forget the honey, Kate. Just swat the bastard. No telling how many potential clients we lost, or how many romances will be derailed this weekend, because of his damned Woofers."

"We don't know it was them."

"We might not have proof, and I'm not saying Duncan himself did it, but his followers are insane."

"I know. Listen, Heidi, I'd better go. My grandmother's given me a good chunk of responsibility for this conference and Duncan's a VIP. He could show up any minute."

"Okay. Text me if he says anything suspicious."

"I will. 'Bye." Kate disconnected the call. Heidi loved conspiracies, but Kate hoped her assistant was wrong about this one. Trading insults was all part of the game, but interfering with a commercial venture was actionable.

Surely the Woofers wouldn't be so stupid as to hack into her dating site on the eve of the conference. She *would* mention it to Duncan and see how he reacted, because he should know that it happened, but she couldn't openly accuse him without evidence.

Not only would that be unfair of her, but Grandma Elizabeth, the Stillman pack alpha and a force to be reckoned with, would be furious. She'd been totally in love with the idea of Kate standing with a sign and a smile when Duncan arrived to collect his luggage. No accompanying staff, no fancy limo. Simple Western hospitality.

The limo wouldn't have worked, anyway, now that the first snow had hit Denver. The storm had begun around noon, dashing hopes that Denver could get through the month of October without the white stuff. Judging from what had already fallen this afternoon, Kate would need the four-wheel-drive capacity of her SUV to navigate the long winding road back to the resort.

The dicey road conditions didn't bother her. She'd been driving on ice and snow ever since getting her license fifteen years ago. But meeting Duncan MacDowell face-to-face worried her more than she cared to admit to anyone, not even Heidi, and least of all her grandmother.

Offering friendly hospitality to the Were she'd called a pigheaded radical who had his head up his ass seemed hypocritical. But treating him like a bitter enemy seemed rude and unprofessional. Online interactions were so much easier. Knowing that Duncan would appear any minute had her pacing the baggage claim area.

She'd responded on Sniffer to his arrogant last statement—*Woofers, it's on. #primedforaction*—with her own challenge—*Bring it, Woofers. Howlers R ready 4 U. #firmlyconvinced*. Other Howlers had added equally feisty comments, which had sparked pushback from the Woofers, although nothing had come from Duncan yet.

Thinking of that, Kate checked her Sniffer feed. Sure enough, there was another Sniff from @DuncanMac Dowell. *Slippery landing in Denver. Can't scare a Scots man/Woofer. #Braveheart*

Kate rolled her eyes. He was so blasted macho it was sickening. Tucking the printed sign under one arm, she quickly typed a response. *Just don't get off the plane naked with your face painted blue, Braveheart.*

The response came almost immediately: *How would you know if I did?*

She answered with a few rapid taps. *Turns out I'm your ride.*

I'm honored.

So he wanted to be sarcastic, did he? She started to type *The honor is all mine* and realized that would be ungracious. Her grandmother would disapprove. As she started a new message, she breathed in the scent of masculine Were.

Glancing up, she had no doubt she was eyeballing Duncan MacDowell, in the flesh. Judging from his purposeful stride and intent focus, he'd figured out who she was, too. His wool topcoat hung open to reveal a cream-colored cable-knit sweater and what looked like wool slacks. His leather dress shoes weren't suited for walking in the snow, but she could work it so he wouldn't have to.

She folded the unnecessary sign with his name on it into fourths and crammed it into her purse.

"Hello, Kate."

Hearing his rich baritone for the first time felt surreal after months of online communication. And the brogue. Damn, it was sexy as hell.

"Hello, Duncan." She kept her tone neutral but pasted on the smile her grandmother had asked of her. "Welcome to Colorado."

"Thank you." His sculpted lips curved in an ironic answering smile.

As she looked into his eyes, she was momentarily distracted by how beautiful they were—soft gray and elegantly fringed with dark lashes. She quickly reminded herself of his arrogant attitude and reckless stance regarding Were security. He was ready to risk everything for some crazy Utopian dream. And his followers might have hacked into her dating site.

He regarded her with a heavy-lidded gaze that probably had more to do with jet lag than any attempt to be seductive. Yet he really was unbelievably gorgeous. She wasn't immune to male beauty, and a quiver of sexual awareness shot through her system.

He was taller than she'd expected. The top of her head, minus her fake-rabbit-fur hat, reached only to his shoulder. And speaking of shoulders, he had broad, powerful ones, the kind that inspired confidence and marked him as a leader.

His hair was longish and his jaw was darkened with new beard growth. He could have shaved on the plane if he'd been so inclined. Obviously he hadn't troubled himself. Cocky Were.

His rumpled appearance only added to his sex appeal, though, as if he were silently demonstrating how he'd look after a long night of fabulous lovemaking. She'd read all the nauseating blog comments from his bevy of female admirers, so she'd expected him to be reasonably good-looking. She hadn't been prepared for sensational.

Not that it mattered whether he was an Adonis. His physical attributes didn't change the threat that he posed to the Were way of life. If anything, they made him a more dangerous opponent.

"I can't say I expected you to meet my plane, lass," he said.

Now would be the time for her to turn on the hospitality spigot as her grandmother had suggested, but sugary words stuck in her throat. "Maybe I wanted to get a preview of what I will be dealing with this weekend."

He surveyed her with those bedroom eyes. "You do realize you're giving me a preview, as well."

"That depends on how much I allow you to see." She hadn't meant that to be a sexual comment, but it sure sounded that way once she'd said it.

His smile widened. "I'm very good at uncovering whatever interests me."

There was that sexual quiver again. She ignored it. "Considering that we're on opposite sides of this debate, I can't imagine I'd be of any interest to you."

"On the contrary. I'm sure you've heard the old saying— *Keep your friends close, and your enemies closer.*"

"I've heard it." But never spoken with a Scottish brogue.

"Is that why you came to pick me up?"

"No." She finally settled on the truth. "I'm here because my grandmother asked me to come. She thought the gesture would disarm you."

"Oh, it has." His gray eyes took on a wicked gleam. "It most certainly has."

"Bullshit."

He laughed. "I'm not kidding. As tired as I am, I'm easily disarmed, which might have been your grandmother's plan."

"Maybe." Kate decided the time for chitchat was over. "We need to get your bags and leave before the snow gets any worse."

"Aye." Turning, he surveyed the luggage circling the carousel. He walked over, retrieved his suitcase with athletic grace, and returned to her. "Ready."

He must have been tired, because she managed to talk

him into waiting inside the building while she brought the Jeep around.

Once they were on their way, he peered past the flapping windshield wipers at the snow that seemed flung by a giant hand. He looked slightly worried. "I'm not sure it's safe to drive in this. Perhaps we should stop somewhere and wait it out."

"We'll be fine." She wasn't about to admit that the snowstorm had become nasty enough to intimidate even her. "I'm used to snowy conditions."

"If you say so." Leaning his head against the headrest, he closed his eyes.

"I wanted to alert you that someone hacked into the Furthebest Web site today, and I—" A soft snore brought her up short. She glanced over at him and sure enough, he had fallen asleep that quickly.

Impressed with his ability to surrender control, Kate drove slowly and kept to the plowed sections of the highway. Traffic thinned once they were outside the city limits, and she began to wonder if she'd made the right call. Hers were the only headlights taking the exit road to the resort. And she had several miles yet to go.

Turning back wasn't an option, because the roads were getting worse and she'd have a problem retracing her path, too. As long as she moved slowly and didn't hit a patch of ice, they'd get there. She'd always been lucky driving on snowy roads.

But not this time. When the skid started, she did everything she'd been taught so they wouldn't flip, but nothing could have prevented them from plowing into a snowbank, nose first.

*   *   *

The impact woke Duncan, who sat up, startled. "What happened?"

She sighed. "We're stuck."

"Can we get out?"

The wind whistled as snow swirled around the Jeep and blocked the view. "I don't know. Maybe not."

Duncan shook his head to clear the fog of sleep from his brain. "Let's have a look, shall we?" He reached for the door handle.

"Hang on. Let me try to back it up and see what happens. Maybe we'll scoot right out." She put the SUV in reverse and tromped on the gas. The motor whined and the wheels spun like crazy, but they didn't move an inch.

She let up on the gas and stared out at the driving snow. "Or not."

"I'll see what's going on out there." Once again Duncan grasped the door handle.

"You can stand out in the blizzard and assess the situation if that makes you happy, but I've lived in this area all my life and I can guarantee that we won't be getting out of here without a tow truck."

He glanced over at Kate. She looked so blasted sweet with her long blond hair and big blue eyes, but he knew better after a summer of trading barbed comments on the Internet. In the interest of getting to know his enemy, he'd decided to read her book, *Sex and the Single Shifter: A Guide to Ultimate Satisfaction*, on his e-reader during the long plane ride.

Kate was about as sweet as a dram of Dewar's. And like that most excellent whisky, she had the potential to addle his brain, and that would be unfortunate. If he'd been lucky, her likeness on the Internet would have turned out to be Photoshopped and her real self would be homely as a hedgerow. Instead she was bonnier than the heather in full bloom.

A blond goddess who'd written a book about sexual satisfaction would tempt any male almost beyond endurance, but he couldn't afford to be tempted. Any weakness in that area could compromise his goals. His followers expected him to stay strong, and he would. He *would*.

Still, he was fighting the effects of jet lag, and he had trouble not staring at her. She looked adorable in her red leather jacket and furry cap. "You know the lay of the land better than I do," he said. "If we need a tow, then perhaps you should call for one."

"Exactly." Pulling off her black leather gloves, she reached for the phone in a holder on the dash, tapped on it, and held it to her ear. After listening for several moments, she frowned. "Automatic message. They're flooded with requests. Let me call another company."

Duncan watched her growing frustration as she tried various avenues to arrange for a tow. When she swore softly under her breath, he couldn't help smiling. She must hate getting herself stuck with him as her passenger.

At last she put the phone in its holder with a sigh of resignation. "I've left messages, but this sudden snowstorm has created emergencies all over the area." She pulled on her gloves and peered out the window. "It's getting worse out there. I can't risk having another vehicle from the resort get stuck while trying to rescue us, so I'm not calling them."

"How far to the lodge?"

"Way too far, if you're suggesting we walk it. Being so remote means we're blessed with privacy, but bad weather makes the resort almost inaccessible."

"What if we shifted into Were form and went cross-country?" He didn't think she'd go for that because they'd have to take off their clothes first. Now, there was a concept that would test his determination to resist his cravings. But if the alternative was sitting in the vehicle all night, they might have to consider it.

"If I thought we could make it up there easily as wolves, then I'd agree to shift, but we'd have a nasty slog that might not turn out well. Still, we can't sit here indefinitely while we wait for somebody to call us back. Folks freeze to death doing that."

"Wouldn't that make a juicy story for Angela Sapworthy?"

Kate let out a martyred sigh. "She's at the resort, you know."

"I assumed she would be. She promised to be the eyes, ears, and nose for her faithful readers."

"She's been good for attendance, so I shouldn't complain, but if I have to read one more reference to the virility of the Wallace brothers, or—"

"The virility of Duncan MacDowell?" he added helpfully.

"Yes, she does go on about you in a rather nauseating fashion."

"I quite like it."

"I'm not surprised."

This was more fun than typing comments on the Internet because he could see her reaction. She developed a cute little jut to her chin when she was irritated. "So, my devastating charm aside, how are we going to extricate ourselves from this cock-up you've got us into?"

"What do you mean, the cock-up *I* got us into? It's very ungentlemanly of you to imply it was my fault."

"If not you, then who? It wasn't me, I can tell you that much."

"It wasn't me, either! It was . . . well, my grandmother suggested this, but I can't blame her for the weather. So I guess it's Mother Nature's fault."

"And . . . so? What are we going to do?"

"I've been thinking about that. Right before we spun out, we passed a turnoff to a cabin. I think we should take our phones and go there. If they're home, they'll give us shelter. If they're not, we'll break in and wait for a towing company to call back."

"Break in? I don't know your local laws, but won't that get us arrested?"

"Not in an emergency like this. Besides, I've met the owners. They're Edith and Bob Stewart, and Bob helped me change a tire when I had a flat on this road last summer."

"That doesn't mean he'll be happy if we break into his house."

"Seriously, he'd understand. Mountain people help each other out like that. This is a summer home, so they're probably not here, but if we can find a number for them, we'll call and tell them what we've done and explain that we'll repair any damage involved in breaking in."

He peered at her in the growing darkness. "Have you ever broken into a residence before?"

"No, but I've seen it done."

"You were an accomplice to a break-in?"

She blew out a breath. "No. I've seen it done in the movies. It looked easy."

"Kate, it was *a movie*. Of course it looked easy! They

used fake glass the actors could easily break or left a door unlocked so the actors could supposedly use a credit card. I'm sure these people have battened down the hatches on their cabin before leaving so no one can break in, at least not without great effort."

"Do you have a better idea?"

"Unfortunately not." Out of necessity, he started thinking like a burglar. "Do you have a torch?"

"Of course not! Why would I carry a torch around? This is the twenty-first century. We use flashlights."

"Sorry. I meant flashlight. We call them torches in Scotland."

"Oh. I vaguely remember that, now that you mention it."

He smiled to himself. "From the movies?"

"Smart-ass." She opened a compartment between the two front bucket seats. "Yes, I have a flashlight." She pulled it out and switched it on.

"Hey, not in the eyes, please." He put a hand on the flashlight and directed it downward so it wasn't blinding him.

"Whoops. My bad." She stuck the light under her chin. "What does this make you think of?"

"*Blair Witch Project*. Which, by the way, isn't a comforting thought as we venture into the cold, snowy woods." But he laughed in spite of himself. He shouldn't allow himself to be so entertained by her.

"It's only a *movie*, Duncan." She mimicked his former patronizing tone. "They made all that up on purpose to scare you. It wasn't real."

"Touché."

"Thanks." She marked an imaginary line in the air with one gloved finger. "Score one for Stillman."

He let that pass. "So we have a flashlight, which we can use to see what the bloody hell we're doing. Do you have a tire iron?"

"Wow, you're gearing up to break some serious glass, aren't you?"

"If we're going to hike over there, we might as well go prepared to get in."

She studied him for a moment. "I'm thinking you might have done this before, Duncan MacDowell."

"If you must know, my brother and I locked ourselves out of the castle one night. It was late, and we couldn't rouse any of the servants, so in order to get in, we—"

"You locked yourselves out of the castle and couldn't rouse the servants? You say that so casually, like everyone lives that way."

"I don't think much about it, really. Is it so different from you living at the resort? You must have staff working there."

"We do, but we don't call them servants. We call them employees and most of them live elsewhere. I think it *is* different. You're like a prince or something."

"Nope. No title. My brother, Colin, has the title— Laird of Glenbarra. I'm just the lowly second son who's a bit of a renegade."

"And who knows how to break into a castle. Why were you giving me an argument before? This cabin will be easy pickings for you."

"It's one thing to break into your own place and quite another to break into somebody else's. So do you have a tire iron or not?"

"I'll take it from the back once we get out."

"Then I guess it's time to become criminals." He pulled on his black leather gloves, which were oddly appropriate for breaking and entering. Then he wound his wool scarf around his neck and turned up his collar. "I'll meet you round back and we'll go from there." He opened the door and snow hit him in the face. "Bollocks! It's cold out there!"

"Wait a minute." She grabbed his arm. "Do you have a hat in your suitcase?"

"No, but I'll be fine. I have gloves and a scarf. Let's go."

"What about boots?"

He closed the door again. "You mean rubbers?"

"Over here we call them condoms, but that wasn't my question." She grinned at him, an imp in a furry hat.

He had the most powerful urge to grab her and kiss that saucy smile right off her face. Bad impulse. Instead he lifted his gaze to the ceiling and sighed dramatically. "I have no *boots*, as you call them." Then he turned to her. "And I saw no need to pack condoms, either."

"And that's another point!" She wagged her finger at him. "If you have Were-Were sex, you don't need those things, either to prevent pregnancy or disease. It's an elegant system. But when you consort with humans, you have to put on a—"

"Spare me the sex education, Kate." Damn it, she almost seemed to be testing him to see if he'd snap. He was too close for comfort. "And for the record, condoms can be sexy, too."

Her cheeks turned pink, but she came right back at him. "I don't believe you. I can't imagine how putting a latex gizmo on your penis can be anything but uncomfortable and ridiculous. As for the female, how horrifying to see something covered in latex coming at you like some alien creature! Ick!"

Time to end this discussion before he did something

he would be sorry for, something that his followers might view as consorting with the enemy. "As they say in the USA, don't knock it till you've tried it. Ready to go burgle this cabin, lass?" Opening the passenger door, he stepped into a snowdrift at least two feet deep and cursed.

At least now he wouldn't have to worry about the erection he'd been trying to control. Five seconds of standing in a snowdrift had taken care of that quite nicely.

Chapter 2

"Oh, God, he's out." When Kate realized Duncan was determined to brave the snowdrifts without boots or hat, she swung into action. He might be part of the enemy camp, but if he caught cold or disappeared in the storm because she hadn't taken care of him, Grandma Elizabeth would not be pleased.

Grabbing her purse and the flashlight, she opened her door and hopped out, too. Then she gasped as the cold and snow enveloped her. She'd worn her best leather jacket and a warm hat, but this kind of cold penetrated all but the most serious outerwear.

She hadn't expected to trudge through snowdrifts, so her outfit was designed to be cute and stylish instead of blizzard-worthy. Even her boots were suede lace-ups instead of vinyl, but they were better than Duncan's dress shoes. He would be miserable until they got inside the cabin.

"Are you coming?" Duncan called from the back of the Jeep. "It's a wee bit nippy out here!"

"On my way!" Activating the flashlight, she soon discovered it wasn't much help. It lit up the incoming snowflakes beautifully, turning her surroundings into a psychedelic light show. But once she and Duncan reached the cabin, they'd need the flashlight. Rounding the back of the Jeep, she found Duncan stomping his feet and flapping his arms to stay warm.

"Here, take my hat, at least." She pulled off her fur hat and handed it to him.

He shook his head, which was already dusted with snow. "I'm secure in my masculinity, but not that secure. Let's get the tire iron and go."

"All right. Your choice." She tugged the hat back over her ears and opened the back of the Jeep. Taking the tire iron out of its storage niche, she handed it to him. "You'll be in charge of that."

"Aye."

"We're going to follow our tire tracks back to the driveway. There's a rural mailbox beside the road. It'll be easy to find." She hoped to hell it would be, because her face felt frozen in place. She was afraid if she tried to smile, her cheeks would crack. "Follow me."

"Right."

The flashlight worked a little better if she pointed it at her feet, so she was able to distinguish the SUV's tire tracks without too much trouble. They'd spun out only a few yards from the driveway leading to the cabin, but the howling wind and blowing snow made the walk seem longer than that. She couldn't hear Duncan's footsteps, and after going several paces, she worried that he might not be behind her, after all.

When she stopped to look over her shoulder, he ran smack into her. With a cry of alarm, she started to go down. Instantly his arm came around her, breast-high, and hauled her against him to prevent the fall.

"Try signaling next time." His warm breath tickled her neck and his body created a firm support for her back.

She'd been in worse positions than being steadied by the muscular arm of a handsome Scotsman who lived in a freaking castle. She tried not to be entranced by that, but she wasn't succeeding. She'd spent too much time watching *Cinderella* as a little girl to be able to ignore the castle connection.

His grip loosened slightly, as if giving her room to breathe, but he didn't let go. "Are you all right?"

"Yes, thanks." In the swirling whiteness of the storm, he was a warm, reassuring presence. A darned sexy one, too. Her body reacted with surprising alacrity to his casual touch. "I stopped because I was afraid you might not be behind me."

"I'm right on your heels, lass."

His Scottish brogue delivered directly into her ear was quite a turn-on, too. "Good. That's good. Let's go on, then."

He released her. "How much farther?"

"Not much." Immediately she missed his warmth. Pointing the flashlight at the ground, she started walking along the tire tracks again. As a mental trick to fight off the cold, she relived their accidental embrace, and soon parts of her became quite toasty.

What a concept. She'd never tried keeping warm in

the snow by thinking about sex, but it worked like a charm, at least for her. Duncan wouldn't be fantasizing about sex with her, though. He wouldn't want to fraternize with the opposition, and he'd also been extremely vocal on his blog about his preference for human females.

Remembering his enthusiasm for Were-human sex cooled her off again, but fortunately they were almost there. She'd never have found the driveway without the mailbox to mark the spot, but she was able to see its vague outline through the snow. Waving the flashlight to signal to Duncan, she turned right.

Once they were off the road, the snow was considerably deeper. She winced at the thought of Duncan navigating without boots, but it couldn't be helped. At least he was behind her and could step in her footprints.

A pale glow straight ahead indicated that the dusk-to-dawn spotlight mounted on a pole near the cabin was working. Kate had known they'd have electricity because the Stewarts chose to leave their heat on low all winter rather than drain the pipes. Bob had told her all about it while he was helping her with the flat tire. Available electricity had been the other reason she'd decided their cabin would make a good safe haven until a tow truck arrived.

The cabin itself was completely dark. No smoke rose from the chimney and no vehicle sat by the side of the house where the Stewarts usually parked their rental. Edith and Bob didn't seem to be in residence at the moment, which was what she'd expected.

The place was small but sturdy looking—a log-cabin structure that blended into its setting. The covered front porch held two rocking chairs all summer, but it was empty now. Double-hung windows on either side of the front door looked out on the porch.

Kate had never gone in, but from the outer dimensions she'd always assumed it was a one-bedroom, one-bath layout. Climbing the porch steps, she trained the flashlight on the door in case the lock might be the kind that would open with a credit card. But sure enough, the Stewarts had installed a dead bolt in addition to the lock on the doorknob.

Stomping his feet, Duncan came up the steps to stand beside her. "Looks like I'll have to use the tire iron."

"Yep, and the sooner the better. I'll bet your feet are frozen."

"They've been warmer."

She walked over to the window on the left. "Guess it doesn't matter which one. With the blinds down, I can't tell what sort of furniture's on the other side."

"But it might matter where I hit it. Use the torch to find out where the lock is, if you can."

"Sure." Now that she knew what he meant, she liked hearing him refer to it as a torch. The word went with his castle persona and his brogue. He was an intriguing Were, and that could be a problem this weekend. She wasn't supposed to be intrigued with the leader of WOOF.

After shining the light around the window casement, she reported that the window seemed to be of traditional design, with the lock in the center, where the two parts of the window met.

"Then I'll try to break it close to that lock. Stand back."

She didn't have to be told twice. Duncan unbuttoned his coat and held the tire iron over his shoulder. Judging from his spread-legged stance, he planned to put everything he had behind the swing.

"And cover your eyes," he added.

"What about *your* eyes?"

"Oh. Good point." Lowering the tire iron, he reached inside his topcoat and pulled out a pair of shades. "They're not exactly safety goggles, but they're better than nothing." He put them on.

"Now you look like a hit man for the mob." She made a joke of it, but he'd taken on a dark and excitingly dangerous air as the shades combined with the scruff on his jaw to produce a breathtaking effect. This was a Duncan MacDowell she'd be hard-pressed to resist if he chose to try seducing her. Good thing he liked humans better than Weres.

"I feel like a hit man for the mob standing here in the dark ready to swing a tire iron at a complete stranger's window. Are your eyes closed?"

They weren't, because she'd been staring at him in total fascination. "Yes." She quickly squeezed them shut and waited to hear the sound of shattering glass. One second, two, and then came the mighty crash.

She opened her eyes. "Good Lord, you've destroyed the entire bottom pane!"

"Didn't mean to, but I don't know how to break glass gently. You have to put your back into it if you want the job done right. At least it was safety glass. No sharp edges." He laid the tire iron on the snowy porch. "Warm air's coming out. Did they leave the furnace on?"

"Yes, on low. That way they don't have to drain the pipes every winter. You know, that hole's almost big enough for me to crawl through without unlocking the window."

"Aye, but I won't have you doing that, lass." Reaching inside, he pushed up the honeycomb shade before flipping open the lock. Then he eased the window slowly upward as small pieces of glass rained down on the windowsill and the porch.

"We'll need to get this fixed tomorrow or the place will be an open invitation to thieves," she said.

"Let's hope that thieves won't be out in this kind of weather. I'm also hoping we can find something to temporarily block the cold air from coming in the house." After opening the window completely, he brushed away the bits of glass from the sill. "Let me have the torch."

She handed it to him, and he crouched down to play the beam over the inside of the cabin. "Looks like a kitchen, and no furniture right next to the window." He handed the flashlight back to her. "Just shine it on the opening while I get inside. Then I'll unlock the door for you."

"You seem to know your way around a break-in, Duncan." Briefly she thought about the hacking incident, but this wasn't the same kind of thing, and besides, she'd been the one who'd suggested breaking in.

He was a big guy and had to maneuver to get through the window. Glass crunched under his shoe. Once he was inside, he stuck his hand back out. "Torch, please."

She gave it back to him and walked over to the door.

Within seconds, the locks clicked and the door swung open. "Welcome to my castle, milady."

"See, now you're even talking like royalty." She walked into the house. Even with the heat on low, the place was ten times warmer than outside. "Wow, that feels nice."

"It does. Let's get some light on the situation." Walking back to the kitchen, he swung the flashlight beam over the walls and settled it on a dimmer switch. "Ah, there 'tis." Crossing to it, he rotated the knob and an elegant little chandelier over the kitchen table slowly came to life. Each bulb was small and shaded, so the effect was romantic.

"So the Stewarts like ambience. I had no idea."

"I'm afraid we just compromised their ambience." Duncan gazed at the chandelier. "I can already tell they love this place, and now we've vandalized it. Not only will I pay to have the window fixed, but—"

"No, *I* will pay." She laid her purse on the table. Then she pulled off her damp hat and draped it on the back of a kitchen chair.

"You ran this errand on my account, so I'll pay."

"Duncan, you're an invited guest." She put her gloves on the back of the chair next to her hat. "I'm paying."

He laughed. "We'll split the cost."

"No, I—"

"Are you really going to stand here with the cold blowing in and argue this point?"

"Well, when you put it that way, I guess not. We'll discuss it later. But just know that I'm going to—"

"Kate."

"Okay. Later." She pressed her lips together to keep from adding anything more.

"In any case, I think they deserve some compensation for us barging into their home uninvited."

"I agree, but because I've met them, I don't think they'll be upset. We haven't ruined anything that can't be replaced." But she felt a twinge of guilt, all the same. The kitchen was charming with its tile countertops, rustic walnut table and chairs, and open shelving for a collection of dishes that looked as if they'd been made by local artisans.

"First order of business is to cover up that window and clean up the broken glass."

She shook her head. "No, first order of business is thawing out your feet. We should probably start by putting them in some lukewarm water so the shock's not too great. Then I'll cover the window."

"Sorry, but I'm not dipping my toes in warm water until that window's sealed up to my satisfaction." He started opening cupboards. "I don't want to waste any more electricity than we have to, and some snow is blowing in."

"I'll take care of it." She spied a turkey roaster in one of the cupboards he'd opened and shut again. Walking over, she pulled it out. "Sit down and take off your shoes before you get frostbite."

"Not yet. Aha. Here's a box of rubbish bags. Now all we need is tape."

"My grandmother will be furious if you end up injured and I could have prevented it." Maybe the thought of an elderly female pack alpha on the warpath would make him more tractable.

"Milady Kate."

His commanding tone would have raised her hackles if he hadn't combined it with that cute title. But she'd be damned if she'd fall in with his game and call him milord, which carried overtones of subservience, in her opinion. Holding the turkey roaster, she stood and faced him. "Yes, Duncan?"

"As you well know, because you sent me a Sniff to that effect, my ancestors fought the British in all kinds of weather while they were naked and painted blue. Don't make a fuss over me. I'm a wee bit tougher than you'd be giving me credit for."

She gazed at him standing there in his open topcoat with his feet braced apart as he held the box of garbage bags. His dark hair was damp and tousled and his collar was still turned up. He'd removed his shades and no longer looked like a mob assassin, but the beard made her think of a dashing highwayman about to kidnap the woman he fancied.

When that image was combined with a sexy brogue, a girl could find herself wanting to be kidnapped . . . and ravished in the bargain.

"I won't get frostbite, lass. We weren't out there long enough. In the second place, I would never allow your grandmother to be angry with you on my account. You spent your valuable time driving to the airport to meet my flight, and you've done your best to assure my survival in a blizzard." He smiled.

Oh, boy. That smile should be registered as a lethal weapon. Dazzled by its magnificence, she felt determination seep away, leaving her ready to surrender without a fight. No wonder Angela Sapworthy couldn't shut up about him.

"You've acquitted yourself well," he continued, "though it pains me to say it, considering that you're the driving force behind the Howler movement."

She blinked as if rousing herself from a trance. The Howlers! They were counting on her to stand firm against this leader of the Woofers, and yet she was allowing herself to be captivated by his Scottish charm. Shame on her!

"Thanks for reminding me of that." She plopped the turkey roaster on the kitchen table. "You can make use of this when you're ready. I'll find some tape for that window."

"Excellent. The job will go faster with two people." He took off his gloves, scarf, and coat and laid them over the back of another kitchen chair.

"You're right, though it pains me to say it, seeing as how you're driving force behind the Woofers." Focus was definitely going to be a challenge when she was in the presence of this Scotsman. By removing his coat and scarf, he'd provided a more comprehensive view of his broad shoulders, massive chest, and narrow hips.

He winked at her. "That I am."

Surely he wasn't flirting with her. At least not on purpose, since she was not his species preference. Maybe flirting was his default setting. She began opening drawers in hopes one would contain tape. "FYI, somebody hacked into the Furthebest Web site today. It was down for hours."

"I hope you're not implying that the Woofers had anything to do with that."

"I'm not accusing anyone of anything." She found a roll of gray duct tape. "But I find it odd that this happened today as everyone's gathering for the conference." She held up the tape. "This should do the job."

"Aye, but let's go back to the other topic. Furthebest is your livelihood. My followers wouldn't jeopardize that to make a point."

"I hope you're right."

"Kate, I know them. That's playing dirty, and that's not what we're about."

"You can't deny that my dating site goes against everything the Woofers believe, so why would they want it to flourish?"

He pulled a garbage bag out of the box. "Is it flourishing?"

"Of course it is." Maybe not as wildly as she'd like, but the site was gaining new subscribers every day. "And I've had wonderful comments about my book. Whether you want to admit it or not, plenty of us prefer Were-Were sex and mating."

"I've read it."

"You've read my book?" She was surprised and a little chagrined that he'd taken the time. She'd totally ignored his.

He nodded. "*Sex and the Single Shifter* is a damned clever title."

"Is that your way of saying the title's great but the book sucks?"

"No, it isn't." He blew out a breath. "Let's tape up the window before the Stewarts have an electric bill to rival the one at the castle."

"Okay. Temporary truce."

His eyebrows lifted. "Are we fighting?"

"It can't be helped, can it? As you conveniently mentioned not long ago, I'm the leader of the Howlers, which means I stand for maintaining our standards. You want to blast them to smithereens."

"I could respond to that outrageous statement, but I won't, because then we'll never get the job done." Crossing to the window, he pushed it back down slowly as bits of glass rained onto the sill. "If we're going to be walking around this area, we should sweep up some of this first."

She hated to admit that he might be thinking more clearly than she was at the moment. "I saw a brush and dustpan under the sink." She handed him the tape. "I'll get it." On her way back to the counter she unzipped her leather jacket and pulled it off. She'd be able to maneuver better without it.

She'd worn her favorite black turtleneck sweater under her coat for this first meeting with Duncan. The sweater was soft and classy, so it gave her a boost of confidence every time she wore it.

Returning with the dustpan and brush, she thought she caught a glimpse of male appreciation in his gray eyes, but she might have been mistaken. She hunkered down and swept up the glass immediately in front of the window. "That should be good enough for now." She laid the dustpan and brush to one side and stood. "We can do a better job later, when we mop up the water we've dripped on the floor."

"Is that sweater angora?"

"Yes." Knowing that he'd checked her out provided a measure of satisfaction. If he rattled her this much, she'd like to think she'd had some effect on him as a way of balancing the scales.

"Thought so. Do you want to hold or tape?"

"I'll tape."

"Nothing like a decisive female, I always say." He handed her the roll of tape.

"For what?" She met his gaze.

"Everything." He turned and stretched the plastic across the top of the window frame. "Whether it's business or pleasure, I appreciate dealing with someone who knows her own mind."

"Even if it's different from yours?"

"Especially then. I don't like shadowboxing. Thankfully, you don't do that. Hey, this is going to blow at the bottom, so maybe you should tape that part while I hold the top."

"Yep. But you'll have to step back so I can get in there." His shadowboxing statement had sounded like a compliment. Interesting.

Maintaining his hold on the bag, he walked his feet backward. "I must look like a perp in a cop show about to be frisked."

"You watch those?"

"Aye. I love trying to solve the case."

"Me, too." Crouching down again, she sandwiched herself between his legs and the wall so she could tape the bag to the bottom of the window frame. The scent of wet wool and warm male surrounded her from behind, while cold, damp air blew in through the broken window.

"At least we have one thing in common." His brogue had an undertone to it that hadn't been there before.

"So it seems." If she didn't know better, she'd think he was getting turned on by working with her in such close quarters. For her part, she was hyperaware that his body hovered over hers. Without really wanting to, she found herself matching the rhythm of his breathing.

"So what's your favorite show?" he asked.

"I love *The Force*. I have a little crush on the guy who plays Adam." Now that she thought about it, Duncan reminded her of that tall, dark-haired actor, who was, of course, human. She'd never consider actually dating him, but he was great to watch on the screen.

"I'm looking forward to some American TV while I'm here." Again, there was a husky quality in Duncan's voice, as if he wanted to sound casual when he felt anything but.

"Stillman Lodge has a flat screen and cable in every room."

"Nice."

There was no mistaking the sexual vibration in that comment.

She picked up the heady scent of arousal. Technically he shouldn't be attracted to her because she wasn't his preferred type, yet it seemed that he wanted her.

The knowledge gave her a sense of power, but it also made her quiver inside. Against all odds, she wanted him, too, despite whom he was and what he stood for. He was her physical type, as evidenced by the fact he looked like the TV actor she liked. But it would be foolish to get involved. She could easily compromise her campaign for HOWL.

Moving faster, she taped each side of the window, but she couldn't reach the top. "I need to stand up to finish. Watch out for your chin."

"All clear."

She stood slowly to make sure she didn't clip his jaw with her head. Once she was upright, she found herself effectively caged between his outstretched arms. For the second time tonight she was being embraced by Duncan MacDowell.

Although breathing had become more difficult, she tried for nonchalance as she ripped off a piece of tape and smoothed it quickly against the window frame. "Well, isn't this cozy?"

"Bloody inconvenient," he murmured.

"I know." She deliberately chose to misunderstand because she wasn't ready to admit what was happening between them. Maybe if they ignored it, the tension would go away. "I didn't intend for us to get stuck here, and I'm sorry." She slapped on some more tape.

"That's not what I meant, and you know it, lass."

So he wasn't going to let her sidestep the issue. She

struggled to stay calm as she put on the last piece of tape. "You can let go now," she said quietly.

"Not yet."

"But we're all finish—" She gasped and dropped the tape as he took her by the shoulders and turned her around.

"No, we're not quite finished." And his mouth came down on hers.

Chapter 3

Sniffer Update: @newshound—WereCon2012 attendees ask—where's Duncan MacDowell? His flight came, but he's AWOL. So is Kate Stillman! #intriguedeveloping

Duncan knew in advance he'd regret this kiss... eventually. But the moment his lips found Kate's, he didn't give a damn about anything except the velvety taste of her ripe mouth. He wanted this kiss, needed it with a desperation that drove him to pull her hard against his throbbing body.

She was every bit as delicious as he'd been imagining she would be, and besides, she was kissing him back. With a groan he shifted the angle and took the kiss deeper. He stroked his tongue against hers and felt her shiver in reaction.

God, but this was good. Of course it would be. She was such an expert in Were sex that she'd written a book about it. Reading her book on the plane had been a tactical error, but he couldn't unread it, and many of her descriptions were burned into his brain.

As a result, her kiss drove him crazy. Wrapping his arms around the soft angora sweater, he envisioned pulling it over her head. He could have it off in a split second. And then . . . as he fell deeper into lustful scenarios, he imagined a soundtrack providing background music, as if they were in a movie. Oh, yes, wild music with a strong beat fit with this moment, this incredibly hot . . .

But for some reason she'd stopped kissing him and was squirming in his arms, and not in a sensuous way. "My phone. It's my phone."

Gradually he returned to the world of blizzards, political differences, and ringing cell phones. He was disappointed that her kiss hadn't made him hear music, after all. But it had been one hell of a kiss, in spite of that detail.

She extricated herself without a lot of help from him, because he really hated to lose the connection with her warm body and that erotically soft sweater. But as the significance of the ringing phone penetrated his passion-drenched mind, he realized they should have called the resort the minute they'd finished taping the window. Someone might be worried about them.

Or maybe a towing company had a free truck available and was about to come and rescue them from the snowdrift. As he listened to the apologetic way Kate was talking on the phone she'd pulled out of her purse, he gathered it wasn't a towing company. Someone, probably her grandmother, wanted to know why they hadn't arrived yet.

In point of fact, they hadn't been free to call until moments ago, when the immediate problems had been solved. He shouldn't feel guilty that he'd delayed that call by less than five minutes. Yet if the phone hadn't rung, the delay might have been longer.

Yes, much longer. Their recent discussion about condoms had reminded him that Weres could have sex whenever they chose to without worrying about birth control. The Were culture celebrated sexual pleasure and encouraged teenage Weres to explore and experiment.

Because their species was naturally disease-resistant, they didn't have to worry about that issue, and no male Were could make a female pregnant unless he'd officially claimed her as his mate. Neither could he impregnate a human female who wasn't his chosen mate, but explaining that to a woman would mean revealing his Were nature.

He couldn't do that in today's political climate. But when Weres could be open about their biology, then he would no longer have to pretend that he needed condoms when he had sex with a human female. Despite what he'd told Kate, he wasn't totally enamored with condoms.

She was correct that sex without them was the most satisfying kind. And while he'd been kissing her, he'd yearned for that kind of satisfaction. He *really* shouldn't have read her book on the plane. Very stupid move.

Running a hand over his face, he encountered the bristle of a day-old beard. He hoped he hadn't given her razor burn. It wasn't a nice thing to do, and in addition to that, he didn't want anyone at the convention to know that he'd been kissing her.

Even for a Were given to spontaneous behavior, which he was, that kiss had been ... possibly the most foolish thing he'd done in a long while. And that was saying something.

While she talked on the phone, he found the trash can and dumped the dustpan full of glass. Then he located the thermostat and turned the heat up a bit. They might not be here long, so he hated to use more than they had to, but now that he wasn't holding Kate, he felt the chill.

Then he remembered his own phone, which he'd tucked into an inner pocket of his overcoat. The charger was in his suitcase, which was in her vehicle, so once he'd checked for messages, he needed to power it down.

None of the e-mails needed immediate attention except one from his brother, Colin, who'd stayed in Scotland with his mate, Luna. A year ago Colin might not have trusted Duncan to represent the MacDowell pack at this conference. They'd butted heads constantly on Duncan's views on Were-human interaction.

But thanks to Colin's love for his half-blood mate, he'd revised his opinions considerably. After all, a human-Were mating had produced Luna, the light of his life. Colin had even given Duncan permission to tell their story in Duncan's book, *Down with Dogma: Benefits of Were-Human Cooperation*. So now all Colin wanted was reassurance that Duncan had arrived safely in Denver.

He sent a quick reply letting Colin know that all was well. It wasn't, exactly, and his brother would shake his head in dismay if he knew that Duncan had allowed himself to get too friendly with Kate Stillman, whose rigid views directly opposed his campaign.

But Duncan believed he could contain that misstep. He'd apologize, back off, and control the damage. No one ever had to know besides him and Kate, and she certainly wouldn't want word to spread, either.

Because she was still on the phone, he checked his Sniffer feed. Woofers who couldn't attend the Denver conference had gathered at various locations for their own miniconferences. His followers were an enthusiastic bunch, but he hoped they wouldn't stoop to sabotaging her Furthebest Web site.

Although he'd promised Kate that no Woofer would hack into her site in order to disrupt it, privately he couldn't be sure. He'd never admit that to her, but she was smart enough to know that he couldn't guarantee all his followers were law-abiding Weres. Any movement had a fringe element.

He sent out a quick Sniff saying he'd been temporarily delayed but should be at the conference site shortly. Then he turned off his phone, tucked it back inside his topcoat, and took a look around the cabin. No walls blocked the kitchen from the living area, which included an upholstered sofa and two overstuffed chairs, all covered in a Native American print.

The furniture had been arranged to face the far wall, which included bookshelves, a stone fireplace, and a flat-screen television tucked into a custom niche. He resisted the urge to pick up the remote from its holder on the bookshelf. He was an intruder, not an invited guest.

On the other hand, if they ended up here longer than an hour or so, he might need that television as a necessary distraction from Kate. Besides, they'd reimburse the owners for any electricity used. A little TV watching wasn't going to add much to the bill.

Wandering to the kitchen window and looking out the unbroken upper half, he saw nothing but snow coming down hard and fast. Intuition told him they might not get out of this cabin tonight. About the time he came to that conclusion, Kate ended her call and glanced over at him.

"We won't be going anywhere for a while," she said. "My grandmother's been watching the news, and several

pileups on the interstate have stretched the city's re-
sources to the breaking point. They're asking that anyone who's not in an emergency situation hold tight until
morning."

"I suppose that would be us." The potent energy created by their kiss remained in the air, a tantalizing shim-
mer that could get them into trouble again if they weren't
careful.

He decided to address the problem immediately. "I
need to apologize for what just happened before the
phone call. I shouldn't have done it, and I can promise
you that such a thing won't be repeated."

She nodded. "Good, because if Angela Sapworthy ever
got wind of something like that, we would both be—"

"Unable to effectively lead. I know. Our followers
would doubt our dedication to the cause if they thought
we were overly friendly, and they'd be justified in that. I
take full responsibility for the incident, but I would appreciate keeping it strictly between us."

"You won't find me telling anyone. But I won't allow
you to take full responsibility. I could have pushed you
away."

He couldn't let himself off the hook that easily. "I was
the initiator, and I don't see how you can be blamed for
simply responding."

Her eyes widened. "What an ego you have, Duncan
MacDowell!"

He blinked, completely taken aback by her statement.
"I don't know what you mean."

"Correct me if I'm wrong, but that comment of yours
implies that once you initiate a sexual encounter, it's a
done deal. Assuming a phone doesn't ring, of course,
which it happened to do in this case."

He rubbed the back of his neck, confused as to why she was so irritated. "In my dealings with females, it usually is a done deal, as you say. We were headed for a wee bit more than a kiss, and I don't think, in all honesty, that you can deny it."

Her rapid breathing stirred her breasts beneath that soft black sweater. "I won't deny it, but that was because, at that very moment, I wanted sex as much as you did. If I hadn't, then I would have stopped you from continuing."

Watching that sweater move was slowly killing him. He focused on her blue eyes instead. "That would have been a new experience for me."

Her mouth opened, forming a perfect pink O of surprise. "No one's *ever* refused your advances?"

"Not that I can recall."

"Oh, my God. No wonder." She continued to stare at him but said no more.

"No wonder *what*?" He had a feeling he wouldn't like the answer, but she couldn't leave her comment dangling like that.

"You're so . . . no, I shouldn't say it. We need to remain civil to each other. We're quite likely trapped together for the rest of the night."

"Either you finish that sentence, or I'll have to retract my statement about your forthright attitude. You've never pulled your punches online, Kate, so why do it now?"

"Because we're face-to-face. Of course everything's different when you're actually looking at each other."

"Then close your eyes and pretend you're typing your response."

"That's the coward's way out."

"So be brave."

"All right." She took a deep breath.

And he wished she hadn't, because she had magnificent breasts and they heaved with a beauty that he couldn't seem to ignore.

"Okay, here we go." She looked him straight in the eye. "No wonder you're so arrogant and sure of yourself. No female has ever rejected you. That's astonishing. Yes, you're very good-looking, and I will concede that you have a certain amount of sexual charisma, but . . . *never*? Seriously?"

"Well, there was one time when I thought the lass wanted me to stop, but it turns out I was mistaken, so we went on to have a very satisfactory time of it."

"Incredible."

"But I'd hate to think my successes have made me arrogant."

"Why else would you insist on taking the blame for making me forget myself just now? Rest assured that if I hadn't wanted to be seduced, no seduction would have taken place. I don't care how good a kisser you are."

"But you did want to be seduced." He shouldn't emphasize that point. He should let the entire matter drop. But she'd accused him of arrogance, and he needed some balm for that wound.

She gazed at him without speaking for several seconds. Then she cleared her throat. "Yes, I did, past tense. I no longer do."

"Are you sure?" Because he wasn't. Her eyes told a different story.

"Let me put it this way. We seem to have chemistry, which, as you mentioned earlier, is damned inconvenient. So although I might still want you, I don't wish for you to seduce me. I lost focus while we were working on the window together. I won't lose focus again."

"Good. That's very good. All we have to do is get through the night. Then tomorrow we'll be caught up in the conference and that should take care of . . . everything."

"Yes." She consulted the time on her phone. "It's a little after six. We only have twelve hours or so, and if we're smart, we'll spend part of that time sleeping."

"Separately."

"Extremely separately. We should also eat something. While I was looking through the cupboards, I noticed they've left some canned food here. But I'd like to contact the Stewarts before we dive into their supply."

"I don't know how you're going to do that. Why would they leave their number somewhere? They don't need to. They know what it is."

"I realize that." Tapping her phone against her chin, she began to roam the kitchen, opening drawers, sorting through whatever she found there. "Here we go." She pulled a small booklet out of one of the drawers. "It's an address and phone book. They won't be in here, but friends will. I'll call around until I get the number."

"They'll simply give it to you?"

She looked surprised that he'd ask. "The Stillman name is very well-known in Denver, so if I pick somebody local, no worries. It would be the same as you using the MacDowell name back in . . . what's the name of your little town?"

"I bide in Glenbarra."

"Right. I'm sure the MacDowell name opens doors in Glenbarra. Besides, I don't have to tell the friend that we broke in. I can just say there's a problem with the cabin and I need to get in touch with Bob and Edith." She flipped a page in the address book, but then she glanced up. "While I'm doing this, I wish you would *please* soak your feet in that turkey roaster."

"It seems I won't need to be soaking my feet, after all."

"Of course you will. You said yourself they were cold."

"They were. But they're not now."

"Why not?"

He smiled at her. "That kiss warmed me all the way down to my toes, lass."

Kate took one look at that smile and quickly began studying the address book as if it contained the secrets of the universe. Now that he'd made that comment, she realized her feet weren't cold anymore, either. In fact, not a single cell in her body was cold.

Earlier she'd watched him cross to the thermostat and turn up the heat, but that had nothing to do with the warmth that had spread through her system. The next twelve hours were going to be a huge challenge. Ironically, although she ran a dating site, she hadn't used it herself in months. Organizing HOWL and writing her book had taken up every bit of her spare time.

Being tucked away with a virile Were like Duncan had reminded her of what she'd been missing. In some ways, even though their interaction had been at a distance until today, he was the male she'd had the most significant contact with recently. Her attraction to him wasn't at all surprising, even given their differences.

But she was strong enough to subdue her urges. She had to be. Taking several calming breaths, she searched the names and addresses in the little book until she found one that looked promising. Someone, probably Edith, had scribbled names of the couple's grandchildren in the margin, so they must be good friends.

Sure enough, the woman who answered was eager to help and supplied a phone number for the Stewarts immediately. Kate thanked her and punched in the number. All the while she was aware of Duncan sweeping glass and using paper towels to soak up water on the hardwood floor. He'd taken off his shoes and socks and she needed to follow his lead so she wouldn't track any more water around.

Sitting on one of the kitchen chairs, she began unlacing one boot as she waited for someone to answer the phone. But it was hard to unlace one-handed. Sticking the phone between her ear and her shoulder, she tackled the laces again and managed to get a stubborn knot in the left boot.

About that time Edith answered the phone, and Kate temporarily gave up on the knot. "Hello, Edith, it's Kate Stillman calling from Colorado."

"Kate! We saw on the news about the blizzard and it looks just awful. Are you calling about the cabin? Please say it's okay."

"Your cabin is fine, Edith." She started working at the knot again with her free hand. "But there is a little matter I need to tell you about. I was returning from the airport with a resort guest when I hit a patch of ice and buried the nose of my SUV in a snowbank."

"Oh, no! Are you all right?"

"Fortunately my passenger and I weren't hurt, but there's no way we're getting a tow tonight. We happened to be right by your cabin, so we—"

"I hope you found a way to get in."

She tugged harder on the knot, but it wouldn't give. "Yes, we did get in. But I have to apologize because we had to break a front window to do it." As she reached down to unlace the other boot, Duncan walked over and knelt at her feet. She waved him off.

"Don't worry about the window," Edith said. "At least you're in out of the storm."

"We'll get the glass replaced tomorrow, I promise. And we've taped a garbage bag over the window. I'll reimburse you for the extra electricity, too."

Duncan wouldn't be waved off. He started working on the knot she'd created, his dark head bent over the task. Unless she wanted to get into a tussle with him while she was on the phone with Edith, she had to sit still and let him finish the job.

"Heavens, don't even think about paying for the electricity," Edith said. "You'll need food. Eat whatever you can find. It's only canned stuff, not very exciting, but there are a couple of bottles of red wine in a cabinet in the living room. Oh, and some beer in the refrigerator, I think. Make yourselves at home."

"Thank you. That's very sweet of you."

Duncan lifted his head and smiled. "You're welcome."

"Not you," she muttered, frowning at him.

"Excuse me?" Edith sounded confused.

"Nothing, nothing. Just trying to do two things at once. I appreciate the offer of food and drink, and we'll replace that, too." She tried not to imagine Duncan undressing her, yet his attention to her boots felt like that. After she'd made such a big deal about his feet, he must assume she was desperate to get out of her boots.

"Please take whatever you need and don't worry

about replacing it," Edith said. "None of it's gourmet fare, I assure you. We don't have TV reception, but there's a DVD player and the bookshelf's loaded with movies. I'm afraid there's only one bed, though. I don't know if you feel chummy enough with your guest to share it, but there's also the couch."

"We'll work it out, Edith. I'm so grateful for your understanding."

Duncan finished with one boot and pulled it off. Then he rolled down her wet sock and tossed that aside. The combination of his capable hands working on her feet and Edith's comment about bed sharing put Kate in the very state of mind she'd been trying to avoid. Why did she have to be snowbound with the sexiest Were she'd met in years when he was also the last one on earth she should lust after?

"Of course I understand, dear. There's a reason we only spend summers at the cabin. It's gorgeous there, but we're not up to battling that winding road in the winter. I'm just glad you're going to be okay. You and your guest, that is."

"Thank you. We're feeling very lucky, too." So long as neither of them *got* lucky tonight, all would be well.

"You'll need a key to lock up when you leave, and also when someone repairs the window. There's a metal key box in the flowerpot by the back door."

"Too bad I didn't know that before. We could have spared the window."

Duncan grasped her calf and pulled off the other boot. After he removed her sock, he began massaging her feet. She told herself to resist, but his touch felt like heaven and she couldn't make herself draw back.

"You can file that information away for next time,"

Edith said. "Also, there's a small supply of firewood under a tarp on the back porch. You should make a fire and
thaw yourselves out."

Kate was more thawed out than she'd been in ages. A
fire might be overkill. But the offer was generous, and
she told Edith so. "And be sure and say hello to Bob for
me. I'll be talking to you soon."

"Don't rush out into that storm again, Kate. Take all
the time you need."

"We will—thanks. Good-bye." She pushed the discon-
nect button and sank against the back of the chair with
a groan. "I thought we agreed on our course of action."

He looked into her eyes. "We did, but you seemed to
be having trouble with your boots, and I couldn't stand
watching you struggle to get them off."

"I appreciate that, but now they're off."

"And your feet were icy."

"They were?" She found that hard to believe.

"Well, chilled. Definitely chilled." He continued his
massage.

He had very talented hands, and she was rapidly losing all interest in being strong, good, and true to the
cause. For one irresponsible moment, she considered in-
viting him to join her in the bedroom so he could put
those hands to good use elsewhere on her body. The
thought of that made her damp and achy with needs that
hadn't been satisfied in too long.

But she'd hate herself later. Summoning what little
willpower she had left, she pulled her foot away. "That
was terrific. But it needs to end, and I think you know
why."

He sat back on his heels and gazed up at her. "Kate,
while you've been talking on the phone, I've been think-

ing. We've already made a pledge not to reveal what's happened here."

"As in what happens in the cabin stays in the cabin?"

His gray eyes flashed with amusement. "Believe it or not, that expression has made it over to Scotland. Aye, that's exactly what I mean."

"I think I know where you're going with this." Her heart thumped crazily at the implied suggestion. She was so tempted to say yes and scratch this maddening itch. But then she'd have to live with herself, and she wasn't sure she could do that.

"The answer is no." She stood and walked away from him.

"I know what this is all about." He got to his feet and swung to face her. "You think it's time some female rejected me, for my own good."

"It's not about that, but now that you mention it, perhaps it will do you some good. However, I'm saying no for me, because I am the leader of Honoring Our Werewolf Legacy, and that means I need to display some dedication and backbone."

He sighed. "I was afraid you'd say that. I admire you for it, lass, but it's going to be a very long and frustrating night, I'm afraid."

"Think of it as character building."

"Aye." He glanced down at his trousers. "But try telling that to my wee man."

"Wee man? Surely not, Duncan MacDowell, seducer of females."

His smile nearly undid her. "Not so wee, then. But you won't be finding out about that, will you, now?"

Chapter 4

**WERECON 2012:
STILLMAN AND MACDOWELL SNOWBOUND!**

**Exclusive *Wereworld Celebrity Watch* report
by Angela Sapworthy**

DENVER—Following a harrowing auto accident in the midst of the worst snowstorm to hit the city in decades, HOWL leader Kate Stillman and WOOF leader Duncan MacDowell have taken refuge in an unoccupied cabin several miles from the conference site. This reporter talked with a visibly shaken Elizabeth Stillman, Kate's grandmother and the Stillman pack alpha.

"I'm so relieved they're all right," Elizabeth said. "This is a killer blizzard and I feared the worst. Thank goodness they found a safe haven."

Other conference attendees echoed that sentiment, although several wondered whether a storm might take place inside the cabin as well as outside! After a summer of battling online, these two are face-to-face at last, with no referee! Emma Wallace, Aidan Wallace's lovely mate and a fellow writer, was heard to say that she would love to be a mouse in the corner of that cabin. This reporter would, too! With luck, Kate and Duncan will inform their followers of the details on Sniffer!

Duncan had made his case and lost. As he'd unlaced Kate's boots, he'd been struck by this new thought — that the snowstorm had isolated them completely. No one could barge in on them to interrupt . . . whatever might be going on. He had some vivid mental images of what could be going on if they allowed themselves full rein.

They'd already vowed to keep their interaction in this cabin private, so they could do whatever they wanted tonight. Maybe that wasn't a noble conclusion to reach, but he wasn't convinced he could be noble for another twelve hours given their circumstances. He wasn't sure that she could, either, and so why make themselves miserable if, in the end, they'd succumb?

Better to succumb sooner rather than later, in his opinion, and reap the rewards of more time alone together. Once they arrived at the conference, they wouldn't dare step out of line. This would be their one and only chance, maybe literally, forever and ever.

He'd even begun to convince himself that fate had thrown them together tonight. They were unlikely partners, and reason said they wouldn't get along. But on one level, the purely physical, sexual level, they could be a perfect match. Now he would never know.

She waved the cell phone she still held. "I'm going to post on Sniffer. Our isolation is making us forget our responsibility, but reconnecting with our followers should help us focus."

"Until our phones go dead. I don't know about you, but I left my charger in my suitcase and my battery's low."

Glancing at her phone, she winced. "Mine, too. So here's a thought. Let's each post something on Sniffer and then turn off our phones so we can conserve battery life and post again later."

"All right." He retrieved his phone from inside his topcoat. "You first. I'll respond to your Sniff."

She looked up from her phone. "Just like old times."

"Except we're not an ocean apart."

"Exactly. And therein lies the problem." She returned her attention to her phone and began typing in her Sniff.

He supposed it was a problem, but he couldn't bring himself to regret a single minute of this adventure so far. Now that he thought back over their Sniffs and blog posts, there had always been sexual overtones. Without acknowledging it to himself, he'd expected them to spark off each other when they met.

And they had. Good Lord had they ever.

"Done." She pushed a final button. "Your turn."

Consulting his screen, he found her Sniff. *Duncan MacDowell claims to live in a castle but says he's no prince. #totallyagree*

Trying not to laugh, he looked at her, eyebrows lifted.

"Well, you did say that."

"Aye." He hid a smile as he typed his response. *Kate Stillman carried a torch for me, but, sadly, she no longer does. #torchextinguished*

She reacted the instant she saw the Sniff on her phone. "Hey, no fair!"

"It's true."

"But they probably don't realize that you call a flash-light a torch! I'm responding to that." Her fingers flew over the surface of her phone.

A moment later, her reply to his Sniff arrived on his phone. *@DuncanMacDowell You're mistaken, Woofer. That torch was a flashlight to keep track of your shenanigans. #clearvision*

He couldn't help chuckling. Sniffs from Woofers and Howlers began popping up in response to the inter-change and the battle was on.

"Ha! The Italian delegate says my posts are *magnif-ico!*" Kate said.

"That's nothing. The Russian delegate just offered to buy me as much vodka as I can hold." He glanced at her. "Guess that woke them up. Feel better now? More fo-cused?" The silly little banter hadn't helped him one bit. It had only reminded him of the fun he'd had sparring with her this summer.

"Sort of." She didn't sound very convinced. "Let's turn these things off and save our batteries." Her phone rang before she could do it. "Oops." She glanced at the screen. "I'd better take this. I won't be long."

Powering down his phone, he laid it on the kitchen table as he wondered who the high-priority call could be from. Not her grandmother. If it had been the Stewarts, she would have said so. He suspected a lover. She ran a dating site, so she must have dozens to choose from.

Her secretive behavior as she walked into the living room and lowered her voice confirmed his suspicions. And yet . . . she'd admitted earlier that she'd responded to his kiss because she'd wanted to be seduced. She must not have an exclusive arrangement with this Were, who-ever he was.

It was none of Duncan's bloody business, but as he went through the cupboards in search of something they could warm up for dinner, he eavesdropped with morbid fascination. Even with his superior hearing he got only snatches of the conversation. Yet because his name came up a couple of times, he was reasonably sure Kate was discussing him.

Her soft laughter that followed a mention of his name pricked his ego. He acknowledged that he had one, although it wasn't as big as Kate seemed to think. Trading punches on Sniffer was one thing, but he didn't relish being the subject of a private joke between Kate and whatever randy Were she was talking to. That was too personal.

By the time she got off the phone and came back to the kitchen, his mood had deteriorated considerably. "I suppose he's worried about you spending the night alone in this cabin with me." As well he should be, considering that scorcher of a kiss.

Duncan took two cans from the cupboard and set them on the counter with a little more force than was necessary. The satisfying clunk of metal cans on the tile counter pleased him.

"Who's worried?" She asked it so innocently, as if she had no idea what he was talking about.

But he wasn't born yesterday. "The Were you were talking to just now." He pulled more cans out of the cupboard without looking at her. "It's plain that you have something going with him, and he can't be happy about this situation you're in, getting trapped for the night with me."

"So you think I was talking to my lover?"

"Pretty damned obvious that you were, lass. I'll wager you didn't mention that kiss, now, did you?"

"I promised you I'd keep that incident private, and I will. But I suppose you don't know me well enough to trust me not to blab."

She sounded so blasted reasonable, so calm. There was even a hint of laughter in her voice. Meanwhile he was seething inside. And for no good reason, either. One kiss didn't mean he had any right to feel jealousy regarding her. He was mostly angry with himself for letting that nasty emotion get its hooks into him.

He'd blame his funk on jet lag, and on finishing her book mere hours ago, which gave him an unrealistic view of how well he knew her. Plus their online contact, though contentious, might have tricked him into thinking he was the most important male Were in her life right now. Stupid.

He reached up to the top shelf for more cans. "I have to trust you. I don't have a choice."

"Duncan, you can stop stacking those cans. That's plenty to choose from and you have some duplicates."

He finally noticed that he'd gathered a grocery market full of canned goods on the counter. In his preoccupation with Kate's phone call from her lover, he'd lost track of what he was doing and why. But he hated admitting that.

"Wanted to make sure we knew all our choices." He waved a hand at the collection he'd created. "What do you fancy for dinner?"

"The chili looks good."

He glanced at her. "That's it? Nothing else, then?"

"One can of chili is more than enough for me, but if you want some, we should open two."

Duncan pretended to study the options carefully, when in fact he'd be happy with warmed-up chili, too.

But he'd hauled all this out of the cupboard, so he picked up two or three other cans and turned them around to read the ingredients as if trying to decide.

Finally he nodded. "Chili would be fine. I'll just put this lot back in the cupboard for now. At least you know what's available, if you get hungry for something else." He began putting the cans back in the approximate order they'd been before, although he couldn't guarantee they were the way the Stewarts had them. Other things had occupied his mind while he'd been emptying the shelves.

"Thanks, Duncan. I'll look for a can opener and a saucepan." There was that hint of laughter again. "I appreciate you being so thorough."

Still irritated with himself for his behavior, and her for enjoying it too much, he paused and turned to her. "I'm glad to be a source of amusement to you, lass. You and your lover, too, in fact. I heard you over there having a wee chuckle on my account."

That brought her laughter bubbling to the surface. "Duncan, that wasn't my lover. That was my assistant, Heidi, reporting that the Furthebest site is back up and wanting to know if you'd said or done anything suspicious. She's convinced the Woofers are behind our site crashing today."

"Your assistant?" Heat climbed up from the collar of his sweater as he began replacing the cans faster now. "Bloody hell." He felt like a fool, but a relieved fool.

"It was bad of me, I know, but I got a kick out of watching you work yourself into a lather over it while you hauled every blessed item out of that cupboard." She put a pan on the stove.

"I wouldn't say I was in a *lather*. I just—"

"You didn't like the idea of me taking a call from my lover right under your nose, after we'd both confessed we were attracted to each other. I get that." She opened the first can of chili. "If the call *had* been my lover, I wouldn't have answered. That would have been tacky."

"Then you have a lover?" To his dismay, he discovered that he still hated the idea.

"Not at the moment." She dumped the can of chili in the saucepan and opened the second one. "And now that we're on the subject, do *you* have a lover?"

"Not at the moment."

She emptied the second can, opened a drawer, and took out a large spoon. "Well, that's good, because to be honest, I don't think a hot kiss like the one we shared should happen unless the two Weres involved are unattached." She turned on the heat under the chili and stirred the contents of the pan. "I realize not everyone agrees with that somewhat conservative view, but — "

"I do."

She glanced up in surprise. "Really? I got the impression from discussions online that you like to play the field, keep your options open."

"Don't believe everything you see online. When I become involved, it's strictly exclusive. And I expect the same from her. You can't get to know someone unless you agree to see only each other."

Her gaze narrowed. "You're not just saying that because you read it in my book, are you?"

"No." He propped a hip against the counter and settled in to what was becoming a cozy domestic scene. After the long plane ride and the drama of their escape from the storm, he was beginning to relax at last. "I was glad to read it in your book, though."

"So you liked at least that part." She went back to stirring the chili.

"I liked nearly all of it. The sexual tips are ... informative."

She laughed. "They're what made it a best seller. I did a lot of research for that section. Even though Weres are taught about sex once they reach puberty, not everyone approaches the subject with imagination."

He wondered if the research was personal or academic but chose not to ask and risk veering off into territory that could get them both in trouble. "That's one of the reasons I advocate dating humans. We can enrich our sexual knowledge by tapping into human imagination."

"But how can humans be of any help when they're limited in their sexual exploration by the threat of pregnancy or disease?"

"Aye, they are, and that's why they have to get more imaginative."

She looked at him with a challenge in her blue eyes. "Okay, name one area in which humans have added to your sexual knowledge."

"Sex toys."

With a wave of her hand, she dismissed his answer. "Weres don't need sex toys."

"We may not *need* them, but why not enjoy them? Why not enhance the experience a little now and then?" He shouldn't be talking about such a loaded topic, but sex toys were a perfect example of how Weres could benefit from interspecies dating and, eventually, mating, too. At least he didn't have any with him so he wouldn't be tempted to demonstrate.

"They're just substitutes for the real thing. They're artificial and ... unnecessary."

If he had a couple of items here and the freedom to make love to her, he'd change her mind in no time, but that wasn't the case, so he had to make the argument intellectually. "You run a dating site for Weres. I can't believe that everyone on your site is successful in finding a partner right away."

"Maybe not right away, but soon enough, I think. There's nothing wrong with being celibate now and then." She turned off the heat under the chili. "It's ready. Do you want to take Edith at her word and open a bottle of their wine?"

He always enjoyed a bit of wine with his food. "Might as well. We'll put it on our tab."

"She said there's a cabinet in the living room. I'll dish the chili if you'll search out the wine."

"I'll be right back." He found the wine cabinet with no trouble. Crouching down, he chose a bottle of red from the small supply and located the corkscrew.

But as he started to close the cabinet, he wondered if drinking it might soften Kate's resolve concerning him. He should probably keep his mouth shut because he wouldn't mind a bit if it did. But his conscience prompted him to glance toward the kitchen. "Aren't you worried that wine will lower your resistance?"

"I'll take the chance. When dinner is a can of chili, you need something to elevate the quality of the meal, don't you think?"

"Aye, I most certainly do." On the way back to the kitchen table, he rotated the dimmer switch. "Mood lighting helps, too."

"Definitely." She gestured toward the two steaming bowls on the table. "I picked her prettiest stoneware, too."

"Then you might as well see if they have any crystal goblets somewhere." He twisted the corkscrew in and opened the wine.

"These will have to do, I'm afraid." She set a plain wineglass at each of their places.

"That they will." He filled each one to the top and put the open bottle in the middle of the table. Then he pulled back one of the chairs and held it for her. "Please be seated, milady."

"Thank you, kind sir." She took her seat with a smoothness that was very Were-like.

Because he'd shared more meals with human females recently, he'd forgotten how fluid a Were could be in her movements. A few humans he'd dated had come close to that kind of grace, but had never quite matched it.

This close to her, he became more aware of her scent, one he'd reacted to from the moment he'd walked into the baggage claim area. He'd been telling himself for the past few years that human females had a more exotic scent, and that might be true. But Kate's aroma excited in him a more primitive response than he'd had to any woman he'd dated.

Fighting the urge to lean down and nuzzle the side of her neck, he let go of her chair and walked around the table to his place on the opposite side. Once he was seated, he raised his glass. "To cooperation."

"If you mean what I think you mean, I can't drink to that."

Stubborn female. But he liked her loyalty and spunk. "Then you propose a toast."

She lifted her glass. "To standards."

"What sort of standards?"

"Werewolf standards, of course." She gazed at him.

"You are a Were, after all, and I assume you have standards, so what's wrong with that?"

"It sounds ominously close to a HOWL pledge, and I don't want to find out later that you've told the Sniffer world I took the HOWL pledge. So how about this—to greater understanding."

She shook her head. "That sounds like a WOOF pledge that could turn into a Sniffer post about me being in favor of greater understanding between humans and werewolves. No, thanks."

He looked into her eyes. "You really don't trust me, do you?"

"I trust you as much as you trust me, Woofer."

"Then let's drink to the blizzard."

"The blizzard? Why?"

"Because, lass, in spite of all we've been through, and in spite of our mutual mistrust and lack of agreement on most things, I wouldn't miss being snowbound with you for anything."

Her lips curved in a wicked little smile. "Same here." She lifted her glass and touched it to his. "To the blizzard."

He held her gaze as they both drank. He could be wrong, and God knew she was an unpredictable female, but he had the feeling she'd begun to reconsider how they'd spend the rest of the evening.

Picking up his spoon, he began eating the chili. "Not bad."

"Anything tastes good when you're really hungry."

He allowed that concept to sink in as they both ate some more. Then he picked up his wineglass, took a sip, and broached a subject dear to his heart. "Speaking of celibacy . . ."

"Were we?"

"You brought it up a while ago, and here we are eating canned chili and relishing every bite. I'm just making a natural connection between celibacy and hunger." He took another drink of his wine before returning his attention to his chili.

"I guess you could say they're related."

He put down his spoon again and looked across the table. She glanced up. Her eyes were luminous in the soft light of the chandelier. He imagined her in wolf form, blond and sleek, and discovered to his surprise that he longed to see her that way. He'd thought the days of Were sex were over for him and that he didn't miss the concept. Not true.

His body tightened as his mind raced ahead of his words. "Would you agree that if you go without sex for a while, you enjoy it more when you finally have some?"

"I suppose."

"So how long has it been, lass?"

"You first." She held his gaze.

"Six months." He picked up his glass and took a fortifying swallow of wine. He didn't often reveal that sort of information. Most male Weres would think he was crazy to stay out of the game for six months.

"Why?"

He shrugged. "Organizing WOOF, writing my book, blogging." And he'd been preoccupied with her since early summer. He could admit it to himself now, although he hadn't realized it before. "Your turn."

"A year."

His blood heated. No wonder she'd kissed him so enthusiastically. "That's a long time."

"My excuses are like yours—organizing HOWL, writing my book, blogging. And then there's Furthebest."

"Which should provide an endless supply of single Weres for your pleasure."

She shook her head. "You might think so, but I've been too busy to take advantage of my own dating site."

"Now, that's just wrong." He paused, hoping she was with him on this. "You're not busy with those things right now."

Surrender glowed in her eyes for a moment, and then she shook her head and smiled. "You're good at this, Duncan."

Damn it, she'd ruined the mood he'd worked so hard to create. "At what?"

"Building an argument, tightening the noose, making others see things your way. No wonder you're the champion of the WOOF movement."

He made one last try, although he knew he'd lost the round. "This has nothing to do with being a Woofer or a Howler. I just think—"

"I know exactly what you think. You've made it very clear that, despite our differences, we're alike in one way. We're both sexually deprived and would be fools not to take advantage of this golden opportunity to experience what would be an outstanding romp after a long layoff— especially long in my case."

"Is that such a bad conclusion?"

"I'm not sure yet." She drained her wineglass. "I need to consider this from all angles."

He groaned. "You're torturing me."

"Maybe so, but according to you, postponing sex makes it sweeter when you finally have it."

"Aye! But that's why we should—"

"Draw out the suspense even more? I completely agree. The rewards will be even greater, assuming we get together in the end." Kate stood. "I'm going to grab some of that wood from the back porch so we can build a fire."

Duncan pushed back his chair. With the frustration rolling through him, he could probably light it with the tip of his finger.

Chapter 5

Kate longed to succumb to Duncan's charms more than he would ever know, but no self-respecting female Were would give in that fast, especially knowing that Duncan was used to easy conquests. If she wanted to stand out in his mind, and no matter how this turned out, she wanted that much notoriety, then she couldn't make a seduction easy for him.

She reserved the right not to give in at all, in fact. Whether she was strong enough to resist his virile Were self was another matter. She'd take it one supercharged moment at a time.

He insisted on helping her bring in the wood from the back porch. They both put their shoes and snow gear back on. The door leading to the porch opened off the bedroom, and they had to turn on a light in there to keep from stumbling against the furniture. Kate had expected the bedroom decor to be similar to the rest of the cabin—tasteful with a Western motif.

She hadn't been prepared for a setup that bordered on sinful decadence. Edith could have at least hinted that the bedroom was a tad . . . erotic. She might have mentioned that the canopy bed was draped in red velvet curtains tied back with gold cords and fancy tassels.

Oh, and she could have made a casual reference to the zillion pillows stacked against the headboard in a manner that made Kate want to dive in, scatter the pillows, and roll around on the fluffy gold comforter, preferably with a certain sexy Scottish Were.

Full disclosure on Edith's part would have included the crystal chandelier hanging from the ceiling that cast rainbows throughout the room, and the thick pile of the fake-fur rug at the foot of the bed, which would also make a nice landing area for a coupling couple. Kate was convinced that she didn't know the Stewarts at all. In fact, she'd never look at Bob and Edith quite the same way again.

"Now, there's a bed that belongs in a castle." Duncan paused beside it and leaned under the canopy as if to check out the interior. Then he let out a low whistle. "*That's* certainly a nice feature."

"What?" Kate poked her head in from the opposite side and her furry hat brushed against the curtains. "You mean the rosy glow?"

"Look up."

She did, and there they were, both rosy, and both reflected in a gilt-edged mirror framed by the top rails of the canopy. Her breath caught. Now she might not be able to face Bob and Edith at all. And they'd always seemed so . . . stodgy.

She cleared her throat. "I don't know what to say."

"I've already had my say, and this bonnie bed adds an exclamation mark to the end of my statement. Ever watched yourself in a mirror, lass?"

"No, can't say that I have. But I'm assuming you've tried it."

"Sadly, I have not."

She expected him to add that here was another opportunity that might never come again, but he didn't. He probably knew that she was already thinking it and didn't need to be reminded. His silence on the matter was more potent than if he'd carried on about having sex beneath a mirror.

She ducked out again and pulled on her gloves. "Let's get the wood." Turning up the collar of her red leather coat, she walked over to the back door and unlocked it. When she opened it, the wind tore it from her grasp. If Duncan hadn't rushed over to block the swinging door, it would have banged into the wall. Gusts of frigid air and swirling snow enveloped Kate and made her wonder what the hell she'd been thinking when she'd suggested bringing in a load of firewood during a blizzard.

She put her hand on the door. "Let's lock up and forget the wood!"

"Nay, we'll have a fire. Hold on to the door. I'm letting go."

She used both hands this time.

Lowering his head, Duncan walked into the teeth of the storm. "Put your weight against it to hold it closed, and open it when I call out."

She did as she was told because Duncan, bless his lust-warmed heart, was out there gathering wood for the fire she'd requested. She couldn't deny his gallantry, even if she suspected his motives.

Soon she heard his command to open the door. She gripped the knob with both hands this time as he came through with his arms full of sweet-smelling cedar and his topcoat and dark hair covered with snow once again. She tried not to think of what his wet shoes and socks had felt like when he had to put them back on. He was sacrificing his physical comfort for her, no doubt in the hope it would win him points. It did.

Throwing her weight against the door, she shoved it closed and locked it.

"Well-done." Duncan turned and walked back into the living room with his armload of wood. He didn't even glance at the velvet-draped bed.

If she didn't know better, she'd think he'd dismissed it from his mind. But she knew better. He was a strategist, and she felt reasonably sure that his goal was to get her into that bed. His current tactic was pretending that he didn't particularly care if he did or not.

The bed and the mirror were added temptations she hadn't counted on. Duncan himself was potent enough without adding embellishments like that. At some point she might have to throw up her hands and accept the inevitable outcome.

But not yet, by God. She, too, ignored the bed as she started out of the room. But then she allowed curiosity to guide her through a door leading to the bathroom. After seeing the bed, she wasn't surprised at the black Jacuzzi, or even the European bidet. Black towels, thick and sensuously soft, hung on heated towel racks, although the heat wasn't on at the moment.

"Kate?" Duncan called out to her as he walked back into the bedroom. "You'll never guess what I found tucked away on the bookshelf."

She turned from the bathroom doorway. "X-rated movies?"

"Aye! How did you know?"

"It goes with my new image of the Stewarts." She gestured to the bathroom. "They're very sensual people. I wouldn't be surprised at much of anything we found now."

"Nor would I." A smile was in his eyes as he held her gaze. "Nor would I."

"You're thinking they have sex toys stashed in a drawer, aren't you?"

His smile reached his sculpted mouth. "Yes, but we won't be looking for them, lass. I'm not above having my way with you in that fantasy bed, but I draw the line at borrowing vibrators."

"Glad to hear it."

"That was a two-part statement. Which part are you glad about? If it's the first half, then—"

"The second half. About not borrowing vibrators."

"Too bad." He winked at her. "If you want to come back into the living room, I've lit your fire."

She couldn't help laughing. "You're incorrigible."

"So I've been told." In silent invitation, he swept an arm toward the door into the living room.

She walked in and discovered that he'd refilled their wineglasses and set them on the coffee table in front of the sofa. She'd halfway expected that he'd have one of the X-rated movies on the flat screen, but it was dark. Maybe he was saving that for later.

"Thank you for the fire." She took off her coat, gloves, and hat.

"I enjoy pleasing you."

She didn't miss the underlying message in that statement, either. After walking into the kitchen and laying her things over a chair, she sat down to unlace her boots.

"Need some help with that?"

"Thanks. I've got it." She paid attention to the damp laces this time so she didn't knot them again. "You've completely abandoned the idea of taking the high road, haven't you?"

"Completely." He sounded unrepentant about it, too. "You're free to battle your conscience if you want to, but mine is clear. We didn't choose to be marooned here together in a cozy cabin with a mirrored bed, and the whole setup has a sense of inevitability to it."

"That's one way to look at it." She pulled off the first boot. And she'd been guilty of having that same view minutes ago.

"Here's another way. I also see this night as a chance to find a meeting place, a middle ground, perhaps, between our two warring factions."

"Now, that's delusional." She pulled off the second boot and glanced over at him. He stood with his back to the fire, his hands shoved into the pockets of his slacks and his powerful shoulders caressed by the flickering light of the flames. He reminded her of a Celtic god who had touched down on earth to bestow his magnificent gifts on a mere mortal.

"Why is it delusional?" His brogue might be the sexiest thing about him, but it topped a long list.

She took off her socks and draped them over the back of the chair, too. "Because there is no middle ground. You're either in favor of Weres mating with humans or you're not."

He regarded her quietly for a moment. "Or to state it

another way, you're either moving forward into the future or you're stuck in the past."

"Or, to state it another way, you're either recklessly endangering your species or you're protecting it from harm and potential extinction." She stood. "Where's your middle ground now, Duncan?"

"Good question." Amazingly, he didn't seem angry at all. "It might be located on that king-sized mattress in there."

"Does it all come down to sex, then?"

He looked thoughtful for a moment, and then he nodded. "It might, at that. It's a concept to be considered. But I'd rather expand on it and include love. The sexual urge is as old as humans and werewolves. So is the urge to connect on a deeper level that goes beyond physical desire. Weres have always wanted a connection with humans. And humans connect with Weres all the time in business, friendship, and sex. They just don't know it." He chuckled. "Damn, I should write this blather down. It's somewhat brilliant."

She couldn't help laughing. They were poles apart in their philosophy, but he was the most entertaining Were she'd encountered in a long time. An unwelcome thought came to her. Would he be half as interesting if they agreed on everything?

Surely that couldn't be part of his appeal. When she finally found her soul mate, he would share her beliefs, and that would be one of the many bonds connecting them. Yet in cruising through the profiles on Furthebest. com, she'd found dozens of Weres who shared her beliefs.

She'd told herself that time constraints had prevented her from contacting any of them. But if she'd been motivated to connect with a like-minded Were, she would have found the time. Could it be that if they agreed with her, she was bored? She hoped not.

"Are you coming over to sit by the fire, then?" Anticipation glowed in his eyes.

She fought the pull of his sexuality. Instinct told her that once she joined him on that sofa, the battle to keep him at arm's length would be over. A warm fire, a glass of wine, soft upholstery, and a hard Were—difficult to resist a combination like that.

"Maybe we should post on Sniffer again, first." She turned back to the kitchen table, picked up her phone, and hit the power button.

"Aye, perhaps we should." His tone was indulgent, as if he knew she was only delaying the inevitable. "Would you mind bringing my phone over?"

"Sure." As she reached for his phone, she glanced at her screen and grinned. "Angela Sapworthy says the cabin score is two–one, my favor."

"How did she come to that conclusion?"

"I guess because I posted two zingers and you only posted one." She carried his phone into the living room, rounded the sofa, and handed it to him.

He gave her a pained look. "I didn't plan on anyone keeping score."

"You should have. Don't you suppose they're making bets on whether we strangle each other before the night is over?"

Understanding sharpened his gaze. "You're right, lass, and that's exactly what we want them to be doing. Our cover story is pretending that we've been fighting ever since we first laid eyes on each other."

"But I thought you were all about love and cooperation?" She perched on the sofa.

"I am, but we're not ready for that, yet. Your Howlers are making that transition difficult if not downright impossible."

"Good! That's our mission!" She tapped quickly on her phone's keyboard. "And the score is now three–one, so you'd better step up the pace, Woofer."

Duncan had never met such an infuriating and sexually exciting female in his life. Nothing was simple with her, and that aroused him in ways that he hadn't believed possible. He wanted her surrender, naturally. He was desperate for it, in fact. Yet by God, the battle was almost as sweet as he imagined her surrender would be.

Powering up his phone, he remained standing by the fire as he waited for Sniffer to load.

She tapped away on yet another post. "Four–one," she announced in a triumphant voice.

That note of triumph charged up his libido. It had done so all summer, apparently, and now he was reaping the result of months of online foreplay.

Consulting his screen, he read the first of her two posts. *Duncan MacDowell enjoys looking into mirrors. #egotoobigforcabin*

She was bloody cheeky. Perversely, that was what he enjoyed about her. She was already posting another Sniff as he turned his attention to the next one: *Duncan MacDowell expects everyone to sing the same song—his, of course. #preferHOWLing*

And a third popped up. *Addendum to previous Sniff. His song out of tune, but what can you expect when he can only WOOF? #harmonioushowler*

With a grim smile, Duncan responded. *Kate Stillman*

is laced up way too tight. Tends to get tied in knots. #1loosewoofer

He didn't stop with one Sniff, though. If Angela Sapworthy was keeping score, he needed to win one for the Woofers. So he typed out *Kate Stillman should see an optometrist. She and the Howlers have tunnel vision.* #far sightedwoofer

Kate was reeling off more Sniffs, too. He ignored hers and kept typing. Another post, and another, and another. His eyes ached from staring at the tiny keys and the small screen.

"Enough!"

He looked up.

Kate had flopped back onto the sofa and closed her eyes. "This is insane. We should quit before we both end up with terminal carpal tunnel."

The sight of her lying against the sofa cushions with her arms flung out stirred him more than a little, but he didn't trust her not to be using exhaustion as a tactic. "You're just saying that because you want to quit while you're ahead."

She opened her eyes, and there was a definite gleam there. "Am I ahead?"

"I think that's an excellent guess considering that you're trying to talk me into quitting."

Mischief danced in those blue eyes. "Okay, I'm one ahead of you. I didn't expect you to catch up so fast, or to keep going this long. Aren't you supposed to be jet-lagged?"

"I *am* jet-lagged, which makes my performance in this contest that much more impressive."

"Braggart."

"Sneak. You thought I'd take pity on you because you're too tired to go on. Well, I'm posting one more Sniff to tie it up. If you really want to quit, then don't post again. Because if you do, I will."

"How much battery do you have left?"

"None of your bloody business." But her question made him think her phone was about to die. He glanced at his and realized that his was also in bad shape. "What do you say, milady? Will you allow me to tie the game so we can give up this crazy enterprise, drink some wine, and enjoy the fire?"

She pursed her lips. "Depends on what you plan to say."

How he wanted to toss the phone aside, go over there, and kiss that saucy mouth of hers. "Tell you what. I'll show it to you before I send it. How's that?"

"All right."

He composed what he hoped was his final Sniff of the night, because he would dearly love to stop doing this and move on to other things, like kissing her until neither of them could think straight. *Kate Stillman is misguided, but she's a worthy opponent. #tiredoftyping*

"Let me see it." She held out her hand.

Walking over, he settled his phone in her outstretched palm and allowed his hand to brush hers. He felt that slight contact right down to his bare toes. He took note that her toes had curled a little, too, and he hoped that was all his fault.

She read the post. "How about taking out the misguided part and just saying I'm a worthy opponent? Would you do that?"

He noticed how sexy she looked sprawled on the sofa, considered the two glasses of wine on the coffee table, and made his decision. "Go ahead. Fix it."

"You'd trust me to do that for you?"

He shrugged. "If you sabotage that post, then I suppose I'll just have to send another one labeling you a dirty player."

"Yeah, you would, too."

"Damn right I would."

Her fingers moved over the keys. "Okay, it's sent. And you have almost no battery left." She held out the phone.

He took it, once again making sure that he touched her soft skin in the process. When he checked the post that came through, it merely said that she was a worthy opponent. She hadn't tricked him.

He glanced up. "I'm going to shut this down. I think there's enough battery left to make a quick phone call if we need to. How about you?"

She smiled at him. "Mine's totally dead."

She'd tricked him, after all. "So I could have won. You would have been literally powerless to stop me if I'd decided to break the tie."

She sat up and reached for her wine. "I don't ever consider myself powerless." She gazed at him over the rim of her glass as she sipped from it.

His groin tightened. "I don't suppose you do. Remind me never to underestimate your power." He busied himself with the fire and decided against adding another log. If the rest of the evening went as he hoped, he wanted this particular fire to die down while a different sort was created under the mirrored canopy.

When at last he joined her on the sofa, he left a civilized distance between them. Cozying up to her right away would lack finesse. He hadn't used much of that when he'd kissed her earlier, so he intended his present approach to be more subtle. Her surrender would be more complete if she came to him. He wasn't sure whether she would.

For the first time in his life, he lusted after a female who was as smart—well, probably smarter than he was. He picked up his wineglass. "Do you suppose we can come up with a toast we agree on, or should we just drink the damn wine and forget about toasting anything?"

"Oh, I think we need a toast." She lifted her glass. "To worthy opponents."

"You consider me a worthy opponent, as well?" That pleased him.

She looked into his eyes. "I do. I confess I enjoy matching wits with you."

"Glad to hear it, because I enjoy matching wits with you. To worthy opponents." He touched his glass to hers and drank.

"I suppose that round of Sniffs will keep Angela Sapworthy busy for a while." Kate took another swallow of her wine.

"I'm sure she'll be dissecting every word for hidden meanings and innuendos."

"But I think we established our mutual antagonism and dedication to our respective causes, don't you?"

"If we didn't, we gave it a good try." He wasn't sure where she was going with her comments, but she might be headed exactly where he wanted her. Anticipation fizzed in his veins.

"Before my phone died, I checked the time." Gazing into the fire, she raised her glass and took another sip.

"And?" Bedtime was what he was thinking.

"And it's morning already in Scotland." She glanced over at him. "You've put up a brave front, but I have to believe you're dead on your feet. I think you should go into that bedroom and get some sleep."

"I agree with some of that statement."

"I'll take the sofa, and—"

"Hold on a minute, there, lass. I think you took a wrong turn. You'll not be bedding down on the sofa. If anyone does, it'll be me."

"That makes no sense. I'm smaller and will fit better. Besides that, I didn't just travel halfway around the world."

"So I'm to go into the bedroom and get some sleep and leave you here on the sofa to do the same." It wasn't going to happen like that, but he wanted to be clear about what she'd said.

She nodded. "It's the intelligent thing to do, and I know you're smart, Duncan. You'll have a big day tomorrow, and because I consider you a worthy opponent, I want you to be at your best. I don't want you stumbling around because you're tired."

"I'd think it would suit your purposes if I'm not up to par."

"Not really. I don't want attendees to start agreeing with your position because your dedication in the face of exhaustion turns you into a hero. I want this fight to be even."

"What if my ability to function is compromised by extreme sexual frustration?"

She laughed. "Nice try. But I'm sure you can subdue your sexual urges in order to be an effective leader in the morning, especially if you get some sleep."

Now it was his turn to drink his wine and stare into the fire. He wondered if she played chess. She'd be good at it if she did. She'd neatly maneuvered him into a corner. He could either walk into that bedroom alone and prove that he placed duty ahead of his appetites, or he would have to admit that he didn't give a hang about duty and had no control over his impulses.

Although he didn't care for either course of action, he had little choice. He had to agree to sleep in that bed—with its red hangings, fluffy pillows, and overhead mirror—without her.

Draining his glass, he stood. "You'll need pillows and blankets. God knows that bed has pillows to spare, and an extra blanket or two must be stored somewhere."

"So you agree to my plan?" She stroked the stem of her wineglass.

He really wished she wouldn't do that, especially now that they wouldn't be rolling around on that big bed together. "I agree with your plan. I don't like it, but you make a valid point about the conference beginning tomorrow. I owe it to my followers to be—"

"That's all I needed to know." Setting her wineglass on the coffee table, she also stood. "You've passed my personal test, Duncan MacDowell. You placed duty to your cause ahead of your immediate personal desire, and I admire that."

"Aye, but admiration is cold comfort when—"

"What do you say we enjoy the best of both worlds?"

He stared at her with no idea of what was coming next. "How?"

"Let's occupy that big bed together. We'll have some fun and then we'll sleep. How does that sound?"

His heart slammed against his ribs. "Good." He was amazed that he had the power of speech. "It sounds good."

No question about it, she was definitely smarter than

he was. But it didn't matter if she was a certified genius. She hadn't had sex in more than a year, and when it came to giving a female pleasure, he'd pit his skills against those of any male, Were or human. Very soon, the scales would be balanced.

She glanced at the fireplace where embers still glowed. "We should bank the fire."

"Aye. I'll do it." And he'd take a moment to rein himself in, as well. She'd invited him to share a bed with her, but if he rushed the process, he could still ruin the experience for both of them. "You go ahead. I'll tend to the fire and turn off the lights."

Her eyes taunted him with the promise of heaven. "I'll be waiting."

He clenched his fists to keep from grabbing her as she turned and walked into the bedroom. "I won't be long."

Chapter 6

**WERECON 2012:
STILLMAN, MACDOWELL CREATE
SNIFFER BLITZ**

**Exclusive *Wereworld Celebrity Watch* report
by Angela Sapworthy**

DENVER—WereCon2012 attendees are buzzing about the recent outpouring of Sniffs from the smart phones of WOOF leader Duncan MacDowell and HOWL leader Kate Stillman. As reported here earlier, Stillman and MacDowell remain trapped in a cabin during the killer storm that continues to buffet the Denver area.

Those Sniffs indicate the antagonism between the rivals is at the boiling point! Stillman accused MacDowell of having a gigantic ego. In response, MacDowell Sniffed, *Kate Stillman is laced too tight.* This reporter spoke with Kate's cousin Neil Stillman, who has known Kate all her life.

"My cousin means well," he said. "But Mac-Dowell's right. It's like Kate has a corset around her mind when it comes to progress. She needs to wake up and realize that change is coming, and my great-aunt, Elizabeth Stillman, agrees with me. I pity MacDowell being stuck in that cabin with her, because she can be a handful. I have the childhood scars to prove it!"

Meanwhile the Howlers rally around their leader and congratulate her on her barrage of Sniffs. Even though the Sniffer battle ended in a tie, Howlers claim victory after MacDowell sent the final Sniff acknowledging that Stillman is a "worthy opponent." His grudging respect demonstrates the class we all expect from that hunky Were!

In related news, sources have revealed that Kate Stillman's popular dating site Furthebest .com was down for several hours today and hackers are the suspected cause. Howlers have been quick to blame Woofers for the apparent sabotage, but Woofers deny all knowledge of the incident.

This reporter is on the edge of her seat as the battle between Howlers and Woofers begins in earnest tomorrow morning! Will Kate Stillman and Duncan MacDowell be in attendance? And will they be in one piece? Watch this space! Or follow me on Sniffer @newshound.

Kate held herself together until she was inside the bedroom. Then she hurried on through and into the bathroom. After turning on the light, she closed the door, braced both hands against the tile counter, and gasped for air.

She'd wanted Duncan to think she was in control of the situation, but in reality she felt like a rookie driver at her first Indy 500. She was not a virginal Were by any means, but she'd never encountered the likes of Duncan MacDowell.

From that first kiss she'd known how much he wanted her, and yet despite the lure of the fantasy bed, he'd been willing to give up sex for his cause. Until that moment, she hadn't been sure how tonight would end. But his sense of honor had seduced her far more effectively than broad shoulders and a dazzling smile. His reluctant sacrifice had tipped the scales.

So now she'd said yes to him, and she was shaking like a leaf, both from nerves and lust. So far she'd held her own by playing mental games. But she couldn't forget that his jet-lagged brain must be operating at half power. She'd been lucky to catch him at a disadvantage.

She had the distinct feeling that once their clothes were off and they'd climbed into that bed draped with red velvet, her advantage would disappear. His sexual prowess wouldn't be affected by jet lag. He'd fall back on his natural abilities that he'd honed while making love to dozens of females, both Were and human.

He might assume that she was equally worldly because of all the sexual tips she'd offered in her book, but she'd gathered those tips by interviewing other female Weres. Only a few of the suggestions came from personal experience. Now was not the time to confess that.

But like the rookie at the Indy 500, she was eager for the race to start. Now that she'd decided to go for it, she acknowledged that having this private time with Duncan in a cabin designed for passion was an opportunity that would never come again. If she'd passed it up, which she'd come close to doing, she might have regretted it for the rest of her life.

As she opened the door and walked back into the bedroom, she heard him shoveling ash over the remaining embers in the fireplace. She wanted him to be thorough because the last thing they needed to do was cause more damage to the Stewarts' love nest.

Although she'd automatically flipped on the chandelier when she'd first rushed in, it created far more illumination than she was comfortable giving to this scene. How odd that the Stewarts had installed a dimmer switch in the kitchen and none in here.

She turned off the chandelier, but there was no alternative, no little bedside reading lamps to give a subdued effect. Perhaps the Stewarts didn't read in bed because they had more interesting things to do there.

Eventually she settled on using the bathroom light and closed the door so only a sliver peeked through. Better. Next she stripped off her clothes, doing it quickly because she wanted to be in bed and under the covers when Duncan came in. Considering the boldness with which she'd suggested this rendezvous, she should greet him with the chandelier blazing while she lounged naked on the bed.

She wished she possessed that kind of daring. It would make him do a double take, and she'd love to see him at a loss for words once again. That moment in the living room when she'd suggested they share the bed had been a real triumph.

But she feared that she couldn't pull off a stunt like greeting him wearing nothing but the rainbows given off by the crystal chandelier. And if she couldn't do it without blushing and trembling, then she didn't want to attempt it at all.

Besides, even though they'd turned up the heat, the cabin was still on the cool side. Presenting herself naked in chandelier light would lose its effectiveness if she was also covered in goose bumps. Consequently, the moment her clothes were off, she dived under the covers, scattering pillows and gasping at the icy feel of the sheets against her warm skin.

Then she rolled to her back, pulled the covers to her chin, and waited, her heartbeat drumming in her ears. Her breathing seemed exceptionally loud, too. She tried taking shallower breaths, but that made her feel dizzy.

Lights flicked out in the other room, and footsteps approached. She held her breath and then caught herself doing it when she grew light-headed again. Passing out wouldn't be a good move right now.

He appeared in the doorway, his impressive bulk in shadow. "Why are you lying here in the dark, lass?"

Good question. By doing so, she'd revealed herself as a nervous Nellie, after all. "I, um, thought the chandelier was a little bright for sleeping."

"I suppose it is bright for sleeping." He flipped the switch. "But when I'm making love, I like to see what I'm doing. Unless . . ." He crossed to the bed and gazed down at her. "Unless you're a wee bit shy, perhaps? You've pulled the covers right up to your chin."

"I was cold." But she wasn't now. His hot gaze had an amazing effect and now she was sweltering under the weight of the blankets. She felt like throwing them off, but that would give the lie to her excuse, and besides, she wasn't a ta-da kind of lover. She was more of the slowly reveal-herself kind.

"Ah." He nodded as if accepting her story. "Let's see

if I can do something about that." And he began pulling off his clothes.

His sweater came first, then the T-shirt under it. His chest, lightly furred with dark hair, expanded as he drew in a deep breath. The more he took off, the higher the temperature climbed under the covers.

"It's always a little nerve-racking the first time with someone new." He unfastened his slacks and took those off, leaving him standing by the bed in knit boxers. The material was stretched over an impressive erection.

Kate thought she'd go up in flames. She felt damp all over, but she was more than damp between her thighs. As she shifted restlessly, she felt the slippery wetness created by watching Duncan disrobe. Her pulse beat frantically as she waited for him to slide off those knit boxers.

He paused, his thumbs in the waistband. "I just remembered something out of your book. You suggest taking each other's clothes off and doing it slowly, so you each get used to being naked with someone new."

"It's only—" She stopped to clear her throat. "Only a suggestion."

"I know, but it seemed like a good one, and without thinking, I've gone and stripped off everything except my boxers. Maybe I should wait on those."

"That's okay." She still sounded like a frog. And she wanted those boxers off ASAP.

"Did you leave on anything for me to take off?"

"No. And you can take off—"

"But see, you removed your clothes and then covered yourself up again. You might have been cold, but you also might have been hoping to take nakedness in stages, like in your book."

She could see that he was hung up on her damned book, so finally she found the courage to do what she should have done when he'd turned on the light. She threw back the covers.

His eyes widened. "Oh, lass." His tone was reverent. "My bonnie lass."

"Please take off your boxers," she murmured.

"With pleasure." He shoved them down and kicked them away.

The blood roared in her ears and she forgot to breathe. Of course he was large. She'd expected that. But she'd never seen such elegant proportions. Released from bondage, his penis thrust forward, anchored in swirls of dark hair. As if carved from marble laced with faint blue veins, it radiated power. Beneath it, in perfect symmetry, hung his testicles. They tightened under her heated gaze.

"I like what I see in your eyes, milady."

She looked up. "And what do you see there?"

"Lust. Anticipation." He settled a knee on the bed. "Much as I'm feeling, I'll wager, when I look at you." His glance swept her from head to toe and his lips curved. "I don't think you're shy anymore."

"No." She reached for him. "Come closer. Let me touch you."

"'Tis all I've been wishing for, to touch and be touched." He moved onto the bed and stretched out, his body close enough to feel his heat, but not yet entwined with hers. "Well, and perhaps a bit more. But let's begin with that. Let's explore."

She smiled. "You read that in my book."

"I did." Resting his head on a pillow, he cupped her face in one large hand. "And I confess that when I read that, I imagined exploring your body, Kate."

"That's quite a confession." Desire sizzled through her as he trailed his fingers along the curve of her throat and caressed her bare shoulder. She followed his lead, brushing her fingertips over the bristles on his jaw.

When he smiled, his teeth were very white against the darkness of his beard. "Are you disarmed by my honesty?"

"Yes, but I'm also disarmed by other things about you."

"Do tell."

"I don't know if that's wise. We both know you have a large ego." She moved her hand slowly down his corded neck and over to his muscled shoulder.

"You've deflated it quite a bit in the past few hours." He laughed softly as he stroked downward and cradled her breast. "While inflating another part of me beyond endurance."

"You were planning to endure. You . . ." She lost her train of thought as he slowly massaged her breast. "Mm."

"Lovely sound, that." He teased her nipple with the pad of his thumb. "I've wanted to touch you ever since you took off your red coat and I saw your breasts outlined under that black angora."

She gripped his shoulder and closed her eyes as his caress made her quiver. "I thought it started with the book," she murmured.

He slid his hand down her rib cage and brushed his knuckles lightly over her tummy. "I think it started with your first post on my blog."

She opened her eyes and gazed into his. "Really? When I called you a pigheaded radical with your head up your ass?"

He smiled at her. "Aye."

"You read that and wanted to get me naked?"

"Aye. You're passionate in your beliefs." His caress moved lower, teasing her moist curls with the very tips of his fingers. "That's very sexy. I thought you'd be passionate in other ways, too."

Anticipation made her breathe faster. She knew his destination and she yearned for his touch there. Desperately she tried to keep track of what he was saying. It could be important, but oh . . . if he would only . . .

She squeezed her eyes shut again. "So you came to Denver knowing that you intended to—"

"Nay. Don't think that." Those clever fingers danced along her inner thigh, tracing patterns in the moisture there. "I didn't admit any of it to myself. I only thought I was learning all I could about the enemy. It's only now that I understand why I was so fascinated by you."

That helped. She gazed at him, needing to reassure herself that this wasn't the endgame of some elaborate scheme to seduce the leader of the Howlers.

"I'm not that kind of Were, Kate. I hope you believe me." His touch became less random. The pad of his middle finger sought out her most sensitive spot.

When he made contact, she gasped. "You're . . . very persuasive."

"Passion drew me to you." He began a slow, deliberate massage of that trigger point. "And I think . . . it drew you to me."

She moaned softly. "Duncan . . ."

"We have that in common, lass." His touch remained slow but relentless as he built her response with a single-mindedness that unraveled all her defenses.

"Yes." She trembled as her body prepared for the climax he was creating with only the pad of one finger and the music of his brogue.

"Whatever happens, the passion will still be there. There are no factions here. Just us."

"Yes." Her breath caught as the first wave hit. *"Yes."* The explosion came, wracking her body as if he'd covered every inch of it with his kisses.

And then he did cover her with kisses. Moving over her, he touched down with his mouth and tongue on her breasts, her arms, and her thighs as she shook with pleasure. Last of all, he held her hips still, parted her thighs, and buried that elegant cock deep within her.

As he thrust with the same deliberate surety he'd used when touching her with only one finger, a second wave gathered. She rose to meet him stroke for stroke and reached for the glory he seemed so willing to bestow on her.

His breathing roughened. "Look up," he said, panting.

She'd forgotten the mirror. Gazing above their heads, she watched in fascination as the muscles of his back, buttocks, and thighs propelled him forward again and again. They were both covered in rainbows, but he more than her. Seeing him ravish her so thoroughly while she felt each powerful thrust brought her quickly to the brink of total surrender.

Arching up against him, she cried out his name as her world shattered into a million pieces of rainbow-colored crystal. Through eyes glazed with pleasure, she watched him rock forward once more before he groaned and his big body shuddered in the grip of his own orgasm. His spasms rippled within her as he filled her with liquid warmth.

Gasping for breath, she continued to gaze upward. She made herself concentrate on the image of their bodies locked together while colored light caressed their skin. So beautiful. This moment would never come again, and when she relived it in the years ahead, she wanted to remember every detail.

Duncan remembered little after experiencing a climax so outstanding that it nearly left him unconscious with the pleasure of it. When he woke up, he stretched as happily as any Were would who'd had great sex the night before. Then he sat up with a start.

He was alone in the bed. Light spilling in the doorway from the other room, the smell of coffee brewing, and a slit of gray light showing under the bedroom window blinds told him morning had arrived, but he had no sense of what time it was. There was no clock in the room, which was logical because the Stewarts wouldn't want to worry about the time as they frolicked in their red-draped bed.

Guilt hit him as he realized that Kate must have gotten up to turn out the light sometime after he'd fallen asleep. He sure as hell hadn't done it. He only hoped she hadn't had to shove his nearly lifeless body off her in order to climb out of bed.

Although he thought the lovemaking had gone well, he wasn't proud of his follow-up performance. A good lover, especially when in human form, needed to stay awake after the event. He should cuddle, murmur sweet nothings, and then get up to turn out the bloody light if necessary.

He should not become comatose, and he certainly shouldn't become comatose while still lying on top of the poor female whose lungs were being crushed by his weight. Duncan was very afraid he might have done exactly that. In addition, he'd probably snored like a chain saw.

With a groan of remorse, he swung his feet to the floor, where he expected to find his clothes lying scattered about. They weren't there. Apparently she'd tidied up after him, too. He had some apologies to make.

"Good morning, sunshine." Kate appeared in the doorway wearing a white bathrobe that was way too big for her. Her hair was piled on top of her head in a fetching way, and with the light behind her, she looked very much like an angel with a halo. She held a mug in both hands, and from the scent of it, she was bringing coffee.

A rush of warmth in the area of his heart told him she'd begun carving out a place there. He was ridiculously glad to see her. Images came back to him, of Kate with the covers pulled up to her chin and a nervous light in her eyes. He smiled as he remembered how her expression had changed as he took off his clothes.

And then . . . then she'd flung back the blankets to reveal a blond goddess even more stunning than he'd expected, and he'd expected quite a bit. But he'd rewarded her by going right to sleep after the sex. "Good morning, Kate. Listen, I'm sorry about—"

"I can't imagine what you have to be sorry about. Are you a coffee drinker or a tea drinker?"

"Either, but coffee's my preference."

"How do you like it?"

"Delivered by a bonnie lass in a gigantic white bathrobe."

Although her face was in shadow, there was a smile in her voice. "Then this is your lucky day. But I meant, do you like it black or with sugar? If you want cream, there's only the powdered stuff, and personally I don't think that's worth the bother."

"Black will do nicely."

"Then here you go." She walked over and handed him the warm mug.

"Perfect. Thanks." He took a sip. "Ah, that helps. By the way, do you happen to know where my clothes are?"

"Everything except your slacks is in the dryer. I found a little stackable unit behind some folding doors in the bathroom. I've already run everything through the washer."

"I slept through all that?"

"You were very tired. Oh, and don't worry. I checked the label on your sweater before I threw it in, but those slacks need to be dry-cleaned."

"And so my slacks are where?" They might be slightly uncomfortable without his boxers, but he wanted to put something on. He'd never been a fan of walking around the house naked.

"Hanging up, but you don't want those yet. They'll be scratchy without the boxers. There's another bathrobe in the closet. Let me get it." Crossing the room, she opened a closet door and pulled out a robe identical to hers.

"They must belong to the Stewarts."

"I'm sure they do, but no worries. We can wash these after our clothes are dry. I'm planning to do the sheets, too." She handed him the robe. "Go ahead and put this on. I've found instant oatmeal we can eat for breakfast." She started out of the room.

"Kate, hold on a minute."

She turned back to him. "Yes?"

"I behaved like a clod last night. You were wonderful, and instead of staying awake to tell you so, I conked out. Did I . . . did I fall asleep while I was still . . ."

"Over, around, and inside me? Yes, you did."

He winced. "Did I snore?"

"Horrendously."

"Damn, that's unforgivable."

"No, it's extremely forgivable." She walked back over and laid her hand on his chest. "I lay there looking up at the mirror while you slept. And snored. I felt your steady heartbeat and I . . . I was simply glad to be there."

He covered her hand with his and pressed it close. "But I weigh twice as much as you."

"At least. So eventually I couldn't breathe and I had to wiggle out from under you. But the feeling of closeness was nice while it lasted."

Curling his fingers around her hand, he raised it to his lips. "Thank you for putting a romantic gloss on my sorry lack of consideration." Her sweet description reminded him of the joy of loving her, which produced a predictable response in his nether regions. "Perhaps I can make it up to you this morning."

"I wish you could." She sighed. "And don't think I haven't thought of it, because I kept hoping you'd wake up sooner so that maybe . . ."

"I wish you'd woken me."

"I did shake you once, but you just moaned and rolled over."

"Damn it. You should have banged a couple of pans together beside my ear. I would have been glad to wake up so I could make love to you again."

She shook her head. "I couldn't do it. You needed your sleep. That was my whole point last night, so forcing you to wake up so you could have sex with me wouldn't reflect very well on my character, now, would it?"

"There's such a thing as being too conscientious." But he respected her values, all the same. "What time is it, anyway?"

"It's nearly seven. The snow has stopped, and the plows will be here before you know it."

"Seven? Really? The conference starts in two hours!"

"That's right, and in order to get this place cleaned up, we'll have to be late, but maybe not too late."

"So that's it." He hadn't expected to feel such deep disappointment that their private interlude was over.

"That's it." She stood on tiptoe and kissed his cheek. "And I'll never forget this time we've had. Now drink your coffee and grab a shower. I found an electric razor and left it on the counter for you. We have to get moving." Slipping her hand from his, she hurried out of the bedroom.

Although her tone had been brisk and businesslike, he suspected from her earlier description of how she'd felt last night that she was as sad about leaving the cabin as he was. But neither of them could let the world know their private feelings for each other. He'd be the most help to her if he adopted her brisk manner from here on out.

He would bloody well do that, even if it killed him. Hurrying through a shave and shower, he put on the robe. The other robe had been huge on Kate and this one was small on him. He wondered if she'd put on the large size in her haste.

No matter. He turned on the light and began stripping the bed. She might think because he lived in a castle and had servants that he didn't know how. He could strip a bed with the best of them. He wasn't sure how good he'd be at making it back up again, but she'd be around to help with that.

After he pulled off the sheets, he held them to his nose and inhaled the sweet scent of making love to Kate. He couldn't seem to accept that it would never happen again. Surely there would be some way that they could—

"Duncan, can I turn on your phone and call the lodge?"

"Sure, go ahead." He dumped the sheets in the bathroom and walked out into the main area of the cabin.

She was talking on his phone while she stirred something in a pan, no doubt the oatmeal. He guessed she'd called her grandmother. "Sure, we'll be ready in about an hour if you can spare . . . Okay. We'll be watching for them. See you soon." She disconnected. "She's sending a couple of snowmobiles down to get us. She tried to call my cell earlier, but of course it's dead."

"Is there enough battery on mine to check Sniffer? We might as well get briefed on what's being said so we don't get blindsided when we head into the conference."

"Good idea. Let's at least try." She tapped on the phone and gazed at the screen. When she glanced up at him, her expression was bleak. "I can't blame you for this, because you didn't start it, but your Woofers have decided to play hardball."

"Kate, I can't believe they sabotaged your dating site. I know it looks bad, but—"

"It's not about the site. They want to know if you used this time while we were trapped together to get all the dirt on my sister."

He gazed at her with a sinking sensation in his gut. He'd avoided this topic on his blog, and he'd been criticized for doing so. In his view, no one should have to answer for the actions of family members. "I'm sorry, Kate. I've never encouraged that discussion."

"I know." She faced him, her expression resolute. "But maybe we needed this to come up to remind us that the battle could get ugly, and we're on different sides."

"I don't feel that way, now."

"You should, Duncan. It's still true, regardless of what happened between us."

He swallowed. "It may be true, but it doesn't have to ruin what we've shared."

"I'll try my best not to let that happen." She handed him the phone.

"Me, too, lass." But as he read the posts, he wondered if they could possibly hold on to the fragile connection they'd forged in that mirrored bed.

Chapter 7

Sniffer Update: @newshound—*What's the story on Penelope Stillman, Kate's older sister? Kate's not talking.* *#skeletoninthecloset*

Kate and Duncan didn't bring up the subject of Penny again, but it hung between them as they ate a quick breakfast, finished up the laundry, and put the cabin and themselves into some semblance of order. The snowmobiles arrived to carry Kate and Duncan separately to the resort.

The staff members driving them agreed to come back for Duncan's suitcase and arrange to have Kate's SUV towed out of the snowbank. Kate used a staffer's phone to call a reputable window company, and the Stillman name got her an appointment for that afternoon. She wasn't sure whether she'd be able to get away from the conference, but the spare key was in her purse if she had to delegate that job.

As the two snowmobiles skimmed over the unblemished snow left behind by the blizzard, the clouds moved off to display a sky so blue it hurt Kate's eyes to look at it. She thought of all the times she and her sister had ridden like this after a storm. Penny, being ten years older, had always been the driver, while Kate was the passenger hanging on for dear life. She hadn't minded at all.

She'd felt privileged that her big sister, glamorous and daring in all things, had wanted her along. Everyone knew that Grandma Elizabeth was grooming Penny to be the next Stillman pack alpha. Their father, Woodruff, sweet though he was, didn't suit, so Grandma Elizabeth was looking to the next generation for a Were to inherit her position. Penny, magnificent Penny, had been the obvious choice.

And then, when Kate was seventeen, Penny had fallen in love . . . with a human. She'd given up everything for him—her family, her position as leader in training, and any hope of inheriting the Stillman millions. But saddest of all, she'd given up her close tie with Kate, the sister who'd idolized her from childhood.

Penny had explained that frequent contact with her Were family would increase the chances that her human husband would stumble upon the truth. Then, assuming he didn't reject her in horror, he would be responsible for keeping the volatile secret. The human community in which she lived had no idea that Weres existed, and they might react violently if they found out.

At first Kate had grieved along with the other members of her family and her pack. But eventually she'd dried her tears and dedicated her life to preventing such tragedies from happening in the future. She'd created her Web site, Furthebest.com, designed to promote the value of Were-Were matchups. She'd founded Honoring Our Werewolf Legacy, and she'd written her book.

Because Penny had dropped out of the Were community entirely, some Weres didn't even remember that she existed. She and her human mate, Tom Rivers, had adopted two human children. Penny had claimed that she had a blood disorder and Tom had apparently accepted that as reason enough to adopt. But Penny was only making sure that she had no biological offspring who might turn out to be Were, which would expose her and them.

As far as the pack was concerned, Penny might as well be dead. Except she wasn't, and somebody in the Woofer movement had decided to make an issue of the fact that Kate Stillman, founder of HOWL, had a sister who'd mated with a human. Kate had dreaded the possibility that someday Penny's name would be mentioned in connection with the Howler movement, but until now, it hadn't been.

She'd gathered from Duncan's reaction that he'd known about Penny, maybe for some time. That only increased her respect for him. He'd known and he hadn't used the information to try to tarnish her cause. But he couldn't control his followers, and someone had decided the time was right to drag Penny and her choice back into the spotlight in an attempt to embarrass Kate.

Well, let them. Much as she loved Penny, she considered her an object lesson in how human-Were mating generated pain and dysfunction. Penny's mate and her adopted children had no idea that they were living with a werewolf. Kate couldn't imagine how a true bond could develop in the face of such a significant deception, but Penny didn't want to burden her husband with the knowledge of her Were nature.

The snowmobiles rounded a curve in the road and

Stillman Lodge, the main structure of the resort, loomed straight ahead. As always, Kate's heart swelled with pride at her first glimpse of the majestic old building that had stood in this spot for more than a hundred years. Built of native stone and weathered cedar, it lifted three stories into the blue sky.

Its solid, enduring bulk was a source of security for Kate, and she imagined it served that purpose for the entire pack. It provided economic security, as well, for the staff consisted entirely of pack members. In days past, the lodge had been open to humans and Weres alike, and Grandma Elizabeth owned a guest book with Teddy Roosevelt's signature on one yellowed page. Teddy had not known, of course, that his hosts had been werewolves.

The lodge's facilities had been expanded, however, when the property was converted into a Were-only resort, one of only two in the world. The other, on a small island off the coast of Washington State, was owned by Duncan's brother, Colin. A Were-only resort could stand in plain sight if it built a reputation for exclusivity.

Humans trying to reserve a room at Stillman Lodge were always told that the resort was booked for months, even years in advance. Kate herself had helped spread the rumor that certain celebrities chose to stay at Stillman Lodge and had requested complete privacy for themselves and their entourage.

This weekend the resort would indeed be hosting celebrities, but of the werewolf variety. Kate had been secretly dazzled by the guest list, which included pack leaders and representatives from around the world. She'd planned to be on hand to greet them all last night, but instead she'd been with Duncan. She didn't regret that particular detour for a second.

She'd requested that her driver take her around in back so she could use a rear entrance and scurry up to her room. She didn't look too rumpled thanks to her laundry project at the cabin, but she wore no makeup and didn't feel particularly pulled together.

Her hope dimmed as she noticed who was standing on the wide walkway leading up to the main entrance. A camera crew filmed Angela Sapworthy interviewing Kate's cousin Neil. Angela's Sniffer tag fit her perfectly. She was a newshound who smelled a story a mile away.

This time, however, she had help from Neil, who'd also inherited the Stillman blond hair and blue eyes. He spotted the snowmobiles and interrupted the interview to come hurrying down the circular drive toward Kate and Duncan.

Kate's driver was forced to stop to avoid running smack into Neil. Kate wouldn't have minded so much. His thinly disguised political ambitions included nudging her out of her spot as Elizabeth's successor so he could have the job. His Woofer leanings didn't help her like him, either, but she had the feeling he'd take whatever side he found politically advantageous.

"Kate, thank God! We were all so worried about you."

"Thanks, Neil." She managed not to roll her eyes. "But we're fine."

"What a blessing." Now that he'd expressed his concern, he walked right past her and held out his hand to Duncan, who'd climbed off the second snowmobile. "Duncan MacDowell. It's an honor, sir."

"Thanks." Duncan shook Neil's hand. "And you are?"

"Oh, sorry. Neil Stillman. Thought you'd recognize me from my profile on the Woofer site. I'm Kate's cousin and Elizabeth Stillman's able assistant."

Kate swallowed her words of protest. Neil wasn't Grandma Elizabeth's assistant, or at least he hadn't been when she'd left yesterday for the airport.

Neil continued to pump Duncan's hand. "Welcome to Stillman Lodge. I've read *Down with Dogma* twice. Brilliant. We're so happy you could make it and that you survived a night with my cousin Kate." He chuckled as if sharing an inside joke. "There's a bunch of Woofers inside waiting to congratulate you on that feat."

Much as Kate wanted to interrupt Neil's ridiculous monologue, she decided that it could serve as a distraction so she could escape and go in the back way as planned. "Ryan." She addressed her snowmobile's driver in a low voice. "Take me to the back entrance as we discussed."

"You got it, Kate." He started off again.

They managed to get partway around the circular drive before Angela Sapworthy blocked their retreat. She'd marshaled her camera crew, as well.

"Kate, may I have a quick word?" Angela usually dressed to startle. Today she'd paired tight silver pants with turquoise boots and a turquoise quilted jacket. Her hair, an improbable shade of red that veered toward magenta, had been waxed and sprayed into a punk style that made Kate think of a scarlet porcupine.

Reminding herself that Angela's tabloid journalism had become all the rage with Weres, Kate squelched the urge to refuse an interview. Even her refusal would become a story or a Sniff, so she might as well try to take control of the news about her. Or about her sister. As she climbed down from the snowmobile, she mentally prepared herself for a question concerning Penny.

Angela motioned to the cameraman and spoke into her handheld mike. "I'm talking now with none other than Kate Stillman, who has just this minute returned from her harrowing adventure. How was your night with Duncan MacDowell, King of the Woofers?"

Kate frowned. "King of the Woofers? When did that happen?"

"I see you're a few Sniffs behind, Kate. When you said he was no prince, his followers crowned him King of the Woofers. Your followers, of course, crowned you Queen of the Howlers. So tell me, does he snore?" Angela's glistening red mouth turned up in a carefully orchestrated smile.

Kate remembered that she had zero makeup on. Oh, well. "I thought I was in the middle of a *Chainsaw Massacre* film festival, Angela. My ears still hurt." She returned the reporter's smug smile.

Angela shuddered prettily. "Dreadful. But then, I'm not surprised. Duncan is such a *beast*." She gave the word plenty of sexual innuendo. "All that testosterone. Sharing a cabin with him must have been an *exhausting* experience."

"You have no idea, Angela. As you can imagine, I'm eager to get back to my suite and freshen up."

"Of course you are. Such an ordeal. Still, I'm sure he's magnificent when he's angry. And you do know how to taunt the beast, Kate."

"He's easier to manage when he's jet-lagged. Now, if you'll excuse me, I really should—"

"One more thing. Have you heard from your sister, Penelope, recently?"

Kate kept her expression and tone of voice carefully neutral. "Yes, of course. We communicate on a regular basis." *Regular* meaning two or three times a year. But she hadn't lied. Penny had sent her a short e-mail last week wishing her good luck with the conference.

That was Penny, always classy. Kate was campaigning against the choice Penny had made, and yet she didn't seem to hold it against her little sister. A familiar ache gripped Kate's heart at the memory of that brief e-mail.

"Woofers have been asking, as I'm sure you would expect, how you can insist that Were-human mating is so terrible when your sister has chosen that route."

"Penelope and I hold different views on the subject. That doesn't mean I love her any less. Now I really must go. The conference has already begun, and I'm expected to be there."

"There's a rumor that Penelope will make an appearance this weekend to support the Woofer cause."

Kate's pulse quickened. Surely not. Penny had dropped out of pack activities completely and distanced herself from her immediate family. God knew what she'd told her husband, Tom, but he must have accepted the estrangement in addition to the invented story about a blood disorder.

The poor guy might even think the rift was his fault because he didn't measure up. In a way, he was right, but it wasn't anything he could fix. Their mother and father would have loved to spend time with Penny, her husband, and her children, as would Kate. But Penny had decided it was safer to minimize all contact.

But Angela was waiting, a gleam of triumph in her heavily made-up eyes, for Kate to respond. Kate gave the only answer that might end this line of questioning.

"I hadn't heard that, but if she comes, I would be happy to see her." She hopped on the snowmobile. "Great talking to you, Angela!"

Ryan responded to that cue and sped off, sending a rooster tail of snow into the air. Kate wondered if some of that snow had landed on Angela. And if the cameraman caught it. She hoped so.

Duncan watched as Kate got caught in Angela Sapworthy's web. At least he assumed that was Angela with the red spiky hair and tight silver pants. He'd never met her in person, but the presence of a camera crew and Kate's obvious reluctance as she climbed down from the snowmobile told him he was right.

He hated seeing Kate waylaid like that, but he couldn't very well go to her rescue. He had his hands full with Neil Stillman, who seemed determined to be his new BFF, as they said in the USA. Climbing off the snowmobile, Duncan thanked the driver and started up the snowy walkway to the main entrance accompanied, inevitably, by Neil.

"Everyone's referring to you as King of the Woofers now," Neil said.

"Everyone?" As a Scotsman, Duncan had a built-in prejudice against the term *king*, which conjured images of British royalty. Centuries had passed, but a true Scotsman never forgot.

"Well, the Woofers, I meant to say. They came up with it after Kate sent the Sniff saying you were no prince. So you've been upgraded."

"That's just silly. I—" A feminine cry of dismay made him turn around. If Angela had caused Kate to cry out like that, he might have to interfere, after all.

But no, Angela was the one who was upset, and covered in snow, to boot. The snowmobile carrying Kate zipped around the corner of the building, but Duncan had no trouble figuring out what had happened. He chuckled.

"That was a bad move on Kate's part," Neil said. "You don't want to make an enemy of Angela Sapworthy."

"I'm sure it was an accident."

"Come on, MacDowell. You just spent more than twelve hours with Kate, so you know what she's like. Think about that for a minute and then tell me her little stunt was an accident."

"She wasn't driving the snowmobile. How could she have engineered that maneuver on purpose?"

Neil studied him. "Surely you're not defending the Queen of the Howlers."

"Of course I'm not, but . . . what did you call her?"

"Once the Howlers found out about your title, they had to give her one. I'm sure she'll love it."

Duncan shook his head. "It's childish. I'm going to put a stop to it."

"Good luck with that. It's all over Sniffer and once something catches on, you can't do much about it. Those titles have taken on a life of their own. I've already seen pictures of each of you with a crown Photoshopped on your head."

"Ridiculous." Duncan sighed. "Well, I suppose I'd better get in there." He started up the walkway again.

"Duncan! Duncan MacDowell!"

His shoulders hunched. Apparently even being covered in snow didn't deter Angela from her appointed rounds.

"Take my advice," Neil said. "Give her a quick interview. She's already leaning toward the Woofer side, and after Kate blasted her with a rooster tail just now, you'll have her eating out of your hand."

"There's an unappealing image."

Neil laughed. "Sorry."

"Duncan, may I have a quick word?"

He turned and did his best to keep a straight face. Angela looked as if she'd been dipped in vanilla frosting. Snow clung to her spiky hair, clustered on her dangly earrings, rested in drifts on the shoulders of her turquoise jacket, and splattered like well-aimed snowballs all over her silver pants.

But to her credit, she retained her poise. "I couldn't let you go inside without one quick interview." She turned to her cameraman and raised her mike. "As you can see, I met with a small accident following my interview with Kate Stillman. She'll be getting the cleaning bill." Angela's laughter had a slight edge to it. "I'm talking now with her counterpart in this battle, Duncan MacDowell, and I'm sorry to tell you he did not arrive in a kilt as I'd hoped. Did you bring your kilt, Duncan?"

"I did, but I won't be wearing it until our formal dinner at the end of the conference."

"Wonderful! I'm sure all the females will be waiting for the moment when they can admire the King of the Woofers in full regalia!"

"Just let me say, Angela, that I'm not comfortable being called a king of anything."

"And he's extremely humble, folks! Is there a sexier combination than a great-looking Were with humility? I think not!"

"Seriously, I would like to ask the Woofers to forgo giving me that title. I—"

"Too late, Duncan. They've already held the coronation. They were positively jubilant at the way you came out fighting during last night's Sniffer exchange. They're also boasting of your gallantry in your last Sniff. Complimenting her on being a worthy opponent made her look ungracious by comparison. At least that's how this reporter sees it." Angela's eyes glittered with malice.

Duncan groaned inwardly. Poor Kate. Her attempt to even the Sniffer score last night had worked against her. Or, if not, Angela Sapworthy would make sure that it did. He began to understand the part Angela would play this weekend, and it wasn't small.

He was in a no-win situation. If he told Angela that he'd wanted to send a more antagonistic post and Kate had talked him into a more civil one, then he'd either arouse suspicion about their relationship or get more points for gallantry. His best bet was to get away from Angela as soon as possible.

"I really should get inside," he said. "I hope they haven't gone ahead with the council elections."

"Of course not. They wouldn't consider having elections without you. Get on in there and claim your place, Duncan MacDowell."

If he hadn't been so irritated with her, he would have laughed. She'd managed to dismiss him rather than the other way around. "Then I'll bid you good-bye." He turned and started up the walkway once again.

"And there he goes, folks. King of the Woofers!"

"Damn it," he muttered, ducking his head.

"Get used to it," Neil said as he opened one of two large and intricately carved entrance doors. "Your subjects await you."

Duncan walked into the lobby and was immediately

surrounded by a crowd of boisterous Weres, both males and females, wearing Woofer buttons and waving Woofer signs. Overwhelmed by the barrage, Duncan didn't read any of the buttons or signs, but he heard the words of welcome. The language was English, the official choice for the conference, but the accents were from all over the world.

As he fought to get his bearings, a female emerged from the crowd bearing a gold crown on a purple velvet pillow. A chant arose from the group. *"King of the Woofers! King of the Woofers!"*

Duncan tried to protest, but he was shouted down. The female Were looked so happy to be presenting him with this crown, which someone must have obtained with a great deal of trouble on such short notice. He couldn't figure out a way to refuse it without crushing her and ruining the mood of the enthusiastic crowd.

And he wanted them all to be enthusiastic. They believed in the cause he held dear, and this weekend he hoped to convince the delegates to adopt a resolution to end the secrecy. Wearing a crown for a few minutes might be the price he had to pay.

Kneeling down, he allowed her to place the crown on his head amid cheers from the group that surrounded him. When he stood again, some instinct made him glance across the lobby. Kate stood there watching the spectacle.

She'd changed into a purple long-sleeved T-shirt with a logo on the front, no doubt the Howler logo. She was too far away for him to gauge her expression, but he could only imagine how she'd react to the idea of him wearing a crown. He wondered whether she'd been offered one yet, and what she would do if she was. Her

gaze locked with his for a brief moment before she
turned away, almost as if signaling that she'd seen
enough.

He had trouble believing that only hours ago he'd
held her naked in his arms while he listened to her cries
of pleasure. It seemed impossible, and the gulf between
them widened with every passing moment. He despaired
of ever bridging it again.

Chapter 8

Kate was eternally grateful to Heidi for running interference with the Howlers. Someone had contacted Heidi about giving Kate a tiara, and Heidi had told them how much Kate would loathe wearing one during the conference. Kate's organization had always functioned democratically, and the concept of promoting her to the status of queen within a group united by an idea seemed wrong. Perhaps one day she'd be a pack leader with all the authority that implied, but the Howlers were a movement, not a pack.

She'd just happened to be in the lobby when Duncan was crowned, and she'd hurt for him. He didn't have someone like Heidi, whose official job was Kate's assistant at Furthebest, but who served as Kate's right-hand Were in so many other capacities, including monitoring the Howler movement. So Duncan had been stuck with a crown. Finally she hadn't been able to watch anymore and had left.

By the time everyone gathered in the lodge's grand ballroom to open the conference and hold the election, she noticed that Duncan had found a way to ditch the crown. Knowing him as she now did, he'd probably done it with charm and grace so the hapless Woofers who'd thought it was such a great idea wouldn't end up with hurt feelings.

Even though Kate hadn't been at the lodge to oversee final preparations for today's session, she was pleased to note that the staff had followed the directions she and her grandmother had given them. They'd set up the room with two blocks of folding chairs facing the dais and an aisle down the middle. A number of chairs were lined up on the dais, as well, and a lectern stood in front of them.

Kate had yet to see her grandmother or any of the other luminaries such as Howard Wallace; his sons, Aidan and Roarke; or Cameron Gentry, the pack alpha from Portland. Howard, whose sons had both mated with humans, was a favorite with the Woofers. Kate assumed Duncan would nominate him. She was scheduled to nominate Cameron, who was friendly to the Howler cause.

Because neither of them was here yet, Kate wondered if some backroom politicking was going on. She wouldn't put it past her grandmother to engineer something like that.

She was curious to meet the Wallace family. They were all registered with the exception of Fiona, Howard's mate. She'd stayed in New York to take care of Emma and Aidan's little girl, Iona.

Kate looked at the crowd of delegates, a few more than two hundred Weres, with a glow of satisfaction. Her grandmother had been the driving force behind this conference, but she'd turned much of the planning over to Kate. Together they'd made it happen, and this room full of colorful accents and excited delegates gave Kate a thrill. By holding the first-ever conference of Weres from around the world, who had gathered to debate the issue of Were-human interaction, they were making history this weekend.

And now it was time to lead her Howler delegates to their seats. Glancing around, she discovered that Duncan and his followers were already heading toward the chairs on the left side of the aisle. By default she led her group over to the right.

She felt strange not being able to go over and talk with Duncan, but she didn't trust herself. She might say something that would let his followers know how much she actually liked him. She dared not let her followers in on that secret, either.

Seeing both groups together for the first time fascinated her, though. Woofer males outnumbered females nearly two to one, and the opposite was true of her group. Her followers were predominantly female. She'd known that about her organization before, of course, but she hadn't realized Duncan's group was the polar opposite.

She noticed other differences, too. Early this summer, her group had adopted a logo and ordered T-shirts, long-sleeved for winter and short-sleeved for summer. Everyone sitting on her side of the room wore a long-sleeved purple shirt with a black howling-wolf logo surrounded by the group's name — *Honoring Our Werewolf Legacy* —

in white. A few had brought signs to wave, and some wore buttons with a red circle and slash over the WOOF acronym. But for the most part, the shirts made the Howlers' statement.

The Woofers, on the other hand, had no shirts, but their side of the aisle bristled with homemade signs, which they waved at the slightest provocation. They also had buttons galore. Someone had been busy dreaming up slogans such as *Lose the Legacy* and *Love Your Human Neighbor*. A few delegates had created lanyards so they could display a long line of buttons. Those with button-filled lanyards clanked when they moved.

Heidi, sitting on Kate's right, leaned toward her. "What a bunch, huh?"

"We really are completely different from them."

"Yeah. We're classy and they're not. Oh, look. Here comes your favorite cousin. Wonder which side he'll sit on?"

"Depends on who he wants to suck up to." Kate turned to her assistant. "Did I just say that out loud?"

Heidi grinned. "Yep. But I don't think anybody heard you except me, and I am the soul of discretion."

"I know, and I appreciate it more than I can say." Kate gave Heidi an affectionate glance.

Heidi laughed. "Must be time to ask for a raise." With her short brown hair and a smattering of freckles across her pert nose, Heidi could pass for eighteen instead of her actual age of twenty-eight. Many underestimated her because she looked so young, but a first-class brain was hidden behind her ingenue facade.

"Neil's not choosing either side." Kate felt a headache coming on as her cousin proceeded up the aisle, climbed the steps to the dais, and crossed to the lectern. "He's commandeering the mike. He must have lobbied for that with my grandmother while I was stuck in the cabin. Damn it."

"Somebody has to run the show," Heidi said. "It can't be you, because you're the leader of one of the factions."

"No, but it was supposed to be Grandma Elizabeth. She hasn't declared allegiance to either side, and she—"

"Are you sure about that? I read an interview where Neil said he supports the Woofers and so does his great-aunt."

Kate's jaw clenched. "He supported the Howlers a few weeks ago. He flip-flops like a spawning salmon. And I know for a fact that Grandma Elizabeth is not taking sides. She made that very clear when I asked her if she wanted a Howler T-shirt."

"I'm just reporting what he said. Or rather, Angela was reporting what he said."

"And of course Angela wouldn't bother to check it out with my grandmother." Kate sat there fuming as Neil fiddled with the mike. "Grandma Elizabeth would have been the perfect MC. She's not going to accept a leadership position in the council and she's respected by everyone. Somehow Neil talked her out of doing it, the rat."

"And now it's a fait accompli, I'm afraid. He's assumed the position."

"So he has." Kate glared at him, hoping he'd look her way, but he studiously avoided doing that. She supposed the delegates would be impressed with him, at least initially. A large Were with broad shoulders and an athletic build, he spent many hours in the gym sculpting his body. He preferred gyms with mirrors.

He tapped on the mike. "May I have your attention? Welcome, delegates! The Stillman Resort and I are proud to host the First Annual Werewolf Conference, known to all by now as WereCon2012. It's an historic event, and you should all give yourselves a hand for being here!"

Kate grimaced. "Barf."

"Put a pleasant smile on your face. Angela's cameramen are prowling around and chances are she'll leap on any chance to catch you scowling."

"I hate it when you're right." Kate plastered on a silly smile. "Better?"

"That looks fake."

"Because it is."

Neil cleared his throat. "Our first order of business this morning is electing a president of what will become the first ever Were Council. Do I have any nominations?"

Duncan stood. "I nominate Howard Wallace, of New York City."

The Woofers greeted that statement with cheers and cries of *woof, woof, woof.*

Kate sighed. "They just upstaged us. We don't have a cheer. We can't very well howl for our candidate, can we?"

"Why not?"

Kate stared at Heidi. "Because it would sound stupid?"

"Couldn't sound any more stupid than *woof, woof, woof.*"

"You have a point. Okay, pass the word around. Are you good at this? Because somebody has to start the howl, and I'll be making the nomination for Cameron." Kate also didn't want to admit that she'd feel ridiculous throwing back her head and howling like an idiot. It was one thing to do it in wolf form, but quite another to do it now.

"Leave it to me." Heidi leaned toward the person on her right, and whispers circulated quickly through the Howler contingent.

Meanwhile Howard Wallace made his way from the back of the room toward the dais amid wild cheering from the Woofers. A barrel-chested Were in his late fifties, he had high cheekbones, a square jaw, and thick, snow-white hair. Kate could understand why Howard commanded respect.

She wished Cameron Gentry had the same noble bearing. In the search to find someone to carry the Howler standard, Cameron had been the only one of any stature in the Were community who was willing to devote the time and energy necessary to fill the position. She and the Howlers had tried to convince themselves he'd be fine.

Neil shook Howard's hand before turning back to the mike. "Do we have any other nominations?"

Kate stood. "I nominate Cameron Gentry, of Portland, Oregon."

Right on cue, her followers began to howl. It made a terrific racket, but an impressive one. Kate fought the urge to laugh as the Woofers, obviously taken by surprise, stared openmouthed at the Howlers, who were ... well ... howling.

For one precious moment she met Duncan's gaze and he gave her a wide smile. He also made a small gesture, one that she doubted anyone else saw. He stuck his thumb in the air for about a second. His approval shouldn't matter to her, but she felt giddy knowing she had it.

Cameron Gentry also walked up the center aisle from the back of the room. As Kate watched him, she swal-

lowed her disappointment and smiled encouragingly
before taking her seat. But Cameron Gentry was no
Howard Wallace. A slim man who was graying at the
temples, he had none of Howard's air of command.

Instead, Cameron looked like an overbred aristocrat.
His glance was haughty instead of warm, as Howard's
had been. He surveyed the Howlers with a superior
smile before mounting the steps to the dais. Although he
shook hands with Neil, and after that with Howard, neither of the other Weres smiled.

Heidi leaned toward Kate. "Methinks our boy is not
very popular."

"Methinks you're right."

"But he supports the Howler position, so we gotta
vote for him."

"Yes, we do."

Neil called for other nominations, and when there
were none, he asked for volunteers to pass out and collect ballots. With only two candidates the voting went
quickly. Kate had arranged for one Howler, one Woofer,
and one undeclared delegate to be present as a staff
member counted the ballots at a table in the back of the
room.

Heidi turned to watch the counting. "If this becomes
an annual event, you might have to introduce a more
sophisticated system."

"Like voting booths and electronic ballots?"

"Well, no, but something more official than four people and a legal pad."

Kate laughed. "You're right, but Grandma Elizabeth
said we didn't have to get fancy this time, so we didn't.
The three watchdogs will keep anyone from challenging
the results, and I can promise you the resort staffer

doesn't care who wins. Grandma Elizabeth won't allow her staff to be political, especially at this conference."

"I hate to tell you, but I think it's a foregone conclusion. Even if all the Howlers vote for Cameron, and there's only about seventy of us, there are quite a few undeclared delegates sitting in the back. The Woofers will give Howard sixty or seventy votes, and I'll bet the undeclared Weres go for Howard, too. He just looks presidential."

"When you're right, you're right." Kate wasn't surprised when Howard was named the first president of the first-ever Were Council. It was a setback for the Howlers, but she'd always heard that Howard Wallace was fair and open-minded. She wasn't giving up hope for her cause, but she grew very tired of hearing an endless chorus of *woof, woof, woof.*

Duncan believed in his cause. Hell, he was passionate about his cause. He'd devoted considerable effort toward building a coalition that would bring a new era of openness and cooperation between Weres and humans.

And yet, he hated seeing Kate's disappointment. He didn't want her faction to triumph during this conference, but she'd worked hard, too, as hard as he had. She'd just suffered a defeat, and he could see in her expression that she wasn't happy.

Sometime in the past eighteen hours her happiness had come to matter to him. But he was on the horns of a dilemma, because in order for her to be happy, he had to give up the fight. He wasn't going to do that, which meant that he was actively working to make her unhappy. Damn.

Once Howard had been declared the president of the

fledgling council, which Duncan had thoroughly expected to happen, the delegates had to elect six council members to serve with Howard. Nominations flew furiously, punctuated by a chorus of woofs or howls, depending on the candidate.

Duncan anticipated that he'd be one of them and so would Kate. He wasn't sure how that would work out, but at least he'd have an excuse to be near her instead of sitting on the opposite side of a large room. That had been no fun at all.

When the dust finally settled and council members had been nominated and voted on, the council consisted of Duncan; Kate; Jake Hunter, from Alaska; Knox Trevelyan, from Seattle; Nadia Henderson, from Chicago; and Giselle Landry, from San Francisco. Duncan was the only international member. He assumed that was because a fair number of the delegates were from the US and would logically vote for US delegates.

Howard had taken over the mike from Neil, thank God. Duncan wasn't sure he could have stomached much more of Neil's self-congratulatory style. Interestingly, Elizabeth Stillman had not yet addressed the conference goers. Duncan hadn't met Kate's grandmother, and he was becoming curious.

He'd had a short but terrific visit with both Aidan and Roarke Wallace during the break to count the votes for the council members. He'd met Aidan's mate, Emma, the novelist he'd interviewed online for his book, and Roarke's mate, Abby, a redhead who was recovering from a bad sunburn after accompanying Roarke on one of his archaeological digs in Africa.

Both Wallace brothers would help Duncan's cause, and with their father as the new president of the Were Council, Duncan considered his chances of success were good. He doubted that Kate had the same confidence. He longed to talk with her, but that might not be possible. Angela Sapworthy prowled the perimeter of the hall, searching out juicy tidbits. He didn't want her to find any that involved either him or Kate.

After announcing the names of the new council members, Howard asked for a recess so that the newly elected representatives could meet and decide on a course of action. Duncan's hopes shot up. He might finally have a chance for a few quiet words with Kate.

Howard motioned his six council members to the front of the dais. "Kate's informed me that there's a small meeting room right through that door." He pointed to his left. "She said the staff has put some coffee, tea, and a few snacks in there. Make yourselves at home and I'll be right along. Those who don't know each other, introduce yourselves."

Duncan glanced over at Kate. "Can I buy you a cup of coffee?"

"Sure." Her smile was brief, as if she didn't dare meet his gaze for too long.

He understood. They had a potentially volatile situation and had to be careful. But he hoped she knew that when he'd mentioned the coffee, he wanted to remind her of the mug she'd brought him first thing this morning, when all she'd been wearing was a robe, and he'd worn nothing at all.

"I know the presidential election didn't go the way you wanted," he said.

"No, it didn't." She gave him a quick glance. "What the heck did you do with that crown?"

"I told them I was afraid it would get damaged, so I

took it up to my room for safekeeping. My plan is to keep it there for the duration."

She laughed softly. "I knew you'd think of something."

"I must have looked like the egomaniac you've accused me of being when I let them put it on me. I saw you on the far side of the lobby taking in the whole damned spectacle."

"I didn't think you looked like an egomaniac. You looked like a Were trapped in an impossible situation."

He sighed with relief. "I'm glad you didn't think I liked the idea. Did the Howlers try a stunt like that with you?"

"They wanted to, but my assistant headed them off, so I didn't have to—"

"Excuse me for interrupting, but I want to make sure I introduce myself to you, Kate." Jake Hunter fell into step beside her. "I hope this isn't a private conversation."

"Not at all," Kate said immediately.

Yes, it bloody well is. But Duncan had no right to say that.

"I didn't join your Howler movement because I live in a fairly remote area of Alaska and my Internet reception is dicey," Jake said. "But I fully support your cause."

"Thank you, Jake. That's good to know."

Duncan found himself bristling. Who did this Jake think he was, butting in like that? Then reason reasserted itself. Jake was a fellow council member and a supporter of HOWL. Of course he'd want to connect with Kate.

Except Duncan didn't want him to do that. Jake had the makings of a rival. From his build, he must be a lumberjack or some other outdoorsy occupation. His dark, wavy hair hung to his shoulders and his green eyes were trained with far too much interest on Kate.

"So, Jake," Duncan said. "Did you leave your mate back home tending to your offspring?"

"No," Jake said. "I haven't been lucky enough to find the right Were. Alaska's population is small, and its population of Weres even smaller. But that doesn't mean I'm interested in mating with a human female. That's just wrong."

"I doubt the Wallace brothers would agree with you," Duncan said.

"I'm sure they wouldn't, but I consider their actions dangerous to the general Were population. As you may or may not know, all the packs in North America, including the Wallaces, are descended from the Alaskan Weres. When Kate talks about honoring our legacy, she's referring to the traditions handed down from those first Weres in Alaska. That's important."

Duncan wasn't about to be intimidated by tradition or Jake Hunter. "As a Scotsman, I'm very aware of the value of tradition. It can be a warm and wonderful part of any culture. But when it becomes a straitjacket that limits the options of that culture, then — "

"MacDowell, you're not going to convince me, so you might as well save your breath."

"And we're here," Kate said as they reached the door. "Shall we go in and have some coffee?" She walked through the door.

Duncan eyed Jake as they stood shoulder to shoulder, neither one ready to let the other go in first.

"Excuse me." A tall, willowy female with dark red hair approached. She wore a purple Howler T-shirt. "I'm Giselle Landry from San Francisco. Is there a problem?"

"No!" Duncan and Jake said together as they quickly separated to allow access to the room.

"I'm Jake Hunter, by the way." Jake held out his hand to Giselle. "And I support the Howler cause."

"Nice to meet you, Jake." She shook his hand.

"And I'm Duncan MacDowell." Duncan extended his hand and wished he'd done it before Jake.

Giselle accepted his handshake. "Oh, I know who you are. Everyone does. I think you're cute, but crazy. Can't go along with your ideas at all. Sorry."

"Well, then, Giselle," Jake said. "You and I have something in common. How about sharing a cup of java with me?"

"I'd be delighted, Jake." The two of them went inside.

"I heard Howard say 'coffee' and I could use a jolt of caffeine." The female who approached was easily as tall as Giselle, but she had long black hair that hung straight down her back and a model's sense of style. She wasn't wearing a purple shirt or buttons proclaiming any allegiance.

By process of elimination, Duncan figured out who she was. "You must be Nadia Henderson."

"I am." Her handshake was warm. "And you're Duncan, of course. Aidan and Emma are big fans."

"You know them?"

She laughed. "I keep forgetting that news doesn't always travel across the ocean. I was pledged to Aidan for years, but then he ended up choosing Emma, instead."

"You don't seem very upset about it."

"I was at first, but they're so happy. Besides, I've found my own true love, Aidan's cousin Quentin. It all worked out."

"So how do you feel about Were-human mating, since you obviously know the Wallaces so well?"

"I'm not sure. If the human is completely trustworthy,

like Emma, or for that matter Roarke's mate, Abby, then fine. But I think there are some dangers there, if the wrong person finds out about us."

"Hey, folks, are we going to debate this issue out here or go in where there's coffee and eats to sustain us?" The last council member came over and greeted them both with a smile. "I'm Knox." He shook hands first with Nadia and then with Duncan.

"Knox Trevelyan." Nadia pointed a finger at him. "You own a commuter flight operation in Seattle, don't you?"

"I do."

"And you were the one who transported that Bigfoot mated pair for my friend Roarke Wallace."

Knox wrinkled his nose. "I was. Smelliest job I've ever had, hands down. Hope never to have to do that again."

"Now, that's something I want to hear about," Duncan said. "Let's go in."

"That was my plan." Knox gestured for Nadia to precede him.

As Duncan started through the door, he was brought up short by Howard's voice behind him.

"Wait a minute, Duncan. I need to ask you a favor."

"Oh?" Duncan stopped and glanced at Howard in surprise. "How can I help you?"

"I've been talking to Elizabeth, and the two of us have come up with a plan. I hope you'll like it."

"Let's hear it."

"We have two strong factions at this conference, and somehow we need to make sure those factions don't divide us before we even have a name for the organization we're trying to form. I think we need a mission statement, and you're a writer."

"I'd be more than happy to take a crack at it." Howard's election as president was already paying dividends. He'd write a mission statement that helped pave the way for more openness between Weres and humans. He began crafting it in his head.

"That's good to hear, but Elizabeth and I thought it would be beneficial if you and Kate worked on it together."

He went very still. "Together?"

"I know it's a bit unorthodox, and of course I have to make sure Kate's willing. But Elizabeth and I thought if the two of you crafted the statement, then both Howlers and Woofers would accept it."

Duncan was no longer thinking about the mission statement. That issue had been eclipsed by the prospect of spending time alone with Kate, time that had been blessed by none other than the council president himself.

Howard studied him. "You seem a bit taken aback. Do you think you can handle the job?"

Duncan had no idea. The potential problems could be enormous. They might end up arguing endlessly about the wording, but at least he'd have a reason to be with her. And maybe, just maybe, they'd actually settle their major differences. Miracles did happen.

He nodded. "Absolutely. If Kate agrees, that is."

"I think she will, especially if I mention that her grandmother recommended her for the job. Now, let's go get a cup of coffee."

Duncan gestured toward the open door. "After you, Mr. Wallace."

"Howard, please. We'll all be working very hard, and I don't want anyone standing on ceremony."

"All right, Howard. But you still get to go ahead of me through that door. That much is bred into me."

Howard chuckled. "Fine."

Once Howard was through the door, Duncan closed his eyes and clenched his fist in victory. He had been assigned to work with Kate. Jake hadn't been assigned the job. Knox hadn't, either. Just him. Life was definitely looking up.

Chapter 9

As Howard proposed his plan to Kate, she carefully avoided looking at Duncan. He stood in a far corner chatting with Knox Trevelyan as the council members waited for Howard to finish his conversation with Kate. No one had taken a seat at the rectangular wooden table for eight that dominated the center of the room.

"I realize I'm asking a lot." Howard sipped black coffee absently, but his gray eyes were trained on Kate and only Kate.

She held a cup of coffee in both hands but didn't drink it. Her tummy was already churning from this unexpected suggestion. Judging from Howard's ability to focus so completely on her, she had no trouble imagining him as the successful head of Wallace Enterprises of New York, one of the wealthiest werewolf conglomerates in the world. His personal charisma aside, he was better-known than Cameron Gentry, so his election as president probably had been assured from the beginning.

"Time is an issue," Howard continued. "Not only is the schedule packed with seminars, but we've had to eliminate most of the breaks to make up for the late start."

"Which is because of Duncan and me. I'm sorry we delayed everything."

"Couldn't be helped, and there was no point in starting until you were both here. Once Elizabeth knew when to expect you, she had everything under control. But I don't think you and Duncan will have any chance to hash this out during the day, and I'd like to have a rough draft by tomorrow. When he agreed to do this, I didn't think to mention to him that it would have to be after hours."

"So you're suggesting we work on it tonight?" She did her level best to make that sound like a sacrifice when inside she was spinning with excitement. They had an excuse to be alone tonight! Yes, they'd have to work on this project, but when they'd finished . . . She pushed the resulting image out of her mind as she felt her cheeks grow warm.

"I hate to ask it of you, but I think it's the sensible solution."

Yes, throw me in that briar patch! "I agree, and I'm sure Duncan will, too." She hadn't a doubt in her mind.

"Good, then it's settled. I want the two of you to get away from the warring factions and just talk to each other about how we can unite this group under one banner. If the two of you can't come to an understanding, then we have no chance to create something worthwhile this weekend."

"We'll do our best." She clutched her coffee cup and worked to subdue the trembling produced by a sudden adrenaline rush.

Howard lowered his voice. "I realize you each have to play to your base with all the Sniffs and so on, but I have confidence in a more meaningful dialogue."

"You mean something that can't be said in a hundred and forty characters or less."

"Exactly. I've known your grandmother for years. She assures me you're an intelligent and sensible Were. I respect your convictions, Kate, but a standoff between Woofers and Howlers wouldn't be constructive for our brand-new organization."

Her joy dimmed a little. Yes, she was being given a chance to spend time alone with Duncan, but what were Howard's motives for that? After all, he had two sons who'd mated with human females. One other Howler had been elected to the council—Giselle—and one Howler sympathizer—Jake.

Nadia wore no identifying buttons, but she couldn't be a strong Woofer supporter or she'd have indicated that somehow. Knox was also without campaign buttons. Maybe Howard thought the scales were balanced in the Howlers' favor and hoped Duncan could change her thinking.

She cleared her throat. "I hope you're not suggesting that I go along with the Woofer proposals. I can't do that. And it's not only because I lead an organization that opposes the Woofers. My personal belief is that we need to maintain Were secrecy."

"I know. I don't expect you to adopt the Woofers' philosophy. Nor do I expect Duncan to abandon everything he believes and take up the Howler cause. I want each of you to get creative. Think outside the box. Get beyond Howlers and Woofers if you can."

Kate knew of only one place where she and Duncan had accomplished that—in bed. Tonight's work session might be more complicated and difficult than she'd thought at first blush. Howard was handing them an important assignment, and he wanted it completed by tomorrow morning, and completed with imagination and flair.

"I can tell you're already considering the possibilities," Howard said with a smile. "That's good." He gave her arm a squeeze. "Let's get this council meeting under way." He turned to the group. "Gather round the table, everyone. We have several important items to discuss before we dive back into the conference events."

Kate chose a seat in the middle of the long side of the rectangular table. She had a feeling Duncan had waited for her to sit down before taking his place opposite and one over from her. That put him across from Jake, who sat on Kate's right. Giselle pulled out a chair on Kate's left. With two remaining chairs, Nadia took the one next to Duncan and Knox sat beside her.

Kate didn't believe for a moment that the seating choices had been random. Her side of the table contained Howler sympathizers, and Duncan sat with the uncommitted members of the council. Howard claimed a chair at the head of the table flanked by Knox on one side and Giselle on the other.

"First order of business," Howard said, "is to thank all of you for being willing to serve for the next year. We'll be feeling our way in the beginning because we don't have any organizational rules in place yet. Nadia, would you agree to be our secretary and take some basic minutes?"

"Of course."

Howard glanced around the table. "Anyone object to that? I happen to know Nadia pretty well, and she's capable. She's also still on the fence regarding the big issue facing us, so I think having a neutral person acting as secretary would be helpful."

"Works for me," Duncan said.

Everyone else, including Kate, voiced their agreement.

Nadia reached into her slim briefcase and pulled out a netbook. "I'll make sure you all see the minutes before they go out to the delegates. Does everyone have a smart phone?"

"Mine's over in the corner getting charged," Duncan said.

"Mine's in the other corner, also getting charged." Kate's statement on the heels of Duncan's made everyone laugh. Apparently they were all thinking about last night's Sniffer war.

The other three council members brought out phones and held them up for Nadia to see.

She nodded. "Great. Make sure I get everybody's contact info before we leave here."

Howard chuckled. "Told you she was efficient. Second big thing is that we have a fledgling organization but no name for it. I'll take suggestions from this group, and if we need to, we'll also take suggestions from the delegates. Something short, easy to remember."

Knox leaned back in his chair. "WOW."

"I grant you that it's an intimidating exercise, and we might not come up with it immediately," Howard said. "We can certainly spend the rest of the day thinking about it, but—"

"No, he means WOW should be the name." Kate looked at Knox with new respect. "Worldwide Organization of Werewolves. Am I right, Knox? If so, I like it."

"That's it." Knox glanced at Howard. "But somebody might have a better idea. I've been thinking about this since yesterday when I realized we had no name yet."

"I like WOW," Duncan said. "In fact, I can't imagine calling it anything else."

Howard nodded. "It fits the criteria of being simple and easy to remember, and it accurately describes us. Anybody have something else?"

"I think WOW is excellent," Giselle said. "I say let's present it to the delegates in the morning. I predict they'll love it."

"They will," Jake said. "It certainly has my vote. Good job, Knox."

"I'm in favor, too." Nadia lifted her fingers from the keys of her netbook and glanced around the table. "I think that's all of us."

"Good." Howard sat back in his chair. "We might as well follow parliamentary procedure, so let's have a motion, a second, and an official vote."

Nadia typed away as the motion was made, seconded, and unanimously approved to propose the new name to the delegates in the morning.

"Excellent." Howard looked pleased. "Next I want to announce that Kate and Duncan will be working together on a mission statement for what we can assume will be called WOW."

"I already knew that," Giselle said.

"You did?" Howard frowned. "I suppose you overheard me talking to Kate."

"No, it was on Sniffer before I came in here. Angela

Sapworthy scooped you, I guess. I'll scroll through and find it again if you'd like to see what she said."

"Yes, I would. Thanks." A muscle twitched in Howard's jaw. "I'm not sure how that was leaked before I'd even talked with Duncan and Kate about it."

"Here you go." Giselle handed over her phone.

Howard read the Sniff and sighed. "I'd like to request that all of you use caution when speaking with Ms. Sapworthy. I'm still not sure how this got out, though. Elizabeth Stillman and I were the only ones who . . . no, wait. I think perhaps Neil might have been in the room, now that I think about it."

Kate started to say something but then decided to hold her tongue. Let Howard come to his own conclusions about Neil. But she would bet anything he'd sent the information to Angela in his continued attempt to curry favor with the reporter.

Howard returned Giselle's phone. "Thanks for making me aware of it. If anything else shows up on Sniffer or the Were Web that you think I need to know about, please contact me. I try to keep tabs on it, but Sniffs have been raining down on us like confetti at New Year's Eve. It's entertaining as hell, but it makes it tough to keep up and have a life."

"I take responsibility for some of that Sniffer blitz," Duncan said.

"Obviously, so do I," Kate said. "I'll dial it back."

Howard gazed at each of them. "I'd appreciate that. In fact, here's an idea. When you settle down to work on that mission statement, I'd advise both of you to turn off your phones and your Wi-Fi. Block out anything that's liable to distract you from the job you need to do."

Turn off their phones and Wi-Fi? Go into total

isolation—*again*—so that nothing and no one could interrupt them? Kate nodded at Howard and hoped that her expression was a complete blank. No way was she looking at Duncan.

Duncan coughed. "What if you or some member of the council needs to reach us?"

"We won't," Howard said. "Writing that mission statement is job number one. Nothing that comes up, short of the hotel catching on fire, is more important right now. The rest of us will handle things so that you two can concentrate."

Kate took a deep breath. "Understood." So maybe she and Duncan wouldn't be playing bedroom games tonight, at least not until they'd finished the mission statement. No telling how long that would take, if they could manage it at all. Their assignment might work better than an old-fashioned chastity belt.

Duncan hoped that Nadia had taken really good notes for the rest of the council meeting, because he barely remembered what was said. Various projects were suggested, including conducting a Were census and creating a central database from the census results. Jake had been against that because he said the very existence of a database would put Weres at risk.

Duncan recognized that kind of paranoia regarding the safety of Weres. He'd dealt with it in Scotland, too. Many Weres couldn't believe that they would be in a power position once their presence was known.

Yet why wouldn't they be? They had economic clout and nearly all Weres were fine physical specimens, as well. They weren't second-class citizens now and wouldn't be once their shape-shifting ability became common knowledge.

He was glad that Kate hadn't joined in Jake's rant about the database being a security issue. But for all he knew, she agreed with Jake. She'd stayed fairly quiet during the council meeting, but then, he had, too.

At first he'd thought the idea of meeting with Kate privately to draw up a mission statement was great. After despairing of ever being alone with her again, he'd been handed a golden opportunity. But there was a catch, a big one. Howard expected them to come up with a mission statement they could both live with.

Duncan knew himself fairly well, and he was beginning to know Kate. They were both conscientious, and neither of them would feel right jumping into bed until they'd written the mission statement. Duncan would love to believe that they could come to a quick and easy agreement on how to word it. He'd love to believe that, but he didn't.

At last Howard adjourned the meeting. Nadia keyed everyone's information into her netbook and all the council members exchanged phone numbers, too. Then they began dispersing to attend one of several seminars taking place in various meeting rooms. Duncan had intended to talk to Kate about plans for tonight, but she was in some deep discussion with Jake.

Oh, well. He could text her later on. Leaving the room, he took out his phone and pulled up the revised conference schedule. He'd promised his brother, Colin, he'd attend the panel discussion titled "Half 'n' Half—the Challenges and Joys of Mixed-Blood Offspring." Colin's mate, Luna, was a mixed-blood Were and she'd just found out that she was pregnant. Colin and Luna's offspring could end up being human, Were, or a mixture of both.

Because Were offspring looked and behaved like human offspring until they reached puberty, their parents had to wait until then before they discovered how the genetics had worked out. Duncan thought it was a fascinating prospect ripe for promoting greater understanding between Weres and humans. But Colin wasn't into the whole grand experiment the way Duncan was. Colin was nervous.

As Duncan consulted a large brass placard on the wall to find out which direction he should go to sit in on that panel discussion, he picked up Kate's scent. Glancing over his shoulder, he watched her approach. She looked damned good in purple. Even if the logo on the front of her shirt stood for the opposition, he liked the way her breasts showcased that howling wolf.

He hadn't had a chance to change clothes, so he was grateful she'd washed everything except his wool slacks. The cabin seemed a million miles away now. Yet he had only to glance into her blue eyes to remember what loving her had been like.

"You look good in that color, lass."

She grinned. "Everyone looks good in this color. That's why we picked it. You'd look good in it, too, Woofer."

"I don't think so." He gazed down at her and fought the urge to stroke her cheek. "The shirt's not so bad, but there's a splotch of something on the front that would clash with my principles."

"Where's your T-shirt?"

"As I'm sure you could tell when we were gathered in the grand ballroom, my crowd doesn't go in for the shirts. They'd rather have the buttons and the signs. The males think T-shirts are too girlie."

"Beats having a bunch of buttons pinned to your chest or hanging around your neck clanking all the time."

"Aye, we agree on that." He gripped his phone to remind himself that he must not touch her. He probably shouldn't even be standing this close, but he couldn't seem to help it. "So what was the deep discussion with Jake all about?"

"He doesn't want me to sell the Howlers down the river. He knows you're a persuasive sort of Were, and he's worried that you'll get the better of me."

"That's because he doesn't know you very well." He could stand here forever looking into her eyes. "You're as likely to get the better of me."

"I doubt it. But we need to come up with a plan for tonight."

"Aye, and don't we find ourselves in a fine fix? We'll be together, but —"

"We'll have one hell of a job to do."

"Couldn't have said it better, lass. I foresee tonight being pure torture, unless, of course, you agree to see things my way from the start. Any chance of that?"

"Nope."

"Didn't think so. So where shall we conduct this test of wills? Howard suggested we block out all distractions."

She rolled her eyes. "Like *that's* possible."

"Little does he know the distraction you present to me."

"Or that you present to me, Woofer. But I suggest we use my suite. It's more like an apartment than a suite. There's plenty of room, almost as much square footage as the cabin, actually."

He lowered his voice. "How big is your bed?"

"It may not matter. We could be locked in battle until dawn."

"I'd rather be locked in a different way." He sighed. "But we have to write that bloody mission statement, and I don't imagine it will be easy."

"Now, there's an understatement. Tell you what. Let's say if either of us has spare moments during the day, we'll start jotting down ideas for the statement. Then we can share what we have. Who knows? Maybe we'll be thinking along the same lines."

He laughed. "You're a dreamer, but I'll jot down some ideas. What time?"

"Let's see." She scrolled through the schedule on her phone. "With the late start, the last session ends at six. Let's meet at seven."

"Sure. That'll give me time to slip into my suit of armor. Where's your suite?"

"Top floor, end of the hall. Thirty-three hundred. I have a fireplace."

"Don't you go making it cozy, Kate. Don't be pouring wine and lighting candles."

"Wouldn't think of it."

"You should also put on something bulky and ugly, if you can manage that."

"Okay." She chuckled.

"And put your hair up in rollers. Wait, I know what you should do. Do you have any of that green glop that females slather on their faces as a beauty treatment?"

Her chuckle had morphed into outright laughter. "No, I don't, but even if I did, you'll show up looking your normal gorgeous self, since I seriously doubt you actually have a suit of armor. And armor would only add to your appeal, anyway. It's not fair if I make myself ugly and you don't."

"I could belch a lot. That should help."

"Oh, my God." She laughed harder. "Yes, that would help. See that you do. And chew with your mouth open. That's especially disgusting."

"What's all the hilarity about over here? Inquiring minds want to know." Angela Sapworthy appeared like an evil queen out of a fairy tale. The snow had been removed from her spiked hair and her makeup was repaired.

Duncan's mind went blank.

Apparently Kate's didn't. "Why, Angela, you're just the one I wanted to see. You have to hear this. You can put it on Sniffer."

"Oh?" Angela's eyes took on an avid gleam.

"I was just telling Duncan the best joke. These three werewolves walk into a bar, and the first one says—"

"Oh, I've heard it." Angela looked disappointed. "That's the one where the punch line is something about a fuzzy navel."

"Yes! Isn't it hilarious?"

"The first time, I suppose. Anyway, never mind. I thought you might be talking about something interesting."

"Nope." Kate shrugged. "Sorry. Just telling werewolf jokes."

"Then I'm off." Angela strolled away.

Duncan glanced at Kate with admiration. "Nice work."

"Thanks."

"I've never heard that joke. How does it go?"

"I have no idea. I was making it up as I went along. I figured there had to be a joke that started out like that. If I'd had to keep going, I was going to make up something stupid, but I got lucky."

He was sure his admiration for her would be obvious for anyone to see, but what the hell. "You're amazing, Kate."

"Don't let Angela hear you say that or we'll be in big trouble."

"Bigger than we already are?"

"Good point. So, I'll see you at seven?"

He nodded. "You will. And God help me, I'm looking forward to it."

"I know." She smiled at him. "Me, too."

After she walked away, he stood staring at his phone as if he had important messages on it, but he didn't see the phone at all. All he could see was Kate's smile. The image of it stayed with him for the rest of the day.

Chapter 10

**WERECON2012:
HOWLERS GAIN MOMENTUM**

**Exclusive report for *Wereworld Celebrity Watch*
by Angela Sapworthy**

DENVER—There's a new kid in town, and his name is Jake Hunter! This reporter admits that she has a soft spot for the mighty Weres in the forefront of the Woofer movement. When confronted by sexy wolves like Duncan MacDowell and the two Wallace brothers, Aidan and Roarke, one can be forgiven for joining the rousing chorus of *woof, woof, woof!*

But the Howlers have a new champion from the wilds of Alaska, the birthplace of all Were packs in North America. If Jake's a typical Alaskan Were, this reporter needs to go north! Jake offers guided tours through the Alaskan wilderness, and note to all Were females—he's single.

He also believes strongly that Weres were intended to mate only with Weres. That's good news for those of us who are worried that the Woofers' doctrine would mean that human females could snap up all the good Weres. No human female will be getting Jake Hunter, and that's reason to celebrate!

Now that Jake is one of six council members who will help steer a course for all Weres in the coming months, you can bet Jake will be advocating a return to Were-Were mating, along with other traditional values. And wherever a six-five, two-hundred-pound Were who looks like Jake Hunter leads, this reporter is willing to follow! And don't forget to follow me, Angela Sapworthy, on Sniffer @newshound—I'm your eyes, ears, and nose for WereCon2012!

Kate spent her day being visible—connecting with Howlers she'd met only online and attending seminars geared toward the Howler movement. In the last scheduled hour of the day, she led a seminar entitled "Letting the Howl Out—Rededicating Ourselves to Werewolf Traditions." The room was filled with mostly females in purple shirts.

Jake Hunter sat quietly throughout the seminar. As the session neared its end, Kate introduced her two fellow council members—Giselle, in her purple Howler shirt, and Jake, who wasn't wearing the shirt but supported the cause.

"May I say something?" Jake asked.

"Be my guest." Kate liked Jake and thought he brought a much-needed strong male presence to the movement.

He stood up, all six-five of him. With his collar-length dark hair and his flannel shirt and leather vest, he looked as if he'd just returned from the wilderness. Every female in the room gave him her full attention, and the males looked at him with obvious respect.

"I think we have a real opportunity here," he said. "Kate got the ball rolling by founding HOWL. As I told her, I would have joined, but where I live, the Internet is still spotty. But I'm here this weekend and was lucky enough to be elected to the council. That gives us three seats out of six."

Applause quickly turned to howls. Kate looked over at Heidi, who was probably responsible for starting the howling. Then she laughed and joined in. Howling was good. It reduced stress and brought the group together.

When the noise died down, Jake continued. "Even more important than the strong Howler presence, though, is the lack of dedicated Woofers on the council. Duncan MacDowell is the only one. The others are still undecided, although I think we all know that Howard Wallace must surely support the Woofers, at least privately."

That news was met with groans. The Wallace pack posed a major threat to the Howlers and they understood that.

"I'm asking all of you to stay strong and promote our cause. Don't be discouraged because Howard won the presidential race. Kate has been assigned to work with Duncan to create a mission statement for the organization, and I know she's going to fight for our position while she does that." Jake challenged her with his piercing green eyes.

"I plan to do exactly that, Jake," Kate said.

More howls greeted that statement, and the session ended. Kate suspected that Jake had intended his little speech to put pressure on her so that she wouldn't cave as she and Duncan crafted the mission statement. Because he was a male Were and very perceptive, she wondered whether he'd picked up on the sexual tension between her and Duncan. She wouldn't be surprised if he had.

Jake would never suggest such a thing, of course. He might not even be completely sure that his suspicions were correct. But instinct told her that on some level, Jake sensed that Duncan had breached her defenses.

But she'd breached Duncan's defenses, as well. Duncan was as susceptible to her as she was to him, and she should keep that in mind. He might want her to greet him tonight looking ugly, but she wasn't about to give him that advantage. When they met, the playing field should be as even as she could make it.

Her meeting with him would take place very shortly. Before it did, however, she wanted to pay a long-overdue visit to her grandmother. Elizabeth Stillman had flitted through the conference all day, but Kate had never managed to be in the same place at the same time. Besides, the questions she wanted to ask couldn't have been voiced with others milling around, anyway.

She thought her grandmother might have some questions for her, as well. She hoped they wouldn't veer too close to the matters Kate wanted to keep private.

After six in the evening, Elizabeth could usually be found having a glass of exceedingly expensive red wine in her suite, a replica of Kate's on the opposite end of the third floor. Kate pressed the doorbell, which sounded a melodious chime. Her grandmother hated buzzing doorbells.

A maid with graying hair dressed in a smart burgundy pantsuit answered the door. "Hello, Kate."

"Hello, Sally. Is my grandmother in?"

The maid smiled. "You know she's always in at this time of the evening, unless she's on a trip. Will you be staying for a glass of wine?"

"No, thank you. I just want a few minutes of her time."

"Sally?" Elizabeth's voice carried well. "Is that Kate? I was hoping she'd come. Send her right in."

A twinkle in her eye, Sally gestured for Kate to head on into the suite's living room.

Kate walked through the entryway and into the living area, her suede boots sinking into rose-colored carpet so plush and soft it would make a perfectly fine surface for sleeping. Her grandmother believed in luxury, from the gold brocade drapes at the windows to the white velvet slipcovers on the furniture, covers that were washed weekly to maintain their pristine condition.

"Kate!" Elizabeth put down her wine and rose from her favorite wingback chair by the fireplace. "I'm so glad you came."

Kate hugged her grandmother, who at seventy-five had the face and figure of a woman at least twenty years younger. She'd lost her soul mate when they were both only sixty, and although Elizabeth could have searched for another, she'd chosen not to. She liked to say she'd had the best and anything else would be trading down.

Elizabeth Stillman was tall, five-nine in her bare feet, and she usually took off her shoes the minute she stepped inside this suite. Her hair was a blend of several shades of blond that looked quite natural thanks to an excellent hairdresser, and she'd had at least one face-lift that Kate knew about. She preferred to dress in jewel tones and loose garments that floated around her when she moved.

She was, as Kate noticed whenever she paused to look with a stranger's eye, a beautiful woman. But anyone meeting her had better not assume that her beauty was the whole story. Elizabeth was extremely intelligent and a skilled politician. She'd run the Stillman pack ever since taking over from her father thirty years ago. She hadn't slowed down a bit, and even though Kate expected to step into the position eventually, it wouldn't be any time soon.

Her grandmother waved her to the companion wingback sitting in front of the fire. "Aren't you having wine? No, of course you're not. Howard told me you're meeting with Duncan tonight to craft the mission statement. Is that a brilliant idea or what? I'm not sure if it was mine or Howard's, but I'm going to take credit for it."

"It is a brilliant idea. Challenging, but brilliant." Kate sat in the chair but didn't settle into it. "And I only have a few minutes. Duncan's coming to my suite at seven, and I've ordered food to be sent up."

"Just food?" Elizabeth's eyebrows arched. "You'll need wine, too. I can't imagine how you'll come to any agreement on the wording if you each don't have a few glasses of wine."

"If I decide we need that, I have some in the suite already, but I think we may be better off just sticking with water and coffee. It could be a long night."

Instead of picking up her own wine, Elizabeth sat in her chair and gazed at Kate for several seconds. "And what of your first night with this Were? How did that go? You know I'm burning with curiosity."

"Fine. It went fine. I got a report from Ryan around

four this afternoon that the Stewarts' window has been replaced."

"I'm not talking about windows. I'm talking about whether you and Duncan managed to get along all right. Disregarding those ridiculous Sniffs, of course."

It was the question Kate had been dreading, and she didn't want to dwell on it for long if she could help it. "Duncan and I have been able to be civil towards each other," she said. "But what I really came to ask you is why Neil was the MC for the opening of the conference and not you. I thought we'd agreed that you'd do it."

Elizabeth laughed. "You didn't like that, did you?"

"Not so much."

"It was for your own good, sweetheart. Neil started pestering me about his role in the proceedings, and I realized he intended to run for the council. I don't know that he would have been elected, but the Stillman name is familiar to so many, and he might have been. I convinced him that being on the council would be boring but being the MC would be fun. He went for it. He's a born ham."

"Now I feel better. If I had to choose, I'd rather have him in the MC position than on the council."

Her grandmother nodded. "So would I. And we can't just ignore Neil. He's family. So I wanted to find a place for him where he couldn't do too much damage. I'm not sure that Howard would have put up with him on the council and I was certain Howard would get elected president."

"Because you pulled some strings?"

"I didn't have to." Elizabeth picked up her wine and took a sip. "I would have, if necessary. I know Cameron Gentry was your choice, but, Kate, that Were has the moral fiber of a dry martini minus the olive. Howard is the better choice."

"I happen to think you're right." She thought of mentioning the incident with the Sniffer leak but, once again, decided that Neil would eventually hang himself and she hated the role of tattletale.

"I love the WOW acronym, by the way."

Kate sent her a sharp glance. "Howard told you?"

"Sweetheart, he tells me everything that's going on. He's like the younger brother I never had."

"You won't tell Neil, though, right?"

"Of course I won't. Howard mentioned the Sniffer leak, and I've already talked to Neil. He denies giving the tidbit to Sapworthy, but I'm pretty sure he did. Both Howard and I should have realized he was close enough to hear our conversation. We'll be more careful from now on."

"Good." Kate hesitated, but they really did need to discuss this. "There's one other thing, Grandma."

"What's that, sweetheart?"

"Do you think there's anything to the rumor that Penny's going to make an appearance at the conference tomorrow?"

Elizabeth greeted the question calmly, so she was obviously aware of the rumor, too. She stared into the fire. "I hope not."

"Have you heard from her?"

"No." She turned to Kate. "Have you?"

Kate shook her head. "Just that one e-mail I told you about, where she wished me good luck with the conference. Nothing more."

Her grandmother sighed. "I checked with your mother and father today, and they haven't heard from her, either. I wish they'd at least be willing to attend the conference for a few hours, just to make an appearance. It's embarrassing that I helped organize this historic event and my own son and his mate aren't here."

"They're torn between Penny's choice and mine. They think if they make an appearance, they'll be expected to take a stand one way or the other, and they can't see themselves doing that."

"Why do they have to take a stand?" Elizabeth looked indignant. "I haven't. Why should they?"

Kate loved her parents, but she understood their limitations, too. "They're not as strong as you are. I'm sure you've been confronted by those who demand that you pick a side."

"All the time. I tell them to bug off. I'm Switzerland. I'd even be willing to run interference for Woodruff and Violet if they'd only show up."

"They hate conflict."

"I know." She raised her glass in Kate's direction. "To tough broads like you who can take the heat."

Kate smiled. "Thanks, Grandma. I'd better go."

"I do think you should offer him wine."

"We'll see. He warned me not to."

"What nonsense. He's a Scotsman. They can hold their liquor."

"I'll see how it goes." She walked over and kissed her grandmother on her smooth cheek. "See you tomorrow. And personally, I think the conference is a smashing success."

Elizabeth brightened. "It is, isn't it? I hear the restaurant's bustling. Later on I'll go down and mingle at the bar, but I always enjoy my quiet time and my wine. It rejuvenates me. Besides, it's good to maintain a certain mystique by absenting oneself now and then."

Kate laughed. "You are my role model, Grandma Elizabeth."

"In that case, you *have* to offer Duncan wine, because in your boots, I would make that the first order of business."

"I'll think about it." With a wave, Kate left the room.

Sally was at the door to show her out. "I want you to see something." She unbuttoned the jacket of her maroon pantsuit. Underneath she wore a purple Howler shirt.

Kate gasped in delight. Then she stepped closer and dropped her voice to a whisper. "Does she know?"

"No. She was so adamant that the staff couldn't take sides, and I'm a member of the staff. But I'm a Were female, too, and I don't like the idea of human females horning in on our territory." Determination glowed in her eyes. "You give that Duncan MacDowell hell, you hear?"

"I will, Sally." She hugged the maid and left.

As she walked down the hallway, she thought about the movement she'd started, and all those who believed in her and in this battle to preserve the traditional werewolf way of life. Duncan might be the sexiest Were she'd ever met, and she might crave his body, but Weres like Sally were counting on her to fight for the cause. She couldn't let them down.

Duncan discarded the idea of taking the elevator to the third floor in favor of climbing the magnificent wooden staircase instead. Each newel post was a carved wolf's head, and the broad stairs were carpeted in red brocade. Duncan loved everything about Stillman Lodge, from its rustic carved chandeliers to the gigantic stone fireplace in the lobby to the stained-glass lamps in the publike bar.

Several Woofers had invited him for dinner in the lodge's luxurious dining room, but when he'd mentioned his assignment, they'd wished him well and promised to buy him a drink later when he was finished. As cozy as the bar was, Duncan didn't expect to be sitting in it tonight. If he and Kate finished before dawn, they would have their own celebration.

He carried a small briefcase containing his laptop as he walked down the long hallway toward her suite. He'd spent a little time during a workshop constructing a rough draft of the mission statement. Since then he'd tried to concentrate on polishing it and failed miserably. He was trying to focus on it now with no success whatsoever.

Instead he was imagining what Kate might be wearing, and whether she'd let him even kiss her, or if they'd work across the room from each other and not touch at all. He didn't think that was possible. They'd become too close the night before to spend hours alone together now and not want to touch, to kiss, and . . . to make love, damn it.

God but he ached for her. This was an impossible situation, but no one knew that except the two of them. Or he certainly hoped no one did. He had a bad feeling that Jake had picked up on the chemistry between him and Kate in the way that only a potential rival would.

From the first time he'd met Jake, he'd been on the alert, and not only because the Alaskan Were supported the Howlers. Duncan had noticed how Jake looked at Kate, as if considering whether to make a move. But he hadn't, possibly because he'd sensed another male had already staked a claim.

Duncan hadn't staked a claim, not really. He'd only

made love to her once, and that was a far cry from staking a claim and miles away from binding her as his mate. Yet he'd reacted to Jake's interest with an inner snarl of warning. He had no right to do that, but Jake might have picked up on it. Bloody hell. That wasn't good.

At the end of the hallway he found a set of carved double doors and a discreet brass plate with the words *thirty-three hundred* on it in elaborate script. Kate's suite was definitely in a higher-rent district than his, which had a single plain door and was in the middle of the hallway on the first floor near the elevators.

He supposed his room would be noisy at night, but he hadn't slept there yet, so he couldn't say for sure. Sleeping there tonight was unlikely, too. Either he and Kate would work all night on the mission statement or they wouldn't, but he could see no scenario in which he ended up back in his own room.

He had, however, tested out the shower not long ago. He'd also shaved and changed into jeans and a slate blue sweatshirt from his alma mater, the University of Edinburgh. He hoped the sweatshirt would inspire him to great heights of verbal genius. Yeah, right.

Her suite had a doorbell, and he pushed it. Chimes sounded inside, and then she opened the door. For a moment they stood there looking at each other. He was glad for the chance to adjust to her beauty before they were behind closed doors again.

As if they'd agreed on a dress code, she'd also put on jeans and a sweatshirt. Hers was gray and said *Stillman Lodge, Est. 1902*. It included a line drawing of the lodge's exterior below the lettering, which curved around either side of her breasts. She'd put her hair on top of her head and, in a winsome touch, stuck a pencil in the topknot.

He wondered how in hell he was going to keep his hands off her.

"Come in." She stepped back from the door, and he noticed her feet were bare.

He could understand the temptation to go barefoot as the soles of his loafers sank into the thick gray pile. Getting naked on a carpet like that would be a sensuous experience. He'd like the chance to find out.

"Go on in." She moved behind him to close the door. "The food's here."

He waited to hear the lock click into place behind him before he turned to her. "I can already tell this is going to be difficult."

"I know." Her shirt quivered with her quick breaths. "Go in and get some food." She made a shooing motion with both hands. "That will take your mind off of sex."

"No, it won't. I wonder if—"

"I mean it." She sounded slightly winded. "Get in there and fix yourself a plate."

He could smell the food, although her scent was the most important one to him at the moment. She looked very earnest and determined, though. He turned and walked into her living area, his steps silent on the thick carpet.

She had windows galore, including a big corner one to his left, and the curtains were open. Although it was dark outside, he could see a row of lights running down a snowy hillside. "What are the lights for?"

"Night skiing. The season came early this year, and they're still setting up, but they turned on the lights tonight and I thought you'd enjoy looking out."

"Thanks." He was strung tighter than a hunting bow and he made a conscious effort to relax his shoulders. "Nice place. Very nice place."

No walls divided the sparkling white kitchen on his left from the living area to his right, probably so she could take full advantage of the views from every window. On the far right wall, a wood fire crackled in a decent-sized stone fireplace flanked by two tall bookshelves. A cushy red leather sofa and two easy chairs faced both the fireplace and a flat-screen television that was about twice the size of the one in his room.

She'd set out the food on a bar-height counter that enclosed most of the kitchen area. Tall stools were spaced along one side. The view from the corner window had to be spectacular in the daytime. She'd fit a good-sized desk neatly into the space in front of it, and when she worked there, she'd have a one-eighty panorama.

He tried valiantly to look at her surroundings as a casual visitor might, but instead he saw everything in terms of whether it would be a good spot for sex. The carpet had already passed muster, and although the red leather sofa might be too slippery, he liked the idea of that cushioned surface. The desk, once cleared, had potential, as did the barstools.

His body grew hard as he cataloged the possibilities. And this wasn't even the main room for what he had in mind. Through a double doorway he glimpsed the edge of her bed. He just knew it was a king. A suite like this wouldn't have anything smaller.

"Let me take your briefcase so you can fix yourself something to eat."

As she walked toward him, hand outstretched, he remembered that he was still holding the damned thing. He'd been standing there like a granite statue, and right now his cock felt as if it had been turned to stone. He allowed her to take the briefcase, but it meant she'd moved close enough for him to breathe in her scent.

Holy hell. She was as aroused as he was.

He cleared his throat. "Look, I have an idea."

She walked over to her desk and laid his briefcase on it. "I know you do." She turned back to him and leaned her hips against the desk. "I can see the evidence in the fit of your jeans."

"Don't be so smug. You're no better off."

"I know it!" Her voice was a soft wail. "I've *tried* to put sex out of my mind. It's like telling yourself not to think about a pink elephant, and then that's all you can think about. I thought maybe if we ate some food . . ."

"I don't care a thing about food right now and neither do you."

Her gaze met his. "No, I don't."

His heart thudded heavily in his chest. "I think we should have sex and get it over with."

"You suppose that will work?"

"I don't know, but I can hardly remember my own name, let alone what we're supposed to be doing instead of having sex. I need you something fierce."

"I guess we could try it." Turning toward the desk, she hit a button, and all the drapes began to close as she walked toward him. "Where?"

He could barely breathe from wanting her, let alone walk anywhere. His voice sounded like gravel running through a chute as he nudged off his shoes. "Right here on the carpet would suit me fine, lass."

Chapter 11

Clothes flew everywhere. Kate couldn't get out of hers fast enough, and she noticed that Duncan apparently felt the same.

"This is not what you recommend in your book." He shoved down his jeans and knit boxers and kicked them aside.

"Ask me if I care. Damn, my zipper's stuck."

"I'll get it. I'm done." He knelt in front of her and grasped the tab on the zipper. "You smell delicious. Hey, it really is stuck."

"That could be a problem."

He continued to work with it, his breathing ragged. "How much do you care about these jeans?"

"Right now? Not at all."

"I'll remind you of that, later." Grabbing hold of the

waistband, he wrenched the zipper forcibly apart, ruining it and ripping the denim.

She couldn't bring herself to care as he pulled both her jeans and her panties to her ankles, slid his hands up the backs of her thighs, and urged her toward him.

"Step out of them." His murmured command ruffled her damp curls.

She clutched his bare shoulders. No sooner had she freed herself from her clothes than he made contact with his tongue. She moaned softly and trembled in anticipation, knowing full well what he intended.

"This is what I was hungry for." Sinking lower onto his knees, he tilted his head back slightly, nuzzled his way between her thighs, and began a slow assault on her sanity.

Closing her eyes, she reveled in the sensuality of a kiss more intimate than any other. Soon she was mindless with pleasure. When he slowed the pace and teased her with featherlight swipes of his tongue, she shamelessly begged for what she wanted, what she desperately needed.

And he gave it. Settling in with his talented mouth and tongue, he gripped her thighs and pushed her closer, and closer still. She began to quiver, and he held her steady, building the tension relentlessly, until at last, with a triumphant cry, she lost all sense of time and place as she tumbled into a raging river of ecstasy.

Guiding her slowly and tenderly to her knees, he kissed her breasts, her throat, and finally her lips. The erotic taste of her climax flavored their kiss, and the thrum of new passion stirred in her veins. Incredibly, she wasn't sated.

His sweet caress, molding her breasts with his palms, sliding his hands over her back to cup her bottom, roused her again. She whimpered and arched her body to brush her sensitized nipples against his chest.

"Aye." His words were rough with passion and his brogue grew thicker. "You'll be wanting more pleasure, lass. And I'll be putting you in charge this time. Spread your legs apart. I long to lie beneath you on this fine carpet while you ride me."

The exotic sound of his voice blended with his explicit request fired her blood in a way she'd never felt before. A wildness overtook her, and when he slid both legs between hers and lay back on the carpet, his eyes glittering with lust, she vowed to give him a ride he'd remember.

But first, she would tease him as he'd teased her. His cock thrust upward, sleek and hard, ready for her to mount. Her womb ached for that connection, but she would delay her need so that she could drive all rational thought from his mind as he'd done with her.

Leaning over him, she swayed back and forth, brushing her taut nipples against his straining erection.

He gasped. "Careful. I might . . ." He sucked in another breath.

"Would that be so bad?" She continued to provoke him, although she paid the price, too, as the urge to take him deep inside her grew stronger with every casual touch.

"Aye, 'twould be bad."

She loved hearing him become more Scottish the lustier he became. "Then let's try this." She used her mouth on him, instead.

His groan was pure male. "I canna stand it, lassie! I dinna mean for you to . . . ah . . . Saints preserve us. . . . You'll do me in for sure. . . ."

She paused to gaze at him. His eyes were squeezed

shut and his jaw clenched so hard the veins stood out in his powerful neck. "You don't like it?"

"I dinna say that."

"Then I'll proceed." She continued to lick and nibble while she cradled his sizable balls, one in each hand.

He breathed rapidly through clenched teeth. "Have mercy on me, Kate. 'Tis enough, now."

"All right. If you insist." Truthfully, she couldn't wait any longer, either. Straddling him, she braced her arms on either side of his broad shoulders and gradually took him in, savoring every magnificent inch, every point of contact that made her body sing with joy.

He remained tense beneath her, every muscle braced to prevent the eruption he'd been fighting, probably ever since he walked through her door. She understood. From the moment she'd opened that door, her body had yearned for this.

When she'd taken every last glorious bit of him, she leaned forward and pressed her lips against his tight mouth. It softened, opened, invited her tongue inside, and as she deepened the kiss, she lifted her hips gently.

He moaned, the sound caught between their seeking mouths.

Lowering her hips again, she began an easy rhythm as she continued to bestow those soul-deep kisses. The sensuality of it washed over her in waves, threatening to bring on her orgasm before she'd meant that to happen.

When he grasped her hips in his big hands, she knew that her illusion of control was about to be destroyed. No matter. She was ready for him to set the pace. And set it he did, with a vengeance.

Soon he was pounding into her with a rapid, steady beat that made her whole body shudder, and she loved it. She abandoned their kiss and lifted her head to discover his eyes were open and he was looking straight into hers with an intensity that sent shock waves through her system.

His lips barely moved, but his words were clear. "Come, lass. Come now."

As if she needed only his command, her body began convulsing around his. He gave her a brief smile, and then he drove harder and faster than ever, before arching upward with a strangled cry of victory. As they collapsed together on the thick carpet, she imagined that same cry could have been on the lips of his ancestors as they charged into battle, naked and painted blue.

She lay with her ear to his chest and listened, for the second time in two nights, to his steady heartbeat. She couldn't have explained why that thrilled her so, but it did. This Scotsman and his endearing brogue, not to mention his virile body, might have spoiled her for anyone else.

As Duncan lay there assessing the situation, he came up with two conclusions, neither of them particularly helpful to his long-term goals. He would definitely replace the carpeting in his quarters at the castle with something more like this. And he doubted that he'd ever find a more passionate female, Were or human, than Kate Stillman.

The first conclusion wouldn't cause much of a problem in his life, but it wouldn't affect his future much, either. The second conclusion was rather more important, because he had always assumed that he'd walk the walk of Woofer principles and prove a fitting example by successfully mating with a human as the Wallace brothers had done. If he hadn't found the right person yet, he'd had no doubt that he would, given enough time.

Now he feared that he could take until doomsday and he still wouldn't come up with a human female to match Kate. That was a problem. And even if he threw over his whole plan and decided to consider her, she wouldn't have him. He was not just a Woofer—he was King of the Woofers, and she wasn't about to pledge her life to someone who opposed her belief that Weres should mate exclusively with other Weres.

Dealing with her convictions would be equally awkward for him. She'd want to push her agenda in every area of her life. She'd made a career out of fostering Were-only dating and mating, and the very existence of Furthebest.com set his teeth on edge. He didn't object to Weres mating with Weres as an option, but her site insisted that was the *only* acceptable option.

And yet . . . she felt perfect in his arms. When their bodies spoke, they did so in perfect harmony. What a cruel joke. Physically, even temperamentally, they fit together. They had a similar work ethic. They just worked for completely different outcomes. Damn it.

"You're thinking." She nuzzled his chest. "I can almost hear it."

"I am thinking. Want to know what I'm thinking about?"

"I'm not sure. Is it going to be helpful to our situation?"

He sighed. "Probably not."

"Then don't tell me. I'm still drifting on a cloud of sexual bliss, and I don't want to be disturbed unless it's good news."

"So you only want good news?" He wrapped his arms

around her luscious body, enjoying the feel of her warm, silky skin.

"Yes, please."

"I haven't had sex that good in years. I might even go so far as to say in forever."

She laughed. "And I'll tell you why."

"I'll wager you will."

"We had Were sex, which means no worries about those silly condoms, no worries about disease. We could enjoy each other in any way we pleased, including oral sex."

"I did especially like that part." He hated to admit that having sex without worrying about the issues that plagued humans had been damned good.

"I know we didn't do this for any reason other than because we couldn't help ourselves, but now I wonder if we didn't just make a good point for my side."

"That's depressing."

She nipped his shoulder lightly. "No, it's not. It's wonderful. I advanced my cause without trying. That makes me very happy."

"Well, very happy lass, are you ready to move your sweet arse and get some work done?" He gave her a playful pinch.

"You claimed that if we did this, we might have a chance of accomplishing something." She braced her arm on his chest and lifted up to gaze down at him. "So it's time to put your money where your mouth is, as they say over here."

He gave her his best evil grin. "That could be interesting, especially if I put my money where my mouth was not too many minutes ago."

"Let's not focus on that, shall we?" But she looked as

if she'd love to. "We have a mission statement to create."
She disentangled herself and stood.

Duncan, however, remained sprawled on the floor
gazing up at her. He couldn't seem to summon the energy to move. The carpet really was comfortable.

"Come on, laddie. Up you go."

He glanced upward. Ah, very nice. "With the view
from here, I may be up in no time."

"That does it." She reached down and picked up his
clothes. "You're officially incorrigible." She tossed his
clothes at him. "When I come back into this room, you'd
better be dressed, or else."

He laughed and sat up. "Or else what?" He found the
pencil that had fallen out of her topknot and tossed it to
her. "We'll get to do this all over again?"

"I think not, Woofer." She caught the pencil and stuck
it back in her hair.

"You look cute with that pencil in your hair."

"I like having a pencil around when I'm working.
Sometimes it helps to write something down. You know,
old-school, on actual paper." She gathered up her clothes.

She was fast taking up residence in his heart without
even trying. "That suits you. A touch of nostalgia."

"It's more than that. It's a useful tool." She hugged
her clothes to her chest. "I don't believe in abandoning
ideas because they've been around for a while."

"I get that. But sometimes—"

"You need to get dressed, Duncan. We can't have this
discussion naked."

"I think it would go much better if we did." He winked
at her, hoping to see her smile.

Instead she gazed at him as if he were a schoolboy
who wouldn't behave.

"I know. We have to get serious." His good spirits began to slip away. "I just hope . . ."

"What?" she asked softly. "That our discussion doesn't change the mood? Because it will."

Maybe they should run away, leave the convention, abandon their respective causes, and . . . be unable to live with themselves. Bloody hell. "Why did we have to end up on opposite sides of the fence, Kate? Can you tell me what sort of karmic debt we owe that arranged for that?"

"No, Duncan, I can't. But it's the reality of the situation, and somehow we have to work it out."

He nodded. "We will, lass." But as the glow from their lovemaking faded, he'd already begun to dread the battle ahead of them.

"Be right back. I need to grab a different pair of jeans and freshen up."

And put on your armor. "All right." He figured she also wanted to create some space, both physical and psychological, between their lovemaking and the task they were about to tackle. That was probably a good idea. "I'll be happy to buy you a new pair of jeans before I leave."

"No, no. I have too many pairs of jeans, anyway." She paused. "When are you flying out? I never thought to ask."

He didn't like thinking about that. It was already Saturday night, which left him far too little time in Colorado with Kate. "First thing Monday morning." He'd been so involved with her that he'd pushed that information to the back of his mind. Their relationship had become so intense so fast that he couldn't get his mind around the idea of leaving her.

"Right. Monday." Her expression became thoughtful, and then she seemed to give herself a mental shake. "Well, the clock's ticking. Be right back."

The clock was indeed ticking, but when he was with her, he lost all sense of time. He couldn't afford to do that this weekend, with all that he hoped to accomplish. He needed to refocus on his goals.

Once she was out of the room, he stood and quickly got dressed. He left off his shoes and socks, though. She'd come to the door barefoot, after all, and wearing shoes while walking on an amazing carpet was a waste of luxury.

The food on the raised counter surrounding the kitchen looked more interesting to him than it had earlier, so he wandered over, picked up a plate, and began filling it. Several platters contained bite-sized items suitable for a cocktail party or a serious working dinner. He'd discovered at the lunch banquet that Stillman Lodge had an excellent chef.

"Good. You're eating."

He turned as she walked back into the living room. No suit of armor, but her resolute expression would serve as well as one. He swallowed the meat-filled pastry he'd been chewing. "It's good. Thank you for providing it."

"There's coffee in the carafe and I set out a couple of mugs."

"I noticed that. Thanks. We'll probably need the caffeine."

"I agree, but Grandma Elizabeth advised me to serve you wine."

"I'll just bet she did." Duncan had met Grandma Elizabeth briefly today and she wasn't at all what he'd pictured. He expected grandmothers, especially ones named

Elizabeth, to look like the Queen of England. Kate's grandmother looked like Meryl Streep.

"Do you want a glass of wine?"

He shook his head. "No, thanks. I need all the inhibitions I can get."

"I hadn't noticed that you had any." Crossing to the counter, she took a plate and began choosing food from the platters.

"That's because you don't know me well enough yet. I have layers. You've only scratched the surface."

She glanced at him. "Don't you dare."

"Dare what?"

"Tease me by suggesting that what we've had is only the tip of the iceberg."

"But it is, lass."

"If you don't stop, I'll begin to think you're being seductive on purpose so I'll be distracted and you'll get your way on the mission statement."

"Hold it right there." Anger stirred for the first time. Trading barbs was one thing, but she'd just impugned his honor. "That's a strong accusation."

She faced him, holding her plate. "Can you deny that you're being seductive?"

"No, damn it, but you're lovely! It's my natural tendency to be seductive when I'm aroused. Every male's natural tendency, in fact. But I would never use sex to hoodwink you into doing something you didn't mean to, and I resent that you even suggested that I would."

Her expression softened. "You're right. That was unfair. I wouldn't be so attracted to you if you didn't have a rock-solid moral code. I *know* you're not trying to influence my behavior with sex, but . . . can you at least try not to be so . . . tempting?"

That made him laugh, and it did wonders for his ego, too. She wouldn't like knowing she'd boosted that ego that she'd lectured him about. "I'll do my best."

"Thank you."

"It won't be easy."

She rolled her eyes. "I appreciate any effort you can make."

He was stating the God's truth. It wouldn't be easy, because instinctively he wanted to tempt her, wanted to make her lust for him. Some of that was self-protection, because his desperate yearning for Kate threw him off-balance. He'd feel a hundred percent better if he thought she was in the same boat.

Chapter 12

WERECON2012:
DELEGATES TAKE TIME OUT FOR FUN

Exclusive report for *Wereworld Celebrity Watch*
by Angela Sapworthy

DENVER—After a day packed with seminars and political jockeying, delegates to WereCon2012 let loose with an old-fashioned romp in the snow, Were-style! A plan hatched in the Stillman Lodge bar resulted in more than fifty delegates shapeshifting and making use of the lodge's special wolf-friendly exits to hit the slopes, minus skis, of course.

This reporter couldn't help but join in the rambunctious free-for-all! Without shirts or slogans, political bias no longer mattered as all enjoyed the freedom to run and slide in the fresh snow with equal abandon. Although this reporter had to call it an evening after only a few minutes of the biting cold, she suspects many Weres are still out there reveling in their freedom to simply be werewolves.

The playful episode provides a brief respite for Weres locked in a heated battle over whether to maintain our time-honored secrecy or risk revealing ourselves to the human community. That question will be the subject of tomorrow's final session, a much-publicized debate between HOWL leader Kate Stillman and WOOF leader Duncan Mac-Dowell. For up-to-the-minute coverage of that historic event, follow me on Sniffer@newshound. You'll have a ringside seat!

Kate glanced around the suite as she evaluated the best way to set up their work environment. Her desk was big enough for them to share it and she had another chair she could bring in from the bedroom. But that would put them tantalizingly close to each other. Bad idea.

She turned to him. "How about if I work and eat at my desk, and you set your laptop up on the counter? There are outlets on the kitchen side of it, so you can plug in."

"That sounds fine." Setting his plate down, he retrieved his briefcase and took out his laptop, along with a trade paperback book. "I brought you this. Don't feel obliged to read it, but . . . I learned a lot from reading yours."

She slid her plate back onto the counter and accepted the book with a pang of guilt. He'd been more open-minded than she had. And smarter, too. They had a debate coming up tomorrow afternoon and it would go a lot better for her if she had read this.

She'd convinced herself she knew what was in it from following his blog, but that was lazy thinking. After spending time with him, she realized lazy thinking could get her annihilated in that debate. He'd done her a favor by bringing his book tonight.

"Thank you." She gazed at the cover. *Down with Dogma: Benefits of Were-Human Cooperation* was splashed across the bottom in vivid red type on a black background. Duncan's name was at the top, and in the middle a human profile faced a wolf profile, each outlined in red. Very eye-catching and dramatic.

"As I said, you don't have to read it."

"But I will." She glanced up. "I should have read it before now, and not doing that shows some arrogance on my part. In fact, when we debate tomorrow, you can ding me for not knowing what's in here."

He shrugged. "I'm sure you've been busy running your dating site and helping your grandmother plan this conference. I didn't read yours until I was faced with a long plane ride, so don't beat yourself up too much."

"All right, I won't. But handing me this tells me that you fight fair." She opened the cover to see if he'd signed it, and sure enough, he had. His inscription read *To my worthy opponent Kate. Affectionately, Duncan.*

"I debated whether that was too incriminating."

"Not if no one sees it but me." She closed the cover and looked at him. "And no one will. I like what you wrote. I'll treasure this. And I'll definitely read as much as I can before our debate."

"Hm." He returned her gaze. "I may have made a tactical error. I'd hate for reading my book to cut into . . . uh . . . your free time."

She smiled. "Diplomatically put."

"I'm trying like hell not to come across as teasing and tempting."

"You're doing better, and I promise that given a choice between reading someone's book or spending quality time with the author, I'll take the one-on-one option every time."

He chuckled. "Good."

"But if we have any chance of finding quality time, we'd better get cracking."

"Aye."

Walking over to her desk, she laid the book on it. Then she hit the button to open the curtains. "Let's see what's happening outside."

"Must we? With the lights on, anyone out there will be able to see in here better than we can see out there."

"Exactly." After reading that inscription, she was feeling way too mellow about Duncan MacDowell.

"You're a determined lass, I'll give you that." With a sigh, he came over to gaze out into the darkness broken only by the lights on the ski slope. "Am I imagining things, or are there a bunch of wolves out there playing in the snow?"

"Are there?" She peered out toward the lit slope. "That's what it looks like to me."

Duncan laughed. "Whoever's out there, they're having one hell of a good time running and sliding. Whoops! That big one just wiped out. I wish we could . . . but we can't."

"Not until we have something to give Howard." But Kate watched the wolves with equal fascination.

"How long since you've shifted?" He was standing close enough for her to feel his warmth and breathe in his scent.

She should move away, but she liked standing here

with him watching wolves romp. "Too long. Like you said, I've been busy with HOWL, my dating site, planning this conference, keeping up with your blog. I forget about shifting and the fun to be had."

"I can imagine how you'd look as a wolf, all blond and fluffy."

"My best time to go out and be camouflaged is when the aspens are turning and dropping leaves. I blend right in."

"I'd love to see that."

"You might have, if this early snowstorm hadn't hit. The leaves were beautiful, but now they'll all be gone." She glanced over at him. "Your coat is pure black, isn't it?" The urge to see him like that overwhelmed her. He would be magnificent, and she might never have the chance to find out.

"Aye. Black as night. I'd stand out in the snow like a blot of ink on a white page."

"But out here we're so isolated that it wouldn't matter. That's why everyone's having such a good time down there. It's safe."

He looked at her. "You want to go out there, don't you?"

"Of course I do, but we have an assignment to finish, as I believe I've mentioned at least a thousand times."

"Or more." He put his arm around her shoulders and gave her a quick squeeze. He didn't linger, as if he wanted to make sure he wouldn't be accused of tempting her. "Let's tackle the job and get it out of the way. Then we can shift and go."

She caught his excitement. "Let's do. I would love that."

"So would I. I haven't shifted in months. Stretching my muscles would feel good."

"I'll get my food and a cup of coffee, and we'll dive in." She headed back over to the counter, poured herself some coffee, and picked up her plate.

"Same here." He followed her over, found a plug on the opposite side of the counter, and connected his laptop cord. "Did you come up with any wording during the day?"

"I did, as a matter of fact." She walked back to her desk and turned on her computer. "How about you?"

"Me, too. I was a little bored in the session on 'Werewolves Through the Ages,' so I used the time to brainstorm."

"Excellent." Kate located the scrap of paper she'd tossed on her desk when she'd come back to her suite at the end of the day. "Let's hear yours first." She picked up one of the cheesy snacks and popped it in her mouth as she glanced at him over her shoulder.

"Maybe you should start." He poured a cup of coffee. "Ladies first, and all that."

She chewed her food and swallowed. "Okay." She didn't want to waste time discussing who went first. "Here it is, and remember, this is rough."

"I understand."

"Then here goes—*WOW Mission Statement: to support the werewolf culture worldwide and protect its traditions, values, and unique benefits through networking and education.*"

Duncan took a deep breath. "That sounds like you."

She turned in her chair to study him. "How do you mean that? In a good way or a bad way?"

"I'm not going to assign good and bad designations at this point."

"You're being evasive, Duncan. You don't like it, do you? I didn't expect you to."

"It's not a matter of liking or not liking. You say some things in there that throw up a red flag for me, and I'm sure you know what they are."

She did know. But she thought of Sally, and of Jake. They expected her to stand firm. "Let's hear yours, then. We need to know how far apart we are."

He cleared his throat and read from the screen of his laptop. *"WOW Mission Statement: to support the interests of werewolves worldwide and expand their influence through networking and unfettered communication with the human population."* He stared at the screen and rubbed his chin. "Comments?"

"We're pretty far apart."

"Granted."

"But we have a few words in common."

He laughed and shook his head. "Damned few."

She sipped her coffee. "We have Wi-Fi hooked up. I'm going to send you mine and you send me yours. Let's look at them side by side and see how they might be blended."

He blew out a breath. "It's worth a try, I suppose."

Within a few seconds, she had his statement pasted under hers.

"If we have Wi-Fi, then we could also go on Sniffer from our computers," he said.

"Yes, but we're not going to do that. Howard asked us to move beyond Howlers and Woofers and get creative so we could hash this out. So let's go for it."

Two hours later, they were still haggling and Duncan couldn't see a solution. They'd eaten most of the food and what was left looked dodgy after sitting there for so long. They'd drained the carafe of coffee and the fire had burned down to a few glowing embers. Neither of them had attempted to build it up again, as if they both kept hoping they'd find a way through the maze and be done.

"Look, you have to give up that word *protect*, Kate. To Weres like Jake, it means some elaborate security system that hasn't even been invented yet. You heard how he went on and on about the database of Weres being a tool of the devil."

"And I'm not so sure it isn't! What if the wrong people got their hands on that database? They could hunt down and kill every Were on the planet."

"It would never come to that. We have numbers, we have economic strength, and we have physical abilities, like a superior sense of smell and hearing. We're experts at surviving, and—"

"You want to put us back into survival mode? We've been there, Duncan, and it's not pretty. You know the word I want *you* to get rid of? *Unfettered.* That implies dropping every safeguard, every precaution, and throwing ourselves on the mercy of the humans. That's nuts. I can't agree to anything that has the word *unfettered* in it."

"So here's what we have so far that we absolutely agree on."

She blinked. "We have something?"

"Of course. I've been keeping track. Here's the mission statement with all the controversial parts taken out. *WOW Mission Statement: to support werewolves worldwide through networking.*"

"That's a very short mission statement, Duncan."

"Granted, but we agree on every bit of it."

"Not hard when there's nothing to it. And now that I think about it, the term *networking* is suspect, because it could be interpreted as suggesting that damned database."

"*Networking* was in your first rough draft!"

"And I'm rethinking the use of it."

Duncan groaned and laid his forehead on the counter. "Now we're backsliding."

"I don't see any more wolves out on the hillside."

Lifting his head, he turned around on his stool and looked toward the window. She'd left her chair. Hands shoved in the back pockets of her jeans, she was staring at a landscape shrouded in darkness except for that pale row of lights on the ski slope.

"They might still be out there." He climbed off the stool and went to join her. "There could be romance happening in the shadows."

Her breath caught. "Duncan, you promised."

"You're right. Shouldn't have said that." But he'd been thinking about it ever since proposing that they take a run in the snow when they finished the damned mission statement. At this rate he didn't think they ever would finish it.

But saying that a miracle happened, and they had a breakthrough, he'd love to take a run with her as wolves and then have a lusty bout of Were sex out there in the snow. Knowing the werewolf mentality as he did, others were doing that tonight, perhaps at this very minute.

He realized that craving Were sex contradicted everything he stood for. He'd written countless blog posts blathering on about how unimportant Were sex was in the grand scheme of things. In his book, which she might read soon, he'd labeled the practice a primitive holdover from the old days.

Yet he wanted to experience it with her. He longed to

see her romping through snowdrifts, exotic in her blond coloring with eyes bluer than the center of a flame. Then, when they'd run themselves until they were panting and pleasantly tired, he would take her as a male wolf takes a female. Warmth shot through his system and stiffened his cock.

And he wasn't alone in thinking about sex. The scent of her arousal drifted toward him, exciting him even more.

She took a long, shaky breath. "Duncan, this isn't good."

"No, it isn't. I'm sorry. My fault." He forced himself to walk away from her, but like a restless wolf, he began to pace.

"It's not all your fault. I was thinking about it, too."

"Let's change the subject." He continued to pace. "Tell me why you're so against the database. Even if we don't have unlimited communication with humans as I envision, a central database would be a very unifying tool. Right now our information is incomplete, but if we had a database, we could send out global messages and coordinate our efforts in ways we've never been able to do before."

"But it's too much like a registration system. I don't like it."

"We could have safeguards, install warning systems. If we had the slightest hint that someone was accessing it in order to round up werewolves, our network, which is still a very good idea, by the way, would alert Weres to the potential danger." The carpet felt good under his feet, the only sensual pleasure he was allowing himself right now.

"Assuming a Were was included in the network."

"But why wouldn't they be?"

She walked over to the counter, picked up the platters, and took them into the kitchen, where she began scraping them into the sink. "A Were might be listed in the database because she's the offspring of other Weres, but she might not be part of the network anymore, maybe by choice because of the risk of discovery."

Then he understood. "Like Penny." He stopped pacing and faced the kitchen area where she was working.

"It's one thing when powerful Weres like Aidan and Roarke Wallace take human mates." She scrubbed the platters vigorously, as if cleaning them would somehow help. "In that case, the Weres protect the humans, and the humans, surrounded by so many Weres, are less likely to betray the werewolf community. But Penny . . ." She stopped scrubbing and looked over at him. "Penny's out there alone, Duncan. Instead of being surrounded by powerful Weres, she's surrounded by humans."

"You're right. It's different."

"You bet it is." Her expression was grim. "If they discovered her secret, I don't know what would happen. Maybe Tom would try to protect her. I want to believe that he would. But he doesn't know her secret, either, and he might feel betrayed and angry." Kate swallowed. "I've had many nightmares about Penny."

"I'm sure you have." He liked to think he was an intelligent Were, but he'd been missing a key point. Were-human mating, if it became a common practice, wouldn't be confined to powerful male Weres choosing human mates. And if female Weres chose a human mate and went to live among humans as Penny had, would it be safe to reveal their Were nature?

Not in the current environment, that was for sure. The

culture still contained too many movies and books that depicted Weres as dangerous beasts who could "turn" a human into a werewolf with one bite. That had never been true, but it made a good story, and the myth had been repeated so many times most people believed it.

Duncan realized that his Utopian dream would take years of reeducation before it had a chance of being realized. And thanks to Kate and her sister, Penny, he had a perspective that hadn't been included in his thinking until now. He'd had male myopia, and he felt a little foolish having to admit that.

"I suppose you've figured out by now that I founded HOWL because of Penny," Kate said.

"Aye. I suspected that, at least on some level, but I hadn't really thought it through. I assumed you were mostly upset because she's no longer close to your family."

"That's part of it. But I'm scared for her. And I don't want other female Weres running the risks she does, so I created my Were-only dating site and founded HOWL for that reason. On the other side of the coin, if male Weres insist on hooking up with humans, then that reduces the number of eligible and safe mates for us."

Duncan massaged the back of his neck, where tension had taken up permanent residence. "I hate to admit that I read that in your book, but it didn't really sink in."

"You were focused on the sex tips."

He nodded. "I fear so."

"What about you?" She stacked the platters in a wire rack so they could drain. "What inspired you to found WOOF?"

The question startled him. He couldn't remember being asked before. "The easy answer is that I want to help create more freedom for Weres in all areas of life."

"But why?" She leaned her hips against the kitchen counter. "Did you lose the human love of your life because of Were prejudice?"

"No. At one time I told myself she was my soul mate, but when my brother, Colin, challenged me on that, I realized that she was only my way to make a statement."

"And why—"

"I'm way ahead of you, lass. Why did I feel such a pressing need to make a statement? Because of the very thing you've accused me of—ego. My big brother is the laird with all sorts of responsibilities. Very important in the grand scheme of things."

"I see."

He was afraid she really did see, and he felt more exposed than ever in his life. But he trusted her in a way he didn't trust most others, and it felt good to get this out in the open. "Plus he and my parents used to bitterly oppose Were-human mating, so of course I had to come out in favor of it."

She smiled. "It takes a humble heart to admit such a motivation. I admire you for telling me, and I don't think your ego is nearly the size I used to imagine it was."

"Maybe you've helped me shrink it down to a reasonable size." There was some truth in that. She was good for him. "Don't get me wrong. I believe in the cause. Inevitably Weres and humans will fall in love, and then you have that *Romeo and Juliet* scenario. I think it's past time that we figured out a way around that."

"Does that mean you're ready to tackle the mission statement again?"

He blew out a breath. "No."

"You're not giving up, are you?"

"I won't do that unless we run out of time, and we still

have some. I think we've been cooped up for too long and our brains are fried. If everyone else has gone inside, let's go out and play in the snow."

"Before we've finished?" She made it sound as if he'd suggested murder and mayhem.

"Howard told us to be creative, and I don't know about you, but my creative well is bone-dry. Some fresh air and exercise is exactly what I need, and then I'll come back in ready to tackle that mission statement."

"As usual, you are a very convincing Were."

"Does that mean you'll go with me? Because even if you won't, I'm set on it. You can sit up here and beat your brains out trying to write that statement if you insist, but I'm heading for the slopes."

"Well, Howard did say we were supposed to work together."

"So let's play together for a little while and then we'll be refreshed and renewed, ready for the task."

"Okay." She still sounded reluctant, though.

He'd coax her out of that reluctance soon enough. His pulse quickened as he imagined them out there together. He might be rationalizing this decision to take a break because he wanted her so desperately. But they wouldn't stay out long, just long enough to play and . . . have a different kind of fun.

Then he'd put his nose to the grindstone. He had no choice. The clock was ticking.

Chapter 13

Kate worried about getting the mission statement finished, but as Duncan had raved on about the wonders of playing in the snow, she'd had a thought. He'd said that shifting hadn't been a priority for him recently. Encouraging him to do that now would remind him of the joys to be found as a wolf, joys he could share only with others of his kind.

She walked over to the desk and pressed the button to close the drapes. "I don't know if anyone's out there, but no reason to take a chance they'd see us taking our clothes off."

"Good thinking." Duncan pulled off his blue sweatshirt. "Before we shift, you should probably show me how we navigate from the third floor. I assume there's some sort of passageway leading down there that we can access in wolf form."

"The other rooms have sloping passageways and revolving doors at the bottom, but the exits from my suite and Grandma Elizabeth's are a bit more sophisticated than that." She loved showing this off and she didn't get many chances.

Walking to the bookcase closest to the window wall, she pushed what looked like a knothole. A carefully matched rectangle of wood the size of a light switch slid back to reveal a control panel with a touch screen. Pressing her thumb to it, she heard the click of a latch. Then she placed her hand against the bookcase and it revolved slowly in response.

"I like it already. Like something out of a murder mystery."

"Wait until you see the rest." Inside was a small platform, and beyond that stood a magnificent glass elevator. The tall panels were etched with scenes of mountains, forests, and wolves. When Kate uttered the voice command of *wolf*, the elevator pulsed with a silvery light.

"That's beautiful." Still wearing his T-shirt and jeans, Duncan walked over to peer at the elevator. "I assume it has a touch pad inside the elevator we can operate after we've shifted."

"I can operate it. It recognizes my thumb or paw print, and my grandmother's, of course. It's the smoothest ride you'll ever have in an elevator. My grandfather had these built a couple of years before he died after Elizabeth complained about the drafty, poorly lit passageways. He had those redesigned, too, so they're much nicer, but he wanted to do something special for his mate."

"This is bloody damned special, all right."

"Grandpa Mitchell told her that now she could descend from their suite like an angel from heaven. And he wasn't being sarcastic, either. He adored her."

"Obviously he did, judging from this elevator. But why build a second one down here?"

"This suite was Penny's back then. She was being groomed to be the next alpha, so my grandfather thought she might as well get the royal treatment, too."

"She gave up a lot to be with the man she loved, didn't she?"

Kate met his gaze. "Yes, she did. I would say she gave up too much, but how do I know? I've never been in love like that. I keep thinking, though, that if she'd never met Tom, none of this would have happened."

"You don't think she was destined to meet him?"

She studied him, intrigued by his comment. "Do you believe in that? Lovers destined to be with each other?" She'd always thought males were more inclined to be practical in such matters. If one female didn't work out, another would be along soon enough.

"Don't you?"

"I asked you first."

"Then, yes, I do, lass. But you have to remember that I'm a Scotsman. We tend to give a little more credit to fate than you might over here."

"I think I like that about you. It's very appealing."

He laughed. "I'm glad, because it's bred into me and I'd be hard-pressed to root it out. So, since you're now in this suite, I take it that you are being groomed for the alpha job?"

"Nothing's been said in so many words, because my grandmother, as you can tell, is still fully capable of leading the Stillman pack. But I believe I'm next in line, and this suite is meant for that purpose. Neil would love to move in, literally, but I don't plan to let him."

"Good. He'd make a terrible pack alpha, but you . . ." He gazed at her with warmth in his gray eyes. "You'd be terrific."

"That's nice of you to say, considering that we don't agree on much of anything when it comes to the future of Weres. Neil seems to be leaning in your direction, though."

"He doesn't strike me as a Were with much integrity. You do, and I'd rather see someone honest be in power than someone who thinks like me, or at least pretends to." He grinned at her. "But enough of that. Ready to shift and go? You still have all your clothes on, milady."

"So I do." Walking over to the red sofa, she started stripping down. She'd taken off everything but her bra and panties when he cleared his throat.

"On the other hand . . ."

She glanced over at Duncan. "You haven't been undressing while I did. What's the deal?"

He stood very still, his gaze hot. "Maybe there are other, easier ways to refill the well."

"Don't go changing the plan, Woofer. You said you wanted a run in the snow, and that's what we're going to have." She was determined now. He probably spent far too much time as a human. He was losing touch with his roots. "Take the rest of your clothes off and be snappy about it."

He shrugged. "I suppose I'll have to do that, regardless." Reaching over his shoulders with both hands, he grabbed fistfuls of his T-shirt, yanked it over his head, and tossed it aside. "You'll soon see the condition you've put me in by taking off yours."

Now it was her turn to stare. She wondered if she'd ever get used to the sight of that broad chest dusted with dark hair and those abs that rippled as he pulled off his T-shirt.

"Presenting Exhibit A." He unfastened his jeans and shoved them down, along with his knit boxers. His cock sprang free, gloriously erect.

She swallowed. "I see what you mean." And the sight of an aroused Duncan created an almost unbearable craving to join with him now, this very minute. But she reminded herself that he needed to rediscover the joys of being a wolf. He might have forgotten what he'd be giving up if he mated with a human who couldn't share that pleasure with him.

"That red sofa looks cozy." He started toward her.

"No." She backed around it, putting the sofa between them. "We're going to shift and ride that elevator down to the ground floor. That was the plan and we're going to work the plan."

"I don't know what will happen if I shift when I'm like this." He gestured toward his groin. "I'm not sure it's safe."

"You'll be fine. Stay right there. I'm going to take off my bra and panties, and then we'll shift together."

"If you say so, but I think when you take off your underwear, I'll be in even worse shape. I seem to have a Pavlovian response to seeing you naked."

"That's funny, considering Pavlov did his experiments with dogs."

"Aye, it's hilarious, isn't it? I'm standing here getting harder by the second, and you think it's funny."

"I also think it's flattering. And you're not the only one who has a Pavlovian response, just so you know."

"Ah." He looked mollified. "Now that you mention it, I can tell by that delicious scent of yours. I was so preoccupied with my own lust that I failed to take note of yours." His glance swept over her. "And your nipples are tight as little pencil erasers. That makes me feel better."

She kicked away her panties. "That's it. I'm ready."

"Me, too. Let's do it on the sofa."

"We're not shape-shifting on the sofa. We'd fall off."

"My wee man has in mind a different activity."

She ignored that comment. "When was the last time you shifted with a female Were, Duncan?"

"It's been . . . a while."

"Years?"

"Maybe. So putting it off for another year is no problem." He held out his hand. "Lie with me on that red sofa, Kate. I promise to make it worth your while."

"You've completely lost focus, Woofer." She held out her hand, too. "Walk around the sofa and lie here on the carpet with me. We're going to shift together. There's something very special about sharing that moment with another Were. Or have you forgotten?"

He hesitated, and then he frowned. "Perhaps I have. It's been a long time since I've done that." He sighed and rounded the sofa. "So if you insist."

"I do. I think it's important." Dropping to her hands and knees, she lay on her side and stretched out on the soft gray surface. Then she patted a spot beside her. "Lie here."

"I'm still hard as a billiard cue. Harder, even."

"I know. Trust me, you'll be fine. And you'll thank me later."

He held her gaze as he came down to lie facing her. He was close enough to reach out and touch her, but he didn't. "I just hope that shifting in this condition doesn't cause me to break something important."

She pressed her lips together to keep from laughing. He wouldn't appreciate that. "If I thought you were in danger of breaking something important, I wouldn't be encouraging you. I do care what happens to you and your important parts."

He smiled into her eyes. "Same here, lass."

She felt a rush of tenderness for this Were. Although he'd given her an argument just now, at last he lay facing her, prepared as she was to be completely vulnerable for the next few seconds. During a shift a werewolf was defenseless.

Trusting each other now would forge a bond. It always did. And maybe that bond would help them bridge the gap between them when they returned to human form. Gazing into his eyes, she concentrated on bringing out the wolf that lived within her and waited patiently to be released.

Duncan was a little rusty, but looking into Kate's blue eyes helped him focus. He sensed the energy flowing through her, a luminous river of change. He felt the hum of it in his own body as her vibrations spread across the space between them and washed over him in a calming wave.

Yes, he'd forgotten the sensation of peace and wholeness that shifting with a Were female could bring. He'd missed the feeling without knowing he missed it, but now that he was here with Kate, he welcomed the shared warmth of moving together into another state of being. His breathing synchronized with hers.

As her body began to glow, he held his hand in front of his face and watched the light enter his fingers. She smiled and held her hand up, palm out. Slowly he aligned his palm with hers, leaving a centimeter of space between. They did not need to touch to be as one. That was the wonder of it.

He'd denied himself this for too long. He gazed in fascination as the transformation began in her, matched by the stretching and tugging that signaled he was shifting in time with her. Like partners in a dance whose bodies never met, they shimmered and slowly transformed, in unison.

He saw her eyes become the incredible blue of a wolf's eyes, and he kept his gaze locked with hers, knowing her change mirrored his. At last, she rose to her feet, a blond wolf with eyes that were Kate's, but different, wilder, shining with a primitive light that beckoned to him.

Rejoicing in the lithe strength of his body, he stood, stretched out his muzzle, and touched noses with her. *Well done, lass.* He'd also missed the telepathic communication possible only between Weres. There was an intimacy about it that couldn't be duplicated with a human female.

Kate had probably meant for him to notice these things. He'd been the one to suggest this, but she'd pushed it once he had. Now he could see how this fit neatly into her plan to convince him her way was superior to his.

She surveyed him from the tip of his nose to the tip of his tail. *Too bad you don't dress like this more often, Woofer. It suits you.*

I could say the same about you, lass.

How are your . . . important parts?

The shift seems to have settled me down some.

Good. She glanced toward the elevator. *Shall we?*

I'd be honored to share an elevator with the next Stillman pack alpha. After you.

She walked ahead of him, her head high. Although she was a large wolf, as all Weres tended to be, he was larger. As a human he'd schooled himself not to care about such things, but as a wolf, he liked knowing that he stood a good five inches taller at the shoulder.

Once they were both inside the elevator, he noticed the control mounted near the floor had two touch pads.

Does this elevator stop at other floors?

That would defeat the purpose of making it exclusive, wouldn't it? This is an express elevator. She placed her paw firmly on the top touch pad, and the bookcase wall swung closed and latched with a soft click. When she pressed the bottom one, the elevator started down.

He'd never imagined what it would be like to be an angel descending from heaven, but he'd be willing to believe this was a close approximation. The glass cubicle glided with a smoothness that told him the mechanism was flawless and probably worth a small fortune. He thought of a love so deep that it would inspire a Were to pay for such an elevator so that his beloved mate could ride from her third-floor suite in luxury.

Duncan wished for a love that deep, but he hadn't found anyone who seemed capable of sharing such an intense emotion. Honesty made him amend that. Kate had that ability, but thinking of her in those terms was laughable. They couldn't even seem to write a short mission statement together.

The elevator came to a graceful stop and a different side of it slid open. When it did, a section of the dark wall in front of them swiveled, letting in a blast of frigid air.

Duncan had second thoughts. Her suite was cozy and warm. They'd let the fire die down, but they could easily build it up again. A wrought-iron log holder by the hearth contained a good supply of firewood.

He nudged her shoulder. *It's cold out there. Maybe this is a bad idea.*

We've come this far. We're going out there. In one bound, she cleared the elevator and leaped through the opening.

He had no choice but to follow. As he sucked in a lungful of cold air, he wondered what he'd been thinking. Fresh air was one thing. But this air was the equivalent of a stroll through a meat locker.

You're lagging behind, Woofer!

One thing about Kate, she knew how to taunt him. Bracing himself against the bite of the wind and the chill of the snow under his paws, he gathered his haunches under him. *Race you to the ski slope!* And he started running through the snow.

He threw up plumes of the white stuff each time his paws touched down, dug in, and launched him forward again. About ten seconds into that exercise, he began to have the time of his life. Shifting was a magical experience, but this, this was what wolves were meant to do. He couldn't believe he'd let so much time go by without racing across the open countryside, his cares forgotten as he abandoned himself to being a wild creature again.

A spray of snow hit him in the nose and he turned to find her running beside him. She kept up with his furious pace with ease. He put on a burst of speed that should have left her well behind him, but no, she was still there, matching him stride for stride.

He shot her a challenging glance as he started uphill

along the row of lights on the ski slope. A climb like this should slow her down. But it didn't. If anything, she was pulling ahead of him.

His male pride was in serious danger of being damaged at this rate. Lungs burning, he ran faster. She kept up, and she was barely panting. But his tongue hung out like a wet pink dishrag.

Fortunately he didn't need breath to send her a telepathic message. *What are you, an Olympic medalist?*

No, I'm a Were who lives above five thousand feet. You, on the other hand, live at sea level, or near to it, I'm guessing. My endurance is bound to be better.

I should have remembered that. I didn't realize I was in a losing battle.

Is this a race, Duncan?

You know it is, lass. You and I, we've been battling for months. It's become a habit for us. He veered off the slope and into the tall pines lining the ski run. *But I'm throwing up the white flag. You bested me, and I'm willing to admit that you have.* He glanced over his shoulder to see if she followed, and to offer a silent invitation.

She swerved, cutting a new path through the snow parallel with his. *You had a good time, though. Don't tell me you didn't.*

I would have had a better time if I'd been able to show off my athletic prowess like the mighty Scotsman that I am. He was poking fun at himself, and he thought she knew him well enough to realize that. But so soon into their relationship, he wasn't quite sure.

Just keeping up with me and my superior lung power proves that you are indeed a mighty Scotsman. I can alert Angela Sapworthy to that fact if you like.

He snorted. So she'd taken his little joke and turned it

back on him. *I don't think we want Angela to know about our midnight run, do you?* He sank into deeper snowdrifts, too deep for what he had in mind. He required firmer footing, but the ski run wouldn't work. Far too bright.

The less Angela knows about anything, the better, she agreed.

Aye. Then he spotted it, a small shelter under the overhanging branches of a giant evergreen. The branches had caught the bulk of the snow, which meant the area under them had gathered only a few inches. *Let's rest over here. There's shelter from the wind.*

And shelter from prying eyes? But she followed him, ducking under the branches as he did.

That little problem I had before we shifted hasn't entirely disappeared. He walked in a tight circle, trampling the snow a little more.

I didn't expect it would. As I recall, it was more than a little problem. It looked like a rather large problem to me.

That's nice of you to say. He faced her and stretched his front legs in a playful bow. *I'm hoping for your assistance in taking care of that problem.* He suspected that Were sex would fall right in with her plans. She'd want him to reacquaint himself with that, too.

As it happened, he was willing to fall in with her plans. He had a strong urge to do so, in fact. One could even say he had a compelling urge that made him circle her as he drew in her musky scent.

But being Kate, she wasn't going to make this easy for him. She bounded to the edge of the snowy enclosure. *Why should I?*

Because you want it as much as I do.

Maybe I do and maybe I don't. She pranced to the

other side of the clearing, flaunting herself. *Maybe I'm too tired after that long run.*

Tired? You were barely panting. I'm the one who should be ready to drop.

Poor Duncan. You need to go back inside and recover.

Not yet. He edged closer.

She danced away.

You're going to make me work for this, aren't you?

Have you forgotten? It's more fun that way.

He circled her again as his blood ran hotter. She was right. It was more fun this way. He feinted left and she leaped right, whirling to put herself out of position.

With a low growl, he stalked her, and she backed up, eyes glowing in the faint light from the ski slope that filtered through the branches.

Come and get me, big boy.

I can't believe you said that.

Always wanted to.

I will get you. It's only a matter of time. He dashed to the right and then whirled back, startling her. With a lightning move he didn't know he had, he mounted her in one swift lunge. *Now.*

I let you catch me.

Liar. He thrust deep and she shuddered with pleasure. Maybe she had let him catch her, after all. And then all thought disappeared as he lost himself in a wild surge of primitive lust. Needs that hadn't driven him in years consumed him now.

He took her again and again and again. Her soft whimper inflamed him even more, and he thrust harder until he felt her close around him, felt her spasms of release. At last he poured himself into her with a ferocity that left him panting.

He'd forgotten. Oh, yes, he'd forgotten. But he would never forget again. And the truth shattered all his carefully laid plans. This was how male and female Weres were meant to connect, and he'd been fooling himself to think he could live without it.

Chapter 14

Kate didn't use her telepathic powers as she rode up in the elevator with Duncan, and neither did he. She didn't need to read his mind to know what he was thinking. He'd immersed himself in the experience, and so had she. And he'd loved it, which created a problem for him. She knew that, too.

But he wasn't the only one with a problem. She'd achieved her goal of reminding him of his Wereness and the joys that sprang from that. She'd also reminded herself of her own Wereness and how little she'd been celebrating that recently. Maybe that would explain why this experience with Duncan had been so incredible.

That would be nice, because otherwise she might have to face the fact that he was the best thing she'd come across in her entire life. If that turned out to be true, they'd created quite a dilemma for themselves. The leader of the Howlers couldn't very well be sweet on the leader of the Woofers and vice versa.

Once back in her suite, they stretched out in the same spot behind the sofa where they'd shifted earlier. Their wolf bodies glowed with blue fire as they slowly transformed again. They lay there, not moving, not touching. But their gazes met. And held.

At last Duncan took a breath that came from deep in his chest and shook his entire body. "Thank you, lass."

"I'm not sure that you should thank me."

"I should." His mouth curved in a soft smile. "We're in a hell of a spot, you and I, but I can't bring myself to regret a minute of my time with you."

"Nor I with you."

He reached out and took her hand. "We're a couple of smart Weres, aren't we?"

"I used to think I was. But I might have outsmarted myself."

"Aye. I know the feeling." He brushed her palm with his thumb. "But I also know our personal complications have to take a backseat to that mission statement. Howard's counting on us."

"Yes, he is."

Duncan raised her hand to his lips and kissed each of her fingers in turn. "So let's do that job, and then . . . we'll talk." He placed a final kiss against her palm.

She shivered, in reaction to both his kisses and the prospect of what they would say to each other once they'd set aside their public duties. Would they agree to give up this special connection, or find a way to continue it? She had no answers and she doubted that he did, either.

"Time to get dressed." Rising to his feet, he helped

her up, too. "I have no chance of concentrating with you looking all rosy and well loved. Makes me want to do it again."

"I know. Me, too." Holding both of his hands, she stood on tiptoe to give him one gentle kiss. "And thank you for loving me so well." Then she squeezed his hands and let go.

Gathering her clothes, she turned away and quickly put them on. She didn't glance over at him as they both dressed, much as she would have liked to. She heard the rustling of denim as he put on his jeans, and ignored the mental image that brought up. They had a job to do, and time was running out.

"I've had a thought about this mission statement," he said.

She shoved both arms into the sleeves of her sweatshirt and popped it over her head. "What's that?"

"We've both approached it with our own agendas." He pulled on his sweatshirt, too, and looked at her. "What if we each put those aside? Let's think of what we would write if we weren't trying to insert our personal philosophy into it."

"You mean lay down our weapons?"

"Aye, something like that."

"But our constituents are counting on us to defend our respective positions in this mission statement." Kate thought of Heidi, Jake, and especially Sally with her stealth support.

"I know, but the entire Were world isn't divided into Woofers and Howlers, much as it seems that way right now. What about the ones who want to drop the secrecy but still think Weres should only mate with Weres? What about those who want to keep the secrecy but allow

Were-human mating under special circumstances? Don't we owe them a mission statement they can be happy with, too?"

She thought about that. "You have a point. Let me put on some more coffee to wake us up." She walked over to the kitchen, where the bare soles of her feet met cool tile. Even the smell of the coffee beans as she ground them helped her focus. She dumped the ground coffee in the basket, filled the reservoir with water, and turned on the switch.

"Got anything sweet to go with it?"

She narrowed her eyes at him.

"I wasn't trying to be cute. I'm looking for cookies, cake, pie. . . ."

"Brownies?"

"That'd be perfect, lass."

She dug around in the refrigerator and came up with a tin of brownies she kept on hand for long nights at the computer. She was ridiculously pleased by his happy smile as she opened the tin and set it on the counter where he could reach it. She liked seeing that smile.

He reached for a brownie and rebooted his laptop. "Let's take a look at each of our mission statements again. There have to be core elements that aren't weighed down by our agendas." He gazed at the screen. "So here's how you start out, nice and neutral— *To support the werewolf culture worldwide.* I'm okay with starting that way."

"Obviously I am, since I wrote it."

Walking around the end of the counter, she stood beside his stool and looked at the two statements, his above hers.

"Then let's take that part and start over." He copied

her opening words down below. "What else is important?"

"Individuals," she said. "How about, *and the interests of each individual*?"

He glanced over at her. "That's bloody brilliant. It leaves room for Weres to choose their own path instead of dictating one. I'm going to move the placement of *worldwide*. So we have — *To support the werewolf culture and the interests of each individual worldwide*."

"*Throughout the world*. I like that better than *worldwide*. The coffee's done. I'll get us each a cup." When she returned, he'd typed in the change and was looking at the statement. He held out his hand and she put the cup into it. He sipped his coffee without taking his eyes from the screen.

"What comes next?" She snagged a brownie from the tin and took a bite.

"I'm not sure anything comes next." He looked over at her. "I think that might be it."

She read the sentence aloud. "*To support the werewolf culture and the interests of each individual throughout the world*. It's very simple. Is it too simple?" She fought the urge to try and insert some of her other wording. But then he'd want to insert his.

"It's not too simple. That's the beauty of it. It allows for protection if that's needed, and for change if that's needed. Everything this organization decides to do can be held up against this statement. Does it support the werewolf culture and the interests of each individual throughout the world? If it does, great. If it doesn't, then back to the drawing board."

She drank her coffee and studied the wording. "After all this, can it be so easy?"

"It can once we each stop trying to push our particular program."

"I wonder if the Woofers and Howlers will be disappointed in it."

He shook his head. "They can't be. As I said, it leaves the door open for more protection and isolation, or for more openness and change. But it addresses the most important consideration, to support the culture and each other. Nobody can argue against that."

She laughed. "Oh, I'm sure someone will."

"Maybe not if we sell it right. You and I don't have to give up campaigning for what we believe. In fact, we can campaign even harder to try to prove that our particular belief system fits the mission statement."

"Howard doesn't want the Howlers and Woofers to be divisive forces."

Duncan took another brownie. "That's where you and I come in. We tell our followers that we support the mission statement, which we came up with together, and we intend to hold all our actions, Woofers' and Howlers' alike, up to that yardstick. If the debate gets too negative, then it won't support the werewolf culture or the individuals in it, right?"

She smiled. "Right. You really are smart, Woofer."

"Not so smart." He looked into her eyes. "I still haven't any idea what we're going to do about us."

She glanced at the time showing in the bottom right of his screen. "I don't have a long-term solution, but I have a short-term one."

Heat flickered in his gray eyes. "Is that so?"

"We finished before dawn." She walked back around the counter and turned off the coffeepot. "And between the night we've had and the coffee I just drank, I'm too wired to sleep."

"I like where this is going."

She chuckled. "I was pretty sure you would. Don't forget to save that document before you come to bed." With that, she winked at him and began flicking off the lights. They'd worked hard and they'd worked well. They deserved a reward.

Despite the anticipation zinging through his system, Duncan carefully saved their mission statement in a new document. Then he even went to his briefcase, took out a flash drive, and backed it up. All of that was probably unnecessary, and the wording should stay in his head, anyway, but he wanted to be sure nothing got lost in the shuffle.

Light from her bedroom beckoned him, and he pulled off his sweatshirt as he walked toward it. "We don't have the authority to release the mission statement yet, but I'm going to write a quick blog before I go down to the conference in the morning to say I support it and the work we did tonight." He expected some response, and got none. "Kate? Would you rather I didn't? If so, then . . ." The rest of his sentence went unsaid as he stood in the doorway and stared.

She sat propped up against a bank of pillows, totally naked and totally engrossed in his book. He stood there a moment so he could etch the scene in his memory. He might need to take it out later to lift his spirits on some cold gray day in Glenbarra.

Surely no reader of his book had ever looked as sexy and lovely as this while turning the pages. She caught her

lower lip between her teeth, and then she chuckled and
turned the page. He'd made her laugh. That was worth
more than fifty rave reviews on the Internet.

She didn't even agree with him, and yet she'd laughed
at something he'd written. Because she'd just begun the
book, she must be reading his description of the first
time he had to use a condom because he was having sex
with a human female and she quite rightly insisted on it.

Kate's chuckle turned to outright laughter that made
her breasts jiggle. Unfortunately, his view of her sweet
breasts was partially blocked by his damned book. Stepping silently back into the shadows, he continued to
watch her read while he took off the rest of his clothes.

At one point she laughed so hard she had to stop and
wipe the tears from her eyes. Then she went right back
to reading. He'd hooked her. He wondered how long he
could stand here before she'd notice that he hadn't
joined her in the bedroom.

He couldn't decide whether to be flattered that she
liked the book so much or depressed because the book
seemed to be taking his place very nicely. In a way, he
was competing with himself for her attention. But watching her lying there in her big, comfy bed soon produced
a now-familiar effect on his cock.

He walked into the room. "You seem to be enjoying
that."

She glanced up, as if surprised to find the author himself, an aroused author at that, standing by her bed. Then
her gaze lowered to his pride and joy, and she grinned. "I
almost wish I had a condom so I could see if you've im-
proved your technique."

"I have." He climbed into bed with her and closed his
hand over the open book. "But you make a good point

about not bothering with one." He started to lift the book out of her hands.

She gripped it tight. "Don't do that. You'll lose my place."

"Then we'll just turn down the corner of the—"

"Don't!" She jerked the book away. "You will not dog-ear a page on my personally autographed book." Her blue eyes flashed. "Are you a dog-ear kind of reader?"

"I suppose I've dog-eared a page or two in my day." He decided not to admit it was his usual habit.

She rolled to the far side of the bed and opened a drawer. "Then remind me never to loan you one of my books." She took a metal bookmark out of the drawer. "This is how civilized readers mark their place." She inserted the bookmark and laid the book on the nightstand.

"I'm honored that you're taking such good care of my book, lass. But there's more where that came from. I had several boxes of them shipped to the hotel last week."

"I know." She scooted around and sat cross-legged, facing him. "I took delivery, which makes me doubly ashamed that I didn't read it before now. But I don't want one of those books. I want the one you gave me."

He was touched by that, more than he wanted to let on. Only an idiot would miss the fact that she was starting to care for him. And he was starting to care for her . . . a great deal. He probably needed to figure out some potential solutions for them, but he'd had a very long day and thinking wasn't so easy when confronted with a naked Kate.

He lay on his side, his head propped on a pillow, and just looked at her. In a moment he would do more than look, but for now he wanted to be still and appreciate the pink and gold beauty of her. Her hair curled around her creamy shoulders, tousled and shining in the light from the bedroom lamps.

He noticed the little pulse beating in the hollow of her throat, and a small freckle above her right breast. Her raspberry nipples tightened under his scrutiny and her breasts moved in rhythm with her breathing. His attention moved lower, past the crescent-shaped shadows beneath her breasts to the sweet little indentation of her navel.

Lower still, a golden triangle of curls nearly covered her treasures, but because she sat cross-legged, she revealed a glimpse of pink perfection. His cock twitched. Perhaps the time for looking was over.

But he hesitated, because she seemed to be engaged in the same sort of study. Her gaze roamed up from his toes, lingered gratifyingly on his erection, and then traveled onward until she reached his eyes.

"I can't decide," she said.

Now, there was a statement to worry any male with his heart set on seduction. "I hope you're not referring to whether we'll have sex or not. Personally, I'm quite decided on that, and in the affirmative, I might add."

She smiled. "Oh, me, too."

That restored his good humor in a hurry. "Then what can't you decide on? Maybe I can help."

"I can't decide if I like you better this way or as a wolf."

"State your preference and I'll be happy to oblige." He'd do handstands and somersaults, too, if it would get him what he wanted, which was his cock buried up to the hilt between her silky thighs.

"I don't want you to shift now." She reached out and

grasped the very part of him he was most happy to have her hold on to. "That would take too long." She caressed him.

At her touch, his eyes nearly rolled back in his head. "That's verra nice, verra nice indeed."

"You look happy."

"Every inch of me is overjoyed, especially that part you're stroking right now." He caught her wrist. "But if you're not careful, I'll become a little too happy, and that would make us both sad." He nibbled on her fingers before tugging gently on her wrist. "Lie down for me, lass. I fancy a tumble."

Laughing, she unfolded her legs and slid down beside him. "You fancy a tumble? That sounds as if you're about to throw me down on a pile of hay and flip up my petticoats."

"What a picture." He rolled on top of her and quickly braced himself on his forearms and knees so he wouldn't crush her as he'd done the night before. "I wouldn't mind trying that someday." He leaned down and kissed her, long and thoroughly, before lifting his head to see the effect of that kiss. Her flushed skin and rapid breathing told him all he needed to know. "We'd have to find a pile of hay, though."

She ran her hands lightly up and down his back. "And I'd have to wear petticoats."

"Aye." He moved between her thighs. "With nothing on underneath."

She quivered beneath him. "Sounds . . . rather scandalous."

"But rather necessary. Otherwise, I canna do this." Holding her gaze, he thrust deep.

Her breath caught and her pupils grew large and dark.

"Note to self." She gasped again as he drew back and shoved home a second time. "Nothing under petticoats."

"At least when I'm around." He began a slow, steady rhythm, and a hum of pleasure rose unbidden from deep in his throat.

She clutched his hips and lifted to meet each stroke. "And when you're not around?"

"A nicely fitted chastity belt would do fine." He smiled to show her he was teasing. Sort of. Not really. He didn't want to think of another male being where he was now.

"I see." She smiled back.

He was afraid she did see . . . that he was besotted and aching to claim her. And he could not, for more reasons than he could count, if he even had the ability to count right now, which he didn't.

But he could do this. . . . He could love her with all that was in him, and hope that she knew that what he couldn't say, what he couldn't promise, was still there, hovering just beyond his reach. Maybe someday he'd find a way to grasp it.

In the meantime, he'd gaze into her blue, blue eyes and watch the climax building there. He'd glory in the heat between them, the urgency of her touch, the satisfaction of plunging into her over and over. Her lips parted and she arched upward, her body asking silently for more.

He shifted slightly and began to pound faster.

"Yes." She clutched him tight as the ride became wild, wilder than any he'd known. "Oh, Duncan, yes. *Yes!*"

"Ah, my sweet lass. My Kate." He watched the fire in her eyes as she came, and then he let her witness the fire in his as he spilled his seed within her. He could not say the words, but he thought she knew. Oh, yes, she knew.

What they would do about it was for another time. He kissed her tenderly, eased away from her, and then drew her, spoon-fashion, into his arms.

She sighed and nestled against him. "So that was a tumble."

"It was."

"I liked it. Even without the hay and the petticoats."

"So did I, milady. So did I."

She slept then, but he could not. He longed to keep the dawn from breaking, because he had a premonition that once it did, their fragile relationship would come under siege. And he was helpless to stop that from happening.

Chapter 15

**WERECON2012:
HOWLER, WOOFER BATTLE, DAY TWO**

**Exclusive report for *Wereworld Celebrity Watch*
by Angela Sapworthy**

DENVER—At a magnificent breakfast buffet in the Stillman Lodge's excellent restaurant, Howlers and Woofers eyed each other with barely disguised animosity as each side worked to recruit members from a sizable number of undecided delegates. But the unanswered question on everyone's minds remains—where are the two leaders of these rival organizations? All attempts to reach them on their cell phones have gone unanswered!

This reporter was able to catch a brief moment with newly elected president Howard Wallace to get the inside scoop on the dynamic duo. "I told them to isolate themselves in order to craft a mission statement that would apply to the entire group, including Howlers, Woofers, and those who are neither," Wallace said. "Apparently they've done that. I look forward to seeing the results of their hard work."

When asked about reports that a blond and a black wolf had been seen on the ski slope at a very late hour, Wallace seemed unfazed. "If it was MacDowell and Stillman out there, they may have needed some fresh air. Whatever they required to get the job done is fine with me."

Rumors are flying, however, that the Howler and Woofer leaders may have a closer relationship than their followers would like! This reporter caught them sharing a cozy moment and a joke in the hallway when most other delegates were attending vital conference sessions. Early this morning, Howler sympathizer and council member Jake Hunter was overheard implying that something was going on between MacDowell and Stillman.

Yet when asked about his suspicions, the gallant Were refused to comment. In this reporter's opinion, a refusal to comment speaks more loudly than words. As the minutes tick by with no sign of MacDowell or Stillman, the evidence mounts that we're not getting the whole story!

But never fear, Sapworthy's here! Watch this spot for breaking news, or follow me on Sniffer @newshound as I sniff out the truth!

Kate woke up with a start, glanced at the clock, and groaned. "Let's roll, Woofer. We're late."

In the bed beside her, Duncan lifted his head. "What time is it?"

"Eight thirty. We've missed the breakfast buffet, but we might just make the opening session if we hurry." She slid out of bed and combed her hair back from her face. "You'd better head down to your room. We'll each get ready faster that way."

"Aye." He climbed from the opposite side of the bed, yawned, and stretched his arms over his head. "I didn't think I'd sleep at all, but I must have drifted off."

He was awe-inspiring, with the body and chiseled features of a Grecian god, except for the slight stubble on his chin, which made him all the more real and adorable to her. As she looked at him across the expanse of the rumpled sheets, she wished with all her heart that they had nothing to do but hop back into that bed and spend the day there. Or shift and run in the snow, as they'd done last night.

His sleepy gaze fixed on her. "I don't know what to-day will bring, but whatever happens, I will be thinking about ..." He gestured toward the bed. "About the beauty of what we've had."

She was surprised by the sudden lump in her throat. "Maybe it's not over."

"It's not over, lass. But we might be in for some rough sledding today."

"We might." She took heart from his assurance that this wasn't the end for them. They didn't have time to discuss it, but he wasn't leaving until the next morning. Time had not run out, not yet.

"I'll get out of your way. And I'll see you downstairs."

"Right."

He started out of the room, giving her an excellent

view of his tight buns. "Oh." He turned back and caught her ogling. His smile was pure masculine satisfaction. "*That* will sustain me through the day."

"I suppose now your ego will swell to twice its normal size."

"Nay, but if you keep looking at me that way, another part of my anatomy definitely will."

"Get out of here, Woofer, before we both get in trouble."

"I will, but I wanted to mention about our blogs. I said something last night, but you were too preoccupied with my book and condom story and you didn't hear me."

She laughed at the memory. "What did you say about our blogs that I totally missed while I was reading about your first condom adventure?"

"I think it would be excellent if we each posted up something in support of the mission statement, without saying what it is, of course. It's Howard's decision when he wants to reveal it. But we can do some advance promo and encourage our followers to greet it with an open mind."

"I won't have time before the opening session."

"Neither will I, but I'll do it as soon as I get a break."

She nodded in agreement. "Sounds good. I'll do the same."

"Good. Go jump in the shower. I'll be gone once I throw on some clothes."

She hesitated, unwilling to end what might be a last moment of intimacy between them for hours. Hurrying over to him, she gave him a quick kiss. "For luck."

He smiled and gave her a return kiss. "For the wisdom to navigate this day."

"Yes, that's probably better than depending on luck. See you soon."

"Aye."

She turned from the bedroom doorway and headed for the shower. This long good-bye could go on forever, and they couldn't afford the time.

"Don't forget to turn your phone on!" he called from the living room.

"Okay, thanks!" She'd left it in her bedside table drawer, shut off as Howard had requested. Pulling it out, she clicked it on, tossed it on the bed, and went in to take the quickest shower in history.

She'd just stepped out and grabbed a towel when her phone rang. A sixth sense told her it was Duncan, although she had no reason to believe he'd be calling her so soon. The readout confirmed it.

She pushed the button and held the phone to her ear. "Miss me already?"

"We've been seen."

"Seen? When? By whom?" Her gut churned.

"I don't know who saw us, but somebody noticed us running on the ski slope and reported it to Sapworthy. She sent out a Sniff sometime during the night, and her first dispatch of the day implies that something's going on between us."

"But she has no proof."

"No, it doesn't sound like it."

"If the Howlers and Woofers think we're sleeping together . . ."

"Aye. It would affect our credibility, the mission statement, everything."

"Then we'd better be more antagonistic to each other, both in person and on our blogs. We can't let anyone suspect that we—" *Are falling in love.*

"No, we can't. I wanted you to have a heads-up."

"Thank you. See you down there in a few." She disconnected and put a hand to her stomach to try to calm the churning inside. A run through the snow was not the same as having sex, and no one had seen that happen.

She and Duncan had been given a tough assignment, so what was so terrible about deciding to shift and take a run through the woods to clear their heads? She knew the answer. It wasn't the run that would raise eyebrows. Everyone would be thinking about the shifting that had to take place prior to the run, shifting that could be done only after removing all their clothes.

They might be leaders of rival organizations, but they were healthy young Weres with normal sexual appetites. No one would believe that stripping down to shift, and shifting back to that naked state, all in complete isolation from the rest of the delegates, was done platonically. And their suspicions would be absolutely correct.

She had several purple Howler shirts, and as she pulled on a clean one, she wondered what sort of reception she'd get from her followers. *She* didn't feel that she'd betrayed the cause, but they might. In her mind, coaxing Duncan to explore his Were nature could reap benefits in the long run, but that might look like a rationalization to others.

Still, she thought his beliefs had been affected by their experience together as wolves. He'd dismissed Were sex as no better, and possibly lesser, than Were-human sex. Surely he didn't feel the same way this morning.

The whole thing was a complicated mess, though, and she wasn't sure how much understanding she'd find among her constituents. She wouldn't accept all the heat from this, either. Howard had thrown them together to come up with that doggone mission statement.

A little voice told her that she should have refused the assignment. If Howard had insisted on having Duncan involved in writing it, then some other Howler could have filled in. Giselle, for example, or even Jake . . . no, not Jake. Duncan and Jake would have come to blows if they'd been forced to work together.

But Giselle seemed smart and capable. Kate could have suggested her, instead, making up some excuse as to why she couldn't do it herself. No reasonable excuse came to her, but anything would have been better than letting the chips fall where they might.

At least they had a mission statement, though. She tried to console herself with that as she hurried downstairs for the first session, her laptop in a small briefcase so she could work on her blog during the next seminar. The mission statement was a good one, too, although if she and Duncan became the target of gossip, acceptance of the mission statement would be in jeopardy. Damn and double damn.

Howard was already at the microphone when she slipped into the room and found a seat in the back. Duncan had made it there ahead of her and sat with his Woofers. Once again they had taken the left side of the aisle and the Howlers had commandeered the right.

Kate gazed at the sea of purple shirts and hoped with all her heart that she hadn't jeopardized the movement she held so dear. Her throat tightened. They'd all been so enthusiastic and loyal. Would they turn on her? Find themselves a new leader? Heidi would stand by her, but she couldn't guarantee that the rest would.

Howard greeted the delegates with warmth and friendliness. He was going to make a terrific president, even if he did have two sons with human wives. Kate thought she'd made progress with Duncan in that respect, too. Apparently he'd been viewing the Were-human mating idea only from the Were male's perspective.

If she were in the mood for laughing, she'd find that funny. Typical, maybe, but funny, all the same. Duncan hadn't considered what the dangers would be for a female Were who married a human, as Penny had done. But he'd considered them now, and it would affect how he approached the issue in the future.

Her close association with Duncan had reaped benefits for the Howler cause, no doubt about it. But she didn't know if she'd get a chance to explain, or if she even could explain without sounding defensive. Some might see only that she'd literally slept with the enemy, and condemn her as a result.

"Thanks to my brilliant council members," Howard said, "I have two exciting proposals for you. The first is a name for our brand-new, bouncing-baby werewolf organization. I present to you the possibility of calling it WOW, Worldwide Organization of Werewolves."

The hall fell silent for a couple of seconds, and then someone began to clap. Soon the applause became thunderous and included howling and choruses of *woof, woof, woof*. The organization had a name.

Even mired down by her personal concerns, Kate realized this was an historic moment. Angela Sapworthy sat two rows in front of her tapping away on her laptop. Kate didn't appreciate the gossip that Angela presented as legitimate news, but at least someone was here recording the event and sending it out into the Were world.

In spite of everything, Kate was glad to be here, to be a witness to the formation of an organization dedicated to making life better for werewolves everywhere. If the mission statement that she and Duncan had worked so hard to create was accepted, she could take pride in being a significant part of this conference.

"And now, for the second exciting development," Howard said. "An organization with a terrific name like WOW needs a guiding principle, a mission statement. I'm happy to say that thanks to the commitment and perseverance of Howler leader Kate Stillman and Woofer leader Duncan MacDowell, we have such a statement."

"Are they shacking up or what?" someone called from the crowd.

Kate cringed. Dear God, this could be a disaster.

"Yeah, what's going on between those two?" someone else shouted. "Maybe they need their own group, the Wofflers!"

The room erupted, with accusations from some and ribald jokes from others. At some point Kate had been spotted, and several Weres turned to look at Kate to see how she was taking it. She straightened in her chair and stared them down, although she could feel the heat in her cheeks.

"Weres! Have some dignity!" Howard banged the gavel several times on the lectern and eventually the crowd settled again.

"Let's be clear," he said in ringing tones. "I will *not* tolerate that kind of behavior in an official session of WOW." He fixed his intense gray eyes on the crowd. "I agreed to serve as your president because I believe in what we can accomplish together. That requires civil discourse at all times. Another outbreak and I will adjourn this session and disband our council."

The delegates muttered among themselves.

His jaw set, Howard banged the gavel again. "You

have an opportunity for greatness today. But you can waste that opportunity by wallowing in petty gossip and innuendo. It's your choice." He continued to glare at the assembled delegates while several squirmed in their chairs.

Now Kate understood why Grandma Elizabeth had such faith in Howard Wallace. If anyone could corral this bunch, it would be a Were like Howard. He hadn't amassed a fortune by being meek, and he hadn't run the Wallace pack through lax leadership. Kate might not agree with the actions of his sons, but she could learn a great deal about being a pack alpha from watching Howard.

Then, to her surprise, Duncan stood. "May I say something, Mr. President?"

"You may, Mr. MacDowell."

Kate's heart thudded painfully in her chest. She had no idea what Duncan planned to say. She prayed that whatever it was, he wouldn't make things worse for himself, or for her, either.

"I realize there are a few rumors circulating about the relationship between Kate Stillman and me," Duncan said. "That's a bloody shame, because there's not a Were more dedicated to the cause she believes in than Kate. During our brainstorming session last night she fought like a tiger, or I should say, like a wolf, for her principles."

Kate's chest tightened with emotion. He was defending her, and that might come back to haunt him.

"Don't misunderstand," Duncan continued. "I fought for my principles, too. Neither one of us has abandoned our position. I'm still in favor of openness and Were-human mating, and Kate wants to maintain secrecy and restrict us to Were-Were mating. Check out our blogs in a couple of hours if you doubt it. Whatever our personal relationship, which, by the way, is none of your bloody business, we remain fierce opponents in this discussion."

She felt attention swing to her once again. He'd tacitly acknowledged that they had a personal relationship. She flushed, but not with shame. She was pleased that he wasn't ashamed of it, either, and he'd had the courage to defend their right to privacy. He'd also set the stage for a continuing battle of principles. All in all, she couldn't have asked for a better declaration.

But he had more to say. "In the end, though, we both realized that the mission statement was separate from our individual agendas. It couldn't be just for Woofers, or just for Howlers. It had to be for all of us, including those who haven't chosen either side. I ask you to listen with an open mind. Thank you." Duncan took his seat amid scattered applause and a few faint woofs.

Everyone, it seemed, was now ready to hear this mission statement that Howard was excited about and Duncan vocally supported.

"Thank you, Duncan." Howard looked pleased. "And I want to commend you and Kate for your fine work. I asked you to put aside your political agendas, and you have. I will now read the proposed mission statement as crafted by Duncan MacDowell and Kate Stillman. *Worldwide Organization of Werewolves Mission Statement: to support the werewolf culture and the interests of each individual throughout the world.*" Howard glanced up and surveyed the delegates.

At first there was silence, and then Jake Hunter stood. "I'd like to speak."

Howard nodded. "Go ahead, Mr. Hunter."

"There's nothing in there about protecting ourselves.

Instead of talking about supporting the interests of each individual, I think we should talk about supporting their safety. Some in this room don't seem to be worried about that, but I, for one, am."

The Howlers clapped enthusiastically. Kate braced herself for someone to start a howl going, but Howard's lecture must have subdued her followers somewhat. No howls were forthcoming, and she was relieved.

She also felt she should answer his objection. She stood. "May I speak in response, Mr. President?"

Howard nodded. "Of course, Ms. Stillman."

She looked at Jake, whose piercing green eyes seemed to take her measure. The stiff set of his shoulders indicated he was disappointed in her. "I understand why you would want the word *safety* instead of *interests*. I argued for that, too. But that word has a connotation that fits the Howler message. Duncan lobbied for his favorite buzzwords, too. We had to leave them out in order to create a mission statement that worked for everyone."

"Well, it doesn't work for me." Jake's angry stance didn't change. "If this mission statement is adopted, then I'm serving notice right now that I'm starting my own organization. And I'll welcome any Howlers who are as unhappy with the direction we're heading in as I am."

"That's your choice," Kate said. "But I'd be sorry to see you do that." She sat down, her stomach churning. Jake had charisma and might very well tear apart the organization she'd struggled so hard to build.

Howard spoke into the mike. "Are you finished, Mr. Hunter?"

"Yes. I'll wait for the vote." Jake took his seat.

"Does anyone else want to speak?"

The room was quiet.

"In that case, that's all the business we have this morning," Howard said. "We're going old-school for the vote on this mission statement. Ballots and a ballot box are out in the hall."

"How do we know it's fair?" called out a Woofer covered in anti-Howler buttons.

"Reasonable question," Howard said. "The vote will be anonymous, but we know how many delegates we have. We'll count the ballots at five this afternoon. If there are fewer ballots than delegates, so be it. If there are more, then we'll have to do it all over again during the ball tonight. So don't try stuffing the ballot box. Please. It'll ruin our party." He banged the gavel. "We're adjourned."

Kate was immediately surrounded by Howlers with questions about how the mission statement would affect them. She was grateful that no one, at least so far, asked about her relationship with Duncan. She did her best to explain to those clustered around her that the mission statement was designed to unify, not divide.

But seminars were beginning, and she didn't want the mission statement debate to pull delegates away from scheduled speakers. She announced that she was going to a lecture titled "Were-Were Sex: Enhancing the Basic Position." She'd interviewed the speaker for her book and wanted to support her talk.

Because of that, she participated in the discussion and didn't have any downtime to write her blog. The second hour, though, she sat in on a session titled "Managing Your Offspring's First Shift." Although it was presented by two of her followers, the topic wasn't relevant to her yet, so she could sneak some time to write her blog. Choosing her words carefully, she told her followers that voting for the mission statement wouldn't jeopardize their cause.

She noticed a few of the Howlers glancing at her while she worked. Maybe they thought she should be paying more attention to the speaker, but she didn't have kids yet, so why worry about it now? She posted her blog just as the seminar ended.

As she shut off her laptop and stowed it in her briefcase, Heidi rushed into the seminar room headed straight for her. She looked upset, and so pale her freckles stood out as if they'd been drawn on with a Sharpie. Kate hadn't spoken to Heidi yet this morning, but she couldn't believe this sudden panic had anything to do with the mission statement.

Worried that something even worse had happened to her dating site, Kate stood, grabbed her briefcase, and met Heidi halfway across the room. "What is it?"

"Duncan's blog. Have you seen it?"

"I haven't had a chance to look, but we both agreed to post something positive about the mission statement. What did he say?"

"He didn't talk about the mission statement, I can tell you that." Heidi pulled out her phone from her purse and clicked a button before turning the phone so Kate could see it.

At first Kate couldn't tell what she was looking at, so she magnified the picture, and then she gasped. The picture was fake, of course, but someone skilled in Photoshop techniques had managed to make it look as if she lay in bed with the male lead of *The Force*, her favorite TV actor and most definitely human. The caption was *Following in Her Sister's Footsteps?* Below that a short blog recounted Penny's choice of a human mate and suggested that Kate was leading a double life by insisting that Weres should have sex only with Weres while she dallied with a human TV star.

Kate felt sick to her stomach. No wonder Howlers had been looking at her during the seminar. They'd probably pulled this up on their phones and wondered what the hell was going on.

One of her first conversations with Duncan came back with perfect clarity. *What's your favorite show? I love* The Force. *I have a little crush on the guy who plays Adam.*

She couldn't believe that the same Duncan who'd loved her so thoroughly mere hours ago could have posted this blog, but she'd confessed her fears about her sister last night, and the night before, she'd confessed her silly attraction to this TV actor.

Swallowing the bile that rose in her throat, she handed the phone back to Heidi. "I have to talk to him."

"*Talk* to him? How about you, me, and the rest of the Howlers lure him into a dark hallway and beat the living shit out of him? How about that?"

"I just can't believe . . . Let me at least see what he says."

"What can he say? He's mounted a smear campaign with a Photoshopped picture! Some Weres will recognize that, but not all of them. We need to take him out." Heidi quivered with rage. "I'm so furious I could do it right now with my bare hands. I don't care if he outweighs me by a hundred pounds. Let me at him."

But Kate had already pulled out her phone and texted Duncan—*How could you post that blog?*

His response came back almost immediately. *We agreed to highlight our differences, remember?*

Not like that!

Kate, I hope you don't expect me to back off from the Woofer position because of last night.

A cold chill traveled down her spine. *You've betrayed me, Duncan!*

How?

If you don't know, then there's no way I could ever explain it to you. A red mist of fury settled over her brain as she looked up from her phone. "Beating the shit out of him is too private a punishment, Heidi. I want the whole of Were cyberspace to know what I think of that slimy bastard."

"Now you're talking!"

"Let's get out of here. I need to go up to my room and concentrate on this." She nearly crashed into Neil as she stormed out into the hall.

"Hey, Kate!" He caught her arm. "Anything wrong? You look furious."

She was in no mood to play nice with her cousin. "Sorry. No time to talk. Heidi and I have something that needs doing immediately." Adrenaline pumping, she headed for her room with Heidi by her side.

Chapter 16

Sniffer Update: @newshound—*Blog attack! Just as WERECON2012 started to bore me, MacDowell and Stillman unloaded . . . on each other! #mesmerized*

Knox Trevelyan stopped Duncan in the hallway between sessions. "I admire all your work and have always admired your dedication to the Woofer cause, but I'm not sure what to think about that blog, buddy. It doesn't sound like you."

"I wanted to make sure everyone knows where I stand." Duncan went back over the blog he'd written and couldn't see why Kate, and now Knox, objected to it.

"Oh, you did that, all right. And she's responded in kind. Can't say I blame her, either."

"Guess I should take a look at her blog, then." He'd written his quickly during the first hour, finished it in about fifteen minutes, and posted it right away. He thought he'd done a decent job of stating the Woofer position while still supporting the mission statement. Her reaction made no sense. Had their time together convinced her that he would never say anything negative about the Howlers again? That was unrealistic and not what he'd expect of her.

"If I were you," Knox said, "I'd issue an apology before this gets any nastier."

"Nasty?" Duncan frowned. "I wasn't nasty."

"Then you and I have different standards. Well, I'm off to another session. I hope you two get this over with before Howard sees it. He'll blow a gasket." Knox headed on down the hallway to one of the meeting rooms.

Duncan found a quiet corner with two easy chairs tucked into it, sat down, and took his laptop out of his briefcase. Something wasn't right. He quickly called up Kate's blog and read it in growing amazement.

OPEN LETTER TO DUNCAN MACDOWELL

Dear So-Not-a-Prince Duncan—I made the mistake of thinking that you had a touch of honor in your soul, but your recent actions have convinced me that you have none whatsoever. I also deluded myself that you had a few brains in that swelled head of yours, but apparently that's not true, either. Otherwise you'd realize that Weres are intelligent beings who will recognize a smear campaign when they see it.

Your opinion of your kind must be exceedingly low if you think they can be duped as you have attempted to dupe them. No wonder you prefer human females. You probably seek out those who are not very bright, so that you can amaze them with your supposed brilliance. I, however, have seen the light, and it does not come from you, Duncan Mac-Dowell. All that I see when I look at you is the dark pit of hell. May you spend the rest of your life roasting in it. Kate

A hive of angry bees buzzed in his head. Smear campaign? Duping other Weres? What was she talking about? He called up his own blog, and there was the reasoned post he'd written.

Now that he thought about it, everyone wearing a purple shirt had been glaring at him for the past hour, and a few had made some rude gestures, too. He'd wondered about that, because he hadn't thought his post was the least bit inflammatory. It still wasn't. Sure, he'd restated his belief in ending the secrecy and allowing Weres and humans to mate without fear, but there was nothing insulting about his argument.

At some point he'd planned a follow-up blog to acknowledge his new understanding regarding Were-human mating. A Were female mating with a human had a different situation, and he'd planned to invite some comments from his followers on the subject and get a civilized debate going. But now . . . Kate had consigned him to hell!

Something was very wrong, but he couldn't find out what it was unless he saw her in person. Taking his phone from his pocket, he texted her. *We need to talk.*

Her response came back quickly. *Not in this lifetime.*

I don't know why you're so upset.

Then you're even more stupid than I thought.

Please, can I meet you somewhere?

No, and hell no.

He sighed and stared at his phone. This exchange was getting him nowhere. Then he noted the time. A lunch break would be next, followed by the autograph session featuring him, Kate, and Emma Wallace, Aidan Wallace's mate and a best-selling novelist.

Earlier today he'd been looking forward to the autographing as a chance to be in the same room with Kate. After the rumors about them he'd been careful to avoid her, thinking that was for the best until they worked out how they'd proceed. Judging from her blog post, there would be no *proceeding* at all, ever. She absolutely hated him. How could that be?

He was thoroughly bewildered and wished she'd been willing to meet him privately to discuss the problem, whatever it was. She hadn't been, but she couldn't duck him forever. They would both be in the room for the autographing, and he'd find a way to talk to her then.

Bolstered by that thought, he admitted to himself that he was exhausted. He needed sleep more than he needed lunch. Returning to his room, he set his phone alarm, pulled off his clothes, and fell into bed. He was asleep instantly.

The alarm woke him thirty minutes before he was due at the autographing. He also had a text from Howard on his phone. *Glad you took that terrible blog post down. Don't know if you did it or one of your Woofers, but you owe Kate an apology. We can't have this kind of animosity on the council.*

Muttering a few swearwords in Gaelic, Duncan treated himself to a very hot shower and clean clothes. Even though he'd showered this morning, he felt dirty. As he dressed in a black turtleneck, slacks, and a sport coat, he thought of something that didn't match up and quickly checked his blog. His original post was still there, so what did Howard mean about being glad he'd taken it down?

If he hadn't known for sure that he was wide-awake,

he'd think this was some horrible nightmare. But he knew what nightmares felt like, and this was real. Too damned real. He intended to get some answers.

The autograph session had been set up in the ballroom, because the debate was to follow immediately afterward and that allowed Duncan and Kate to remain in the same room. Delegates were already lined up outside the door waiting for the autographing to begin. The Woofers gave him a grin and a thumbs-up, but the Howlers simply glared.

"Don't think you're off the hook because you took it down," one female in a purple shirt called out to him.

"Yeah, better stay out of dark alleys," said another.

Frustrated, he turned to them, hands outstretched. "I don't know what you're talking about!"

One Howler turned to another. "Short memory."

"That's a Woofer for you."

"Hey!" A male with a long lanyard full of buttons gestured to the two Howlers. "I'm glad MacDowell finally took the gloves off. It's about time. If I had my way, we'd—"

"That's enough, my friends." Howard came down the hallway with Emma, his daughter-in-law, and Aidan, his son and heir to the alpha position. Emma, a curvy blonde, was dwarfed by the Weres flanking her.

Duncan finally had the two Wallace brothers straight in his mind. Aidan, who was now striding toward him, had brown hair and eyes that were almost golden. Roarke, who had blond hair, was not with the others at the moment.

"The blog has been taken down," Howard said to the

Weres standing in line. "And I'm sure Duncan plans to make amends, don't you, Duncan?"

"First I have to find out what I'm supposed to have done."

Howard gave him a sharp glance. "That wasn't quite the response I was looking for." Then he turned back to the lines of autograph seekers. "I warn you, we can't have arguments breaking out during what's supposed to be a pleasant author event. The doors will open shortly. Please be civil to one another." He walked forward and held the door for Emma, Aidan, and Duncan.

"We need to talk," he said in a low voice as Duncan walked through the door.

"I'd like that very much." Maybe the mystery would finally be solved. He glanced to the front of the room where Kate had already ensconced herself at a table piled high with books. A petite brunette stood by her side, and he made a guess that was Heidi, her assistant.

Howard motioned him toward the back of the room. "I'll admit I was surprised and disappointed to see your blog this morning," he said. "I thought you understood that inflaming the opposition wasn't going to help this organization function."

"I fail to see how my blog inflamed anyone. In fact, I was afraid that my followers would accuse me of pulling my punches."

Howard studied him for a long moment. Then he sighed. "I wondered if that's what had happened."

"What?"

"I'm afraid somebody hacked into your blog, Duncan. They posted something really offensive as if it had come from you."

A trickle of cold sweat worked its way down Duncan's spine. "Tell me about it."

"This morning, sometime before the end of the first round of seminars, your blog post included a picture of Kate in bed with a TV star. He's on one of those cop shows. Emma would know it."

Duncan's jaw dropped. "No, it didn't. I don't know what blog you were looking at, but I'd sure as hell like to find out. That's outrageous. It's . . ." He trailed off. "Is that what she thinks was on my blog, too?"

"She doesn't just think, Duncan. She knows. She saw it. We all did. There's no doubt it was your blog."

"It couldn't have been."

"Well, it was. A couple of us might have been mistaken, but when nearly all the convention delegates say they saw it, then it was there. And it was yours."

Duncan swallowed. "What . . . what else was on there?" He listened in horror as Howard described the rest of the blog's contents.

"So you see why she was so upset," Howard said. "Why we all were, except some of the Woofers."

"I didn't do it. By all the saints, I didn't put up that blog." Duncan turned toward the front of the room. "I have to go tell her. I can't let her think that I—"

"Hold on a minute, son." Howard laid a heavy hand on his shoulder. "I doubt she'll believe you, and you'll only cause more of a commotion."

Duncan glanced back at him. "Do you believe me?"

"Yes, I do. But before you go trying to convince Kate or anyone about your innocence, let me put Aidan on the job. He handles security for Wallace Enterprises, and when it comes to something like this, he's the best. Let him nose around and find out what happened with your blog."

Duncan scrubbed a hand over his face. "I hate for her to go on thinking I would sabotage her like that. No wonder she wants me to burn in hell."

Howard gave Duncan's shoulder a squeeze and stepped back. "We'll get it fixed. Let me have a word with Aidan. Right now it's time to open those doors so you three can sign some books."

"Aye." Duncan walked up to the front of the room feeling like a condemned man going in front of the firing squad. An innocent condemned man, at that.

Kate glanced up once and then turned to talk with her assistant.

His heart ached at the disdain he'd glimpsed in her blue eyes before she turned away. Her assistant didn't turn away, though, and she had more than disdain in her eyes. Duncan would describe what he saw there as bloodlust.

He didn't blame Heidi for that, either. In fact, he was happy to know that Kate had such a loyal friend on her side. In Heidi's place, he'd feel the same. He'd want to kill whoever had hurt Kate.

Three rectangular tables had been lined up across the front of the room. Kate was on the far right and Duncan was on the far left. Emma sat at the middle table, and she gave him a tight smile. Howard had already pulled Aidan over into a corner, leaving Emma alone at her table.

He glanced at her and sighed. "I didn't do it, Emma," he said as he walked around behind the table with his name tent on it. "Howard's asking your mate to investigate a potential blog hijacking."

Some of the tenseness left Emma's expression. "Really? You didn't put that up there?"

"No, I didn't. And I wouldn't. That's not my way."

"I didn't think so, either, but . . . who would want to hijack your blog?"

"I don't know." But he was already lining up suspects in his mind. Anyone who had reason to want the rivalry to continue had a motive. That included Jake, who pretended not to be much of a tech-savvy Were, but that could be an act. Angela Sapworthy needed a steady supply of juicy stories to keep her readership. Besides those two, he wondered if any of his Woofers might be that crazy.

If Jake wasn't the culprit, then perhaps some other Howler wanted to make sure that Kate didn't go soft on the Woofers. Then he remembered that on Friday someone had hacked into Kate's Furthebest dating site. Although the doors had opened and delegates were pouring in, he quickly left his chair.

Emma glanced at him in surprise. "You can't leave, Duncan. Your fans are arriving."

"Please tell them I'll be right back. I have one more piece of information for Aidan." He covered the distance in a few long strides and spoke quickly with Aidan, who seemed glad to get more evidence that someone was up to no good in cyberspace.

"Don't worry," Aidan said. "We'll figure this out."

"I hope so. I have a lot riding on it." He'd said that without thinking, but it was true. If he couldn't convince Kate that he would never knowingly do anything to hurt her, he'd carry that sorrow with him for the rest of his life.

On that cheery note, he returned to the table to greet

the first delegate in line to have a book autographed. He managed a smile and picked up his pen. For the next hour, he tried to focus on the steady stream of Woofers who wanted a signed book as a souvenir.

But his thoughts kept drifting to Kate, sitting so near, yet so far away. Then he thought about Aidan, and whether he'd learned anything yet. If Aidan was a fast worker, maybe he'd be able to resolve the issue by the end of the hour. If not, the scheduled debate could be torture. But an hour wasn't a lot of time. And it was going fast.

Kate wasn't having a good day. The shock of seeing Duncan's blog had shattered her composure. She'd fired off that response without thinking it through, and Grandma Elizabeth had not been pleased. She'd literally called Kate on the carpet over it, but at least the lecture had been a private one in Elizabeth's suite.

Duncan's behavior was reprehensible, she'd said in words that still rang in Kate's ears, *but you stooped to his level with your out-of-control response. A leader can't afford to have a hissy fit in public.*

Kate had wanted to argue that she had good reason for her hissy fit. But she knew her grandmother would be unmoved. She also knew her grandmother was right. After years of watching Grandma Elizabeth handle any crisis that came her way, and after recently observing Howard dealing with unruly delegates, she knew how she should have responded.

Anger was fine so long as it was controlled and directed like a laser at the offending party. She'd spewed vitriol over the entire Were Internet. She'd also sounded like a teenager when she'd added that part about hoping

Duncan roasted in hell. Saying it had felt oh-so-good, but now it was everywhere, which felt oh-so-bad.

She'd taken her response down but hadn't decided what to put in its place. After very little sleep last night, and not a whole lot more the night before, she was mentally and physically exhausted. She wasn't sure how she'd have survived the autograph session if Heidi hadn't been there giving her moral support.

Most everyone who came to the table had some comment to make about Duncan's blog. The majority understood that the picture was fake, but a few didn't and wanted to know what that actor was like in person.

"I don't know," she'd answer each time the question came up. "I've never met him."

The Were would look confused. "But . . ."

"The picture was a fake. He and I have never been in the same room together, let alone the same bed."

"Oh." The questioner usually left looking vaguely disappointed.

"You'd think they'd be more concerned about you abandoning your principles to sleep with the guy," Heidi muttered. "I guess if the human's a celebrity, then all bets are off."

"How much longer until we're done here?"

"We're almost there."

Kate couldn't even rejoice in that, because her debate with Duncan started after a short break between events. She'd grabbed spare minutes to speed-read the rest of his book, but she hadn't laughed at any of his attempts to be funny this time. For all she knew, he'd made up every story he told, anyway. She felt like such a fool as she remembered all the times she'd complimented him on his integrity. Yeah, right.

And yet, while she hated him with a white-hot passion, she couldn't stop thinking about him sitting over there only one six-foot table away from her. She'd noticed his little confab with Howard before the event started and assumed Howard had read him the riot act.

Yet Duncan had made no move to speak to her, no attempt to apologize for his egregious behavior. Not that she would accept his apology, but now that he'd been forced to take down that blog, he must realize what an ass he'd made of himself by putting it up.

Well, good. Let him suffer. If he was too proud to apologize for what he'd done, then she'd mark that down in her growing list of his sins. And when they had their debate, she would do her very best to eviscerate him. In a classy way, of course, so Grandma Elizabeth wouldn't give her another lecture. She wanted his blood on the floor, if not literally, then figuratively.

"That looks like the last of them," Heidi said.

Kate tossed down her pen. "Then I'm going to disappear into the ladies' room for five minutes. I need a moment."

"You bet." Heidi gave her a quick smile. "I'll tidy up here and haul out your notes for the debate. Go take a few calming breaths so you can come back and kick his ass."

"You know it, girlfriend." Leaving her chair, Kate headed for the nearest exit. From the corner of her eye, she saw Duncan get up, and she moved faster. She did *not* want to deal with him now.

Unfortunately, he had longer legs than she did and he beat her to the door. "Kate, please listen for a minute."

"I don't care to listen." She avoided his gaze. "Now please move so I can take a bathroom break."

"It wasn't me, Kate. I didn't put that blog up there. I don't know who did, but Aidan is looking into it."

Rage gripped her and she finally looked into his eyes. "Of course you put it up there." Her chest tightened and she had trouble breathing, but she wasn't going to let him wiggle out of this disaster by claiming he'd been the victim of a hacker. "After last night you had all the information about Penny. And on Friday night, I conveniently mentioned my crush on the guy who stars in *The Force*. My picture's on my blog, and I'm sure his picture is everywhere on the Internet."

Pain flashed in his gray eyes. "I didn't do it. I would never deliberately try to hurt you, Kate."

"You seem sincere enough, but then so do all psychopaths. Everyone thought Ted Bundy was a nice guy, too."

"Kate! My God! How can you say something that horrible, lass?"

"How could you put that picture on your blog, Duncan? And then drag my sister's name into it? How could you?" Unshed tears made her eyes ache and if she stood here much longer, she was liable to cry. Damned if she'd let him see that. "Either you move or I'm calling for help to physically move you. I'm sure I could find several Howlers who would love to do that."

"Aye. I'm sure you could." He moved aside. "But search your heart, Kate. You're a good judge of character. You didn't misjudge me before, but you're doing so now."

"I wish that were true." She hurried past him and out the door before his soft, low voice could seduce her into believing in him again. He'd fooled her once, but he wouldn't fool her a second time.

Chapter 17

Duncan's vain hope that Aidan would arrive in the nick of time and make some grand announcement about the hijacked blog didn't materialize. None of the Wallaces were in the room for the debate, so maybe they were all working on the problem, including Emma. He appreciated that, but he wished they'd hurry up.

Elizabeth Stillman sat in the back of the room looking regal as always. When her gaze fell on him, he expected to feel a chill wind blowing his way, but her expression was neutral. Maybe Howard had told her that Duncan appeared to be innocent. That would be helpful.

A second lectern had been brought in so that he and Kate could each have one from which to speak. Or to hide behind, in his case, if angry Howlers started throwing things. He'd never experienced standing in front of an audience where some of the listeners were openly hostile.

He spent most of his time looking at the Woofers, who gave him smiles of encouragement. The Howlers continued to stare at him as if he were the spawn of Satan and would sprout horns at any minute.

At least Neil, the moderator for the debate, liked him. Or, more accurately, Neil fawned on him. Duncan was willing to accept fawning as opposed to outright hate.

Neil had managed to find a small lapel mike with a battery pack attached, so he wasn't tied to any certain spot. As the crowd settled, he paced in front of the audience, making cute little jokes with those in the front row, who included Angela Sapworthy tapping away on her netbook.

No doubt Angela was sending those jokes out on Sniffer. Because Neil's mike was on, his comments and knowing chuckles were also broadcast throughout the room, whether the audience cared to hear them or not.

He preened and strutted like the cock of the walk. After Duncan had that negative thought, he chastised himself for it. Neil was an ally, but bloody hell, the Were had a narcissistic streak a mile wide.

At last Neil paused dramatically and intoned in a deep voice, "It is time."

Duncan couldn't stop himself from looking over at Kate, and he discovered she was looking back. He could read her expression perfectly, and he was sure she could read his. For one sparkling moment they were in complete agreement once again—Neil was a first-class jackass. Then Kate glanced away, ending the brief flash of mutual disgust with Neil.

"Throughout the weekend we've gathered questions from the delegates," Neil said. "We'll get to as many as we have time for. I'll alternate between the debaters, allowing Kate to answer first and then have Duncan rebut, and switch around the next time. I'll be timing your answers." He held up a stopwatch.

"Before we begin asking the questions," Neil continued, "our president has suggested that we give Kate and Duncan each two minutes for an opening statement, to set the stage, as it were. I'll toss a coin to see who goes first. Heads it's Duncan, tails it's Kate." He tossed a quarter in the air and caught it behind his back. "Heads! Give it up for the King of the Woofers!"

Duncan winced. He'd hoped that title had died on Saturday morning, but no such luck. His supporters gave him a rousing welcome interspersed with *woof, woof, woof*. He gazed at his cheering followers and wondered if one of them, or more than one, had conspired to hijack his blog today.

Neil held up his stopwatch. "Two minutes, Duncan. And . . . go!"

Duncan hadn't prepared an opening speech, but he knew what he wanted to say. "Earlier today many of you saw a blog post with an inappropriate picture in it. I want to take this opportunity to tell you I had nothing to do with that post or the blatantly fake picture. Whoever hijacked my blog, whether you did it because you support me or because you don't, I am sadly disappointed that you chose to do so. You've distressed me, and you've greatly distressed my worthy opponent."

When he fell silent, Neil turned to him. "That's it? You have time left."

"That's it."

Neil shrugged. "Then next up is Kate. You have two minutes, Kate. And . . . go!"

She cleared her throat. "Duncan would have you believe that he's innocent in this business of the blog post, but I have good reason to think that he's not."

Duncan knew he shouldn't look at her while she tore him to shreds, but it was like watching a train wreck. He couldn't turn away. She gripped the lectern so hard her knuckles and the tips of her fingers were white. He remembered kissing those sweet fingers, and regret burned in him like lava.

Her voice rang out, clear despite the way she was trembling. "On Friday night, when Duncan and I were snowbound, we had a conversation about television shows, and I told him of my fondness for *The Force* and my silly crush on the lead actor. It's no coincidence that actor was chosen for the Photoshopped picture of me."

Angry murmurings rose from the purple-shirted bloc.

"That alone might be enough to incriminate him, but in addition, on Saturday night while we worked on the mission statement, I confided my concerns about my sister, Penny. He may have known something about her situation before, because it's no big secret, but he got all the details last night. He used the information I trustingly gave him to create that abomination of a blog post. That's all I have to say. Bring on the debate."

The discontent from the Howlers grew louder. Duncan began to appreciate how someone might feel facing a lynch mob. If this Howler group thought they could get away with it, they'd find a rope and a tall tree. He thought about his brother, Colin, and how much he would hate having the family name covered in mud.

Then he forced himself to settle down. He was innocent, and eventually he'd clear himself of suspicion, somehow, and all would be well. He had to believe that.

His entire reputation and that of the MacDowells would not be ruined because of one crazy hacker.

"All righty, then." Neil consulted a stack of index cards in his hand. "First question, which goes to Kate because Duncan won the right to the first opening statement. Here we go: If Brad Pitt were the last male on the planet, either Were or human, would you mate with him? Why or why not? And don't worry, Duncan. The question is altered for you. We're not going to ask you whether you'd have sex with Brad Pitt."

It was a question designed to break the ice, and a ripple of laughter eased the tension before all delegates focused on Kate.

"Of course I would mate with him," Kate said. "You're talking about the future of both Weres and humans. In that case, there is no choice. But ask me if I'd choose Brad Pitt, who is gorgeous, over an old, somewhat mangy Were who is not, and I'd choose the Were every time. Our kind needs to band together, and that includes mating."

The Howlers cheered and howled their approval.

Neil turned to Duncan. "Substitute Angelina Jolie in that question and give me your answer."

"I doubt there's a male alive, Were or human, who hasn't at some point fantasized about having sex with Angelina Jolie. And if she's the only female, then, as Kate said, the future of our species, as well as humans, is at stake. We'd have to help each other repopulate the world. Which is an interesting thought, because we'd be doing so in partnership with humans. What a different world that would be."

"But not better!" called out a Howler.

"How do you know?" responded a Woofer.

That challenge was answered by shouted insults from the Howlers and corresponding jeers from the Woofers. Neil tried to quiet them, but he didn't have the kind of personality that could handle a rowdy group.

Duncan finally decided he'd had enough of the chaos. It was really Neil's job to control it, so Duncan decided he'd have to take over Neil's job for a moment. Stepping out from behind the lectern, he closed the distance separating them.

Neil's eyes widened as Duncan reached over and unclipped the mike from Neil's lapel. It was still attached to the battery pack so he and Neil were linked together, but that couldn't be helped.

"Silence!" Duncan's command, delivered with his strong Scottish brogue, sounded like the battle cry of a warrior. Even Neil jerked in surprise.

And silence descended on the group.

"Now." Duncan pitched his voice low on purpose. "Kate Stillman has labored for months, along with her grandmother Elizabeth Stillman, to plan this historic meeting of Weres from around the world. You would think that we would all be grateful to be here and would want to take full advantage of the opportunity. You would think that we would refrain from wasting our valuable time in Colorado by squabbling like children. However . . ." He surveyed the audience.

Neil cleared his throat and leaned over to speak into the mike Duncan still held in his hand. "Let's try it again, shall we?"

That suggestion was greeted with a smattering of applause.

With one last survey of the group, Duncan gave Neil

his small mike and returned to the lectern. Not long ago he'd been nervous about the possibility of mob rule, but something had shifted in him, and now he'd be damned if he'd let that crowd run the show. Kate had put her heart and soul into this event, and she deserved to have it turn out better than the circus it had become.

"Next question," Neil said. "And this one goes first to Duncan. Although Were-human mating is not common, it has taken place. Half-bloods are among us. If they mate with Weres, they still have a fifty percent or better chance of producing Were children. If they mate with a human, that percentage goes down. Logically, isn't it possible that, with interbreeding, the Were strain could eventually die out?"

"Yes, I suppose it's possible." Duncan knew that wouldn't be a popular answer with his Woofers. "That's where our mission statement comes in. And to be honest, that's where dating sites like Furthebest can help. We do need Weres to mate with other Weres, provided it's a love match. We can encourage that, but please, let's not forbid Weres to marry the humans they've fallen in love with."

Neil nodded and turned to Kate. "Your rebuttal?"

"I think Duncan has made my point for me. There are far more humans in the world than Weres. The more we accept Weres mating with humans, the more it will happen and the more half-bloods will be born, then quarter-bloods, and so on. It may take hundreds of years, but eventually, the Were strain will die out and we will have lost . . . everything."

"But what about Weres like your sister, Penny?" Neil asked. "Would you deny her the love of her life?"

Kate flushed and lifted her chin. "Was that question on your cards, Neil?"

"As the moderator I have the privilege of inserting questions of my own, and this seemed the perfect opportunity to do so."

Duncan's fist clenched. He longed to plant it right in the middle of Neil's smug smile. The bastard had planned the order of the questions precisely so he could put Kate on the spot.

Kate straightened her shoulders and looked Neil in the eye. "If my sister had never met Tom Rivers, she might have mated with a Were instead. The more we encourage Weres to become intimately involved with humans, the more likely these conflicts will arise. Why not encourage Were-Were mating instead? The Were population still provides plenty of mates to choose from, but if we continue to mate with humans, that will change."

Neil paced in front of the audience, grandstanding, as usual. "With all due respect, Kate, you haven't answered the question. Would you deny your sister the love of her life?"

Kate took a deep breath. "I don't believe in that concept."

Duncan blinked in astonishment. Truly, she did not? He went back over their brief conversation about it. She'd said that she liked him for believing that lovers were destined for each other, but she hadn't mentioned her opposite view on the subject. It made sense if she was determined to stamp out Were-human mating. She couldn't let a silly thing like destiny interfere with that campaign.

"I thought you might say that," Neil said. "In the interests of hearing the whole story, I've asked Penny to speak on the subject."

"No!" Kate went white. Then she whirled toward

Duncan, her blue eyes blazing. "You knew about this, didn't you?"

"No, lass, I did not." His heart ached for her.

"I don't believe you. I think you and Neil cooked this up as a stunt to win the debate for the Woofers."

"No, he didn't, Kate." A tall, striking blonde with shoulder-length hair walked down the center aisle toward them. She wore a black jersey dress, four-inch black heels, and simple gold jewelry. "I only spoke with Neil."

Duncan could easily see why Penelope Stillman had been the first choice to take over from Elizabeth. She carried herself like a leader, and intelligence gleamed in her hazel eyes. Kate would make a fine pack alpha, but another ten years of seasoning would give her the kind of confidence Penny had now.

"Oh, Penny." Kate's voice shook as she came out from behind the lectern and went to her sister. "It's so good to see you."

Penny opened her arms and the two sisters exchanged a fierce hug. Anyone watching would know that they hadn't been together in a long time, and, despite their differences, they were devoted to each other.

Duncan was so engrossed in the reunion that he didn't immediately notice that Angela Sapworthy had motioned her camera crew over so they could film the whole thing. He could interfere, but that might create more problems than it would solve.

As Kate and Penny drew apart and wiped their eyes, Neil moved in. "I believe you wanted to add something to this discussion, Penny."

"I do want to add something." She glanced over at Duncan. "But first I want to denounce that Were." She pointed an accusing finger in his direction. "His unscrupulous behavior dishonors all of us. My sister would *never* go against her principles. I don't agree with them, but I've never once questioned her loyalty to her beliefs."

"Nor have I," Duncan said quietly. He doubted it mattered what he said, but he refused to stand there mutely, as if he'd done something wrong. Where the bloody hell were the Wallaces?

Penny turned to Kate. "Mind if I borrow your spot for a few minutes?"

Kate shook her head, her eyes still teary.

Duncan longed to walk over and gather Kate into his arms. She looked utterly destroyed by this surprise visit. After hearing of her fear for her sister, Duncan could only imagine what was going through Kate's mind. He doubted she was worried about losing the debate. She was probably far more worried about the danger Penny had placed herself in by coming here.

She would have had to make up some story to tell her mate, Tom, and their children, some really good excuse for why she'd gone to the lodge. He wondered how many of those lies had piled up over the years, and what it had done to their relationship. Maybe he was about to find out.

Penny took her place behind the lectern and adjusted the mike, because she was taller than Kate. "I'm glad to see that this conference is so well attended, and I congratulate my grandmother and my sister on a successful event."

Everyone could applaud that uncontroversial statement.

"You are dealing with some tough questions, and although I have to be very careful how often I check the news in the Were world, as you can imagine, I've followed this growing debate as much as I dared. I have a huge investment in the outcome."

Woofers gazed on her as if she were an angel from heaven, while the Howlers remained openly suspicious.

"As some of you may know, when I married Tom— excuse me for using human terminology, but I've grown used to it—I made the decision not to reveal my nature, which would force him to keep the secret from his family and friends." She gazed around the room. "In my mind, it was that or give him up."

Then she looked over at Kate. "Begging your pardon, little sister, but you don't know what the hell you're talking about when you say there's no such thing as one true love. Tom is mine, and if you're lucky, you'll find yours. I hope for your sake he's Were."

Kate said nothing, but her jaw tightened. Duncan also hoped her one true love would be Were, because he couldn't imagine the conflict in her heart and soul if he happened to be a human. It could tear her apart, and he couldn't bear the thought of that.

"I will say, though," Penny continued, "that having this lie between Tom and me gives me great pain. Many times I've been on the brink of confessing everything, but then I realize that would be selfish. I'd only transfer the burden from me to him. But I would love to think that someday I'll be able to tell him the truth because Weres and humans will have come to accept each other. I pray for that day. Thank you."

The Woofers cheered, woofed, and stomped their feet as she made her way back to Kate. They exchanged another tight hug, and then Penny walked back down the center aisle. She paused to embrace her grandmother before leaving the ballroom.

The Howlers sat there as if they'd all been shot with a stun gun. For that matter, Kate didn't look much better. As she took a deep breath, her body quaked in reaction. Duncan decided enough was enough. She could barely stand, and he couldn't in good conscience continue this debate.

He no longer cared whether he was following protocol or Neil's schedule as he spoke into his microphone. "I don't care if you're a Howler, a Woofer, or someone who's in between—you have to be touched by Penny's story. To me, it illustrates the complexity of this issue and the problems Weres face, especially female Weres, when they choose to mate with a human. Forget the slogans and the sound bites. We need to go back to the drawing board and brainstorm real-life solutions, not just concepts that sound good on a blog or in a book."

Kate walked back to her lectern and spoke into her mike. "Does that mean you're conceding this debate?"

She was one plucky lass, all right.

"You can't concede," Neil said. "From my perspective, Penny's touching story put you way ahead of Kate."

Duncan shook his head. "No, it did not. That's what I just tried to say. This issue is not as simple as I've made it sound, or as simple as Kate's made it sound, for that matter. Let's lay down our weapons and just talk to each other."

"But . . . but we still have time left." Neil waved his stack of index cards. "We still have questions. I'm sure everyone would like Kate to respond to her sister's heartfelt plea for openness and sharing. I'm sure—"

"I concede." Duncan turned to her. "I concede because I have nothing more to say until I've considered the matter more thoroughly. The debate victory is yours, milady." He hadn't meant to add that last endearment, but she tugged at his heart as she struggled to cover her vulnerability with righteous indignation.

Her blue gaze challenged his. "You're not deliberately taking a fall, are you?"

He lied with a clear conscience. "No."

"Because if you think that surrendering in this debate will make up for that blog, you're sadly mistaken."

"I know it won't." He was afraid nothing would. She might listen to the Wallaces if they came up with proof that he wasn't guilty. But once Kate got an idea into her head, she didn't let go easily. It was one of her best traits, but also one of her worst.

"Then I accept your concession," Kate said. "Any Howlers who care to come are invited up to my suite for a victory celebration." She gathered up her notes and started down the aisle trailed by Heidi and a group of Weres in purple shirts.

Elizabeth stood. At first Duncan thought she might go with Kate, but instead she walked up the side of the room toward the front row and took a seat. A few other delegates left, but most of the Woofers stayed in the room. Duncan didn't have a suite to invite them to, so he was about to suggest buying a round of drinks in the bar.

Before he did that, the Wallace contingent arrived through a door at the front of the room, the same one where Duncan had intercepted Kate earlier when he'd hoped to have her listen to his story. Howard led his two sons, Aidan and Roarke, and their mates, Emma and Abby, inside.

The cavalry had arrived, but they were too late, at least for this round. Kate and her followers were on their way upstairs, and he wasn't going to chase them down, especially when he didn't know what Howard had to say. He and Aidan might have found nothing at all.

Elizabeth came to join the group at the front of the room, too. "What's going on, Howard?" she said. "Looks like you have the whole family here." She smiled at Roarke and Abby. "Good to see you two. I've been so busy we've barely talked."

Abby smiled back. "No worries. We've been well taken care of."

Howard gestured to Aidan. "My son did most of the work on this, but we all did some digging, background checks, Internet searches, anything we thought would help. As you can imagine, this issue is dear to our hearts, and we didn't like the ugliness that developed today."

Aidan stepped forward. "First of all, Duncan, your blog is ridiculously easy to hack. I could have put up anything I wanted in a matter of seconds. You need to fix that, and I'll give you some suggestions about it later."

"Thanks." Duncan wished to hell Kate could be here for this, but surely she'd get the information eventually.

"Anyway, the short answer is yes, someone hijacked your site and posted that unauthorized blog. With a little more time, I should be able to identify the hacker or hackers, depending on how well they covered their tracks."

"I'd be very interested to know that information," Duncan said.

"I'd say it's likely to be one or more of the Howlers," Neil said.

Duncan himself had suspected Jake, but something in Neil's attitude made him study the blond Were more closely. "Why would you think that?"

"Makes sense. Howard was elected president and the

mission statement leaves plenty of room for the Woofer agenda. The pendulum's swinging that way. I even wondered if my cousin might have done it."

Duncan's instincts sharpened. "You think Kate would post up a picture of herself in bed with a human?" That was so far removed from the Kate he knew as to be laughable. Yet Neil was offering the possibility with a straight face.

"Why not? She looks like an innocent victim and you look like a jerk. Great for her, lousy for you."

Except that Duncan knew that Kate didn't play the game that way. She wasn't a double-dealer. Neil was, though. He wouldn't trust Neil further than he could throw him, which wouldn't be far, because the guy was packed with muscle.

Then everything clicked into place, and he felt like an idiot for not seeing it before. Neil, who wanted to steal the pack alpha position from Kate, would do whatever it took to rattle her this weekend and make her look bad. Neil surely knew about her favorite TV actor. And he had all the information on Penny, too.

"It was you, wasn't it? Or you and some tech-savvy delegates, because I doubt you have the brains to pull off something like that without help." Rage began to bubble deep in his gut.

Neil gave him a wary look. "That's ridiculous. Of course it wasn't me."

"That's a strong accusation, Duncan," Howard said. "You might want to retract it until Aidan does some more sleuthing."

"I don't care to retract it." Duncan held Neil's gaze and he could see guilt lurking there. "I know who it was sure as I'm a Scotsman." The rage filled his chest now, demanding release. He swore he could hear the pipes playing.

Neil sneered. "You don't know a damned thing, Mac-Dowell. You're bluffing."

"Nay, I'm not bluffing. And to prove it, I challenge you to settle this the traditional way, as Weres."

Elizabeth sucked in a breath. "Let's not be hasty."

"She's right, MacDowell. Don't be hasty. You'd have no chance against me. I outweigh you, and I can outfight you."

He was probably right. Duncan was a lover, not a fighter, and he could well get beaten to a pulp. But although the MacDowells lived at sea level these days, the blood of brave Highlanders ran hot in his veins. By all that was holy, he would be Kate's champion and defend her honor. Whether she wanted him to or not.

He faced Neil and imagined all those ancestors standing behind him, urging him on. "Meet me outside in fifteen minutes."

Chapter 18

**WERECON2012:
WOLF FIGHT!!**

**Exclusive report for *Wereworld Celebrity Watch*
by Angela Sapworthy**

DENVER—A stunning development took place Sunday afternoon following the scheduled debate between HOWL leader Kate Stillman and WOOF leader Duncan MacDowell. MacDowell accused Kate's cousin Neil of hijacking his blog and posting the incriminating picture of Kate in bed with a well-known TV actor!

Neil, great-nephew of pack alpha Elizabeth Stillman, denies the charge. Security expert and certified hunk Aidan Wallace is hot on the trail of the culprit, but MacDowell refuses to wait for confirmation. He's challenged Neil to a traditional battle, Were to Were!

This reporter expected philosophical battles

this weekend, but she had no idea that the fight would become physical! Pack alpha Elizabeth is understandably concerned about potential bloodshed and the effect on WereCon2012's reputation as a peaceful venue. "I've known Neil all his life," she said. "And he's been a fighter all his life. He's big, and he's brutal. I think Duncan MacDowell made a tactical error. He should have engaged Neil in a battle of wits."

For another viewpoint, this reporter caught up with Nadia Henderson, a young but confident leader for the Henderson pack in Chicago and Duncan's fellow council member. "I haven't known Duncan MacDowell long, but while serving with him on the council I've been impressed with his intelligence and creativity. I never did believe he was responsible for that terrible blog. But I can't speak to his fighting skills. I hope he uses his intelligence out there, because Neil looks as if he could make mincemeat of Duncan."

Dear reader, don't make the mistake of thinking Duncan MacDowell is small. He weighs in at 210, according to his profile on the Were Web. But Neil Stillman is listed at 250! His profile names more than twenty Weres he's defeated in wolf-to-wolf combat. Duncan MacDowell has no list at all! Will he survive? Follow me on Sniffer @newshound to find out!

Kate submerged herself in the welcome chatter of Howlers enjoying one another's company. None of the male Howlers had shown up, as if they'd known this would be a female-centered event in Kate's suite.

She had considered making a special point to personally invite Jake Hunter as a goodwill gesture, but he'd slipped out of the ballroom before she could do that. And frankly, she was too exhausted to care. If the mission statement was adopted when the votes were counted and posted at five this afternoon, which was only thirty minutes away, Jake would abandon ship anyway.

Heidi raised her wineglass. "Down with Woofers!"

Someone else raised hers. "Up with Howlers!"

A chorus of loud howling followed, and Kate joined in. She'd had one crappy day, and she was ready to unwind with her supporters. She wanted to forget about mission statements, Photoshopped pictures, lectures from her grandmother, surprise visits from her sister, and, most of all, Duncan MacDowell.

Of course he realized now that he should never have posted that blog, and he was trying to get back in her good graces by handing her the victory in the debate. No matter what he said, he'd done it to try to mend the rift between them. Howard must have told him he had to because they were both on the council and needed to work together.

She would work with him, though, despite hating his guts. That's what a leader had to do, and she understood that far better after this weekend. She'd had a real object lesson in leadership. Yes, she'd made a couple of mistakes, maybe more than a couple, but she'd learn from them and go on.

She'd have a chance to demonstrate her new understanding tonight at the gala ball to mark the end of the conference. In an hour or so she'd leave this private party and go check on the preparations for that. Once she knew everything was going according to plan, she'd come back upstairs and get into her red sequined dress.

She'd rather not go at all, but a leader didn't sit up in her room because she didn't feel like making an appearance at the final event of a conference she'd helped organize. A leader put on her big-girl panties along with her sparkly clothes and attended with a smile.

"How do Woofers get human females into bed?" shouted someone on the far side of the suite.

"I don't know," someone called back. "How do they get them into bed?"

"They spike their drink with woofies!" That was greeted with more enthusiastic howls.

The noise became so deafening that Kate didn't hear the doorbell until whoever was out there leaned on it for several seconds. She raised her voice. "Hey, everyone! Pipe down a minute! Someone's at the door."

Carrying her wineglass, she went to the door still laughing about the woofies joke. Maybe this was just a late-arriving Howler who'd decided to join the party. She opened the door, and her smile of welcome faded.

Her grandmother stood on the other side looking upset. She wore a coat and boots over her elegant conference outfit. "I called your cell, but you didn't answer."

"Sorry, Grandma." She stepped into the hall so she could hear. "What's wrong?"

"You have to get downstairs. Duncan's going to fight Neil, Were to Were."

"*What?* Why would he do that?" She tried to make sense of her grandmother's hurried explanation. It seemed that the Wallaces had confirmed that Duncan's blog had been hijacked, and Duncan was convinced Neil was the culprit.

The moment her grandmother said it, Kate saw the situation clearly at last. Neil would have known about the TV actor, and he certainly knew about Penny. Neil wanted to throw her off her game and the blog was one more way to do it.

"Go get your boots and coat," Elizabeth said. "We'll take your elevator."

"Right. Open the bookcase. I'll be right there." Kate turned and ran back into her suite. "Everyone! Duncan and Neil are going to fight. I want everyone down there so we can stop it."

"Why stop it?" Heidi sounded mystified. "We hate Duncan, and we don't much like Neil, either. Sounds like a great fight to me. I'll bring popcorn!"

Kate raced into her bedroom, yelling over her shoulder, "Duncan didn't put up that blog! Neil did!" Throwing open her closet door, she pulled out her coat and a pair of short boots without laces. Carrying them, she ran back into the living room and over to the corner where the bookcase stood open, revealing the elevator behind it.

All the Howlers stared at the elevator except Heidi, who had seen it in operation. Kate clutched her coat and boots and followed her grandmother inside the etched glass cubicle.

"I'll lead the charge down the stairs," Heidi said. "Meet you there, Kate."

"Thanks, Heidi." Kate leaned against the glass and pulled on her boot as the elevator started down.

"He cares for you, Kate." Elizabeth buttoned her coat.

"That doesn't mean he should make this kind of sacrifice." She pulled on the other boot. "It's ridiculous!"

"Apparently he doesn't think so."

"Well, I do. Neil will crush him." She shoved her arms into her coat sleeves. Riding in the elevator brought back memories of the late-night run with Duncan. "He's not used to the altitude and Neil is. Besides being lighter, he'll get winded faster."

"I hadn't thought of that."

"Well, he should have. He found out when we raced last night. And I thought he was so smart. But he's stupid, stupid, stupid! He should never have challenged Neil to a Were fight."

"Maybe we'll make it in time."

"I hope to hell we do." Her chest tightened with fear at the thought of Duncan ending up bloody . . . or worse. "What if Neil cripples him? He's capable of that. He fights hard and he fights dirty. I should know."

Elizabeth sighed. "I remember those days. You two fought all the time."

"And he didn't fight fair, either. If the fight wasn't going his way, he'd grab a stick, or throw a rock, or pretend to give up and then turn around and slug me. I know his tricks, but Duncan doesn't."

The elevator slid to a stop. Opening the door, she glanced back at her grandmother with a silent question.

"Go ahead. Go! You can move faster than I can. I'll be right behind you."

Kate didn't need any more urging. She pushed through the revolving exit door, and emerged into the sharp cold of late afternoon. To her right, a crowd formed a circle around a small clearing behind the lodge. She ran toward that crowd.

The site had been used for such challenges in the past, but Kate had never seen that happen. She knew the spot only as a place for playing lawn games in the summer and having snowshoe races in the winter. She did not want to remember it as the field upon which Duncan MacDowell spilled his precious blood.

It *was* precious, especially to her. As she pushed her way through the circle to the front, she admitted just how precious. The apparent betrayal of his blog wouldn't have hit her so hard if she hadn't already begun to care for him.

She would stop this fight. She had to. But the sight that greeted her when she was finally able to see what was happening inside the circle turned her blood to ice.

She hadn't seen Neil in Were form in a long time, and he looked even bigger than she remembered. Even his blond fur puffed out and seemed to add to his bulk. Nothing about him was small—not his massive chest, his broad head, his powerful jaws, or his immense paws.

Yet Duncan faced him without apparent fear, his head held high, confidence shining in his gray eyes. His lustrous fur gleamed like polished ebony against the white snow. Kate imagined that white snow flecked with blood and shuddered.

"Stop it!" She walked toward the two wolves, her boots crunching on the snow. "I forbid this!" She wasn't sure she had that authority, but it was worth a try. She stepped between the wolves, but she faced Duncan and looked into his eyes.

"I don't want you to do this." She knew he could understand her spoken words, even though he couldn't respond. Telepathy worked only between Weres in wolf form. No doubt he was exchanging heated messages with Neil. "Please, Duncan. It's not worth fighting over. Let

Howard and the council decide what sort of punishment Neil deserves. It's not up to you."

Behind her, Neil snarled.

She glanced over her shoulder and her temper flared. "Don't you dare snarl at me, you bastard."

Neil snarled again and bared his teeth.

A low, rumbling growl told her that Duncan was ready to answer that snarl. She turned back to him. "Do *not* fight him, do you hear me?"

He met her gaze, and she thought she saw a twinkle of amusement in those gray wolf eyes.

"Elizabeth thinks you're doing this because of me. That better not be true."

He simply stared at her.

"So help me, Duncan MacDowell, if you challenged Neil because of some stupid Scottish code that says you have to defend my honor, forget about it!"

He backed up a few paces.

"Good. You're rethinking this. That's good. Just keep backing up and leave the circle. Physical violence solves nothing. It— No!" Too late she realized he'd backed away only so that he could dodge around her.

Turning quickly, she watched in horror as he launched himself at Neil. "Damn you, Duncan! I'll never forgive you for this!"

He gave no sign that he'd heard her. The battle was on. Snarling, tumbling, struggling to use his sharp teeth, Duncan knocked his opponent down in a spray of white.

Hands pulled her away from the arena and into the protection of the crowd. She didn't bother to find out who had done that. All her attention was locked on the blond and black wolves as she began pleading silently for Duncan to find the strength and the stamina to survive this fight.

No, she wanted more than survival for him. If she couldn't stop him from fighting, then he had to *win*. Balling her hands into fists, she sent every bit of energy she possessed hurtling toward the black wolf with a heart bigger than she'd ever given him credit for.

But after that first lunge when he'd been lucky enough to catch Neil slightly off-balance, the fight went all Neil's way. The blond wolf surged to his feet and threw all his weight at Duncan, who went sprawling. He bounced back up, but Neil hit him again, this time pinning him to the ground.

Kate's nails dug into her palms as Neil strained his neck to reach a tendon in Duncan's back leg. Woofers yelled encouragement to their leader, begging him to throw off his attacker and escape those powerful jaws. Even a few Howlers joined in.

Instead Duncan went limp.

Kate cried out, begging him to fight back.

Neil momentarily lost his balance when Duncan stopped resisting him, and in a lightning move, Duncan scrambled out from under the big wolf and leaped on his back, his jaws clamping down on his neck.

Yes! Use your brains, not your brawn! Kate's pulse hammered as she recognized that Duncan was doing exactly that.

Woofers roared their approval of the clever move, but their joy was short-lived. Neil threw Duncan off his back with apparent ease, sending the black wolf to the ground again. This time he didn't get up quite fast enough, and

Neil was on him immediately, still going for the crippling hold on his back leg.

As Neil's jaws inched closer to that vulnerable spot, Kate started forward. She had to keep Duncan safe. Had to. But strong arms restrained her. She fought them as she watched in horror. Neil opened his jaws.

Drawing on some unseen reservoir of strength, Duncan wrenched free at the last minute and rolled. He came to his feet snarling, fangs bared. And there was something different about his stance this time.

Kate looked on in amazement as Duncan hunched his shoulders. A low, menacing growl rumbled in his chest, and he seemed to take on more bulk. He was no taller, no broader, and yet . . . she sensed the pride of his ancestors in every line of his body. So this was how a Scottish Highlander had faced the British army. A shiver ran down her spine.

The two wolves circled, never taking their eyes off each other. Neil was still the bigger wolf, and undoubtedly the stronger wolf. But Duncan was the braver wolf.

A hush fell over the crowd, as if they, too, saw that the contest was no longer lopsided. What Duncan lacked in size and strength, he made up for in valor. His eyes seemed to flash fire as he circled, and circled again.

The low growl sounded once more, and then he struck, sinking his fangs into Neil's throat with such speed that the big wolf failed to dodge away in time. With a howl of rage, he tried to shake off his foe. Duncan held on.

Neil tossed his head and slammed the black wolf to the snow. Duncan held on. He held on as Neil rolled and tumbled, leaving drops of blood in his wake and smashing Duncan's body to the ground over and over.

At last, Neil lay on his side, panting, as if he'd given up.

Duncan braced himself above him, head down, still gripping his opponent's throat. The blood didn't gush from the wound, which meant the jugular had not been pierced. But if Duncan chose to, he could easily do it now.

With a wail of distress, Elizabeth ran into the center of the circle, arms outstretched in supplication.

Slowly, Duncan unclamped those powerful jaws and stepped back.

"Thank you," Elizabeth said as she knelt in the snow beside Neil. "I can't let you kill him."

With one last glance at Neil, Duncan turned his back and started to walk away.

In that instant, the blond wolf leaped to his feet, knocking Elizabeth over as he launched his big body into the air and drove Duncan to the ground.

Kate rushed to help her grandmother. "Stop him!" she cried. "The fight's over! He surrendered!"

But Duncan had already squirmed out from under that crushing weight and both Weres were on their feet, circling once again. No one seemed inclined to get in the middle of wolves locked in a life-and-death struggle.

Kate pulled Elizabeth back to the shelter of the crowd.

Her grandmother's gaze followed Neil. "He used my compassion. He used me." Disbelief laced her words.

As he's used you all along. But Kate couldn't waste words or thought on Neil. She was too busy praying for Duncan. Incredibly, he was still on his feet.

But so was Neil. He might be bleeding, but he stalked Duncan with deadly purpose. Duncan's flanks heaved from the exertion of breathing at this elevation. He was a courageous Were, but he was in a battle where the odds were stacked against him.

Then one of his Woofers began to chant—*woof*, *woof*, *woof*. The rest picked it up, filling the air with support for their leader.

Kate could see the effect on Duncan as the weariness left his body. She joined in, chanting with all her might—*woof*, *woof*, *woof*. Next to her, Elizabeth did the same. Kate glanced over at Heidi across the circle and Heidi followed her lead. Soon all the Howlers added their voices to those of the Woofers.

Then Kate realized Howard had arrived along with his family. They began chanting with the rest. She spotted Knox, Giselle, Nadia, and even Jake. Duncan had given them all a cause to support, regardless of allegiances. They believed in honesty and fair play.

The noise was deafening, and Neil paused, as if confused by the racket. That encouraged the crowd even more as the cry of *woof*, *woof*, *woof* rose into the cold mountain air.

Neil's haunches bunched as if to spring at Duncan. Duncan coiled his body, preparing for the assault.

Woof, woof, woof! The chant rolled in waves around the circle, as if weaving a net of protection for the black wolf with the valiant heart.

Neil's gaze darted from Duncan to the shouting crowd, as if he wasn't sure where his enemy lay. At last, with a snarl, he ran straight toward the crowd, which scattered to let him pass. He ran up the ski slope as if yearning to put distance between himself and the endless chanting. Soon he was no more than a small smudge against the white snow of the ski run.

Tears streamed down Kate's cheeks as Duncan stood on wobbly legs and accepted the cheers from a circle of Weres finally united by his unwavering courage. She started forward as his gaze met hers. She saw the warning there. Noticed the slight shake of his head.

He was telling her not to come to him. Whether that was for his sake or hers, she couldn't know. Turning away from her, he walked unsteadily out of the ring.

Elizabeth came up beside her. "You didn't go after him. Why not?"

Kate swallowed the tears lodged in her throat. "Because he didn't want me to, Grandma."

Chapter 19

WERECON2012:
SOLIDARITY HERE, THEN GONE

Exclusive report for *Wereworld Celebrity Watch*
by Angela Sapworthy

DENVER—In a small clearing behind Stillman Lodge, Duncan MacDowell became a hero today. For the first time since the conference began, Woofers and Howlers joined forces in support of MacDowell's courageous battle with suspected hacker Neil Stillman. Dear readers, the atmosphere was thrilling! This reporter had goose bumps!

Alas, the sense of cooperation didn't last long. Delegates returned to the lodge and discovered that the mission statement crafted by MacDowell and Kate Stillman has passed. That news was cheered by some and booed by others. Supporters of the mission statement seem evenly split between Howlers and Woofers, as are the detractors.

"Middle-of-the-road delegates and compromisers like Howard Wallace think the mission statement is fine," commented former Howler supporter Jake Hunter. "But you know what happens when you stand in the middle of the road? You get run over by oncoming traffic in both directions."

Jake, whose rugged good looks still get my motor running, was observed in the bar trying to recruit disenchanted Howlers to his new organization, Werewolves Against Random Mating, or WARM. Jake says he's already submitted his resignation to the Were Council, which he claims has "stacked the deck" in favor of Woofer principles.

When asked his opinion about Kate Stillman and HOWL, Jake was refreshingly blunt. "I respect Duncan MacDowell and Kate Stillman, but they've become too cozy for my tastes. Kate's personal involvement with MacDowell renders her HOWL movement irrelevant. WARM is the new standard-bearer for the cause."

Jake said he may or may not attend the gala scheduled tonight. But this reporter will be there, hoping to see Duncan MacDowell in a kilt! As for Neil Stillman, is he gone for good? Or not? Follow me on Sniffer @newshound for all the news on glitter, glamour, and celebrity sightings!

Duncan staggered through the lit tunnels and back to his room before the crowd recovered its wits enough to come after him. He was grateful for that, because if they'd wanted to do something symbolic like carry him off the field on their shoulders, he might have passed out. Bloody hell, how he ached. He hoped the pain in his left hind leg was a sprain and not a break.

Kate had told him not to fight Neil, and no doubt he should have listened to her. Now that WOW existed, werewolves had a governing body that could deal with the behavior of renegades like Neil. Choosing to call him out had been a demonstration of the ego Kate had railed about when they'd first met.

Apparently she was right about the size of it, and now he was paying for his overblown sense of honor. Worse yet, she'd almost committed political suicide out there when she'd started toward him. He couldn't allow her to damage her standing with Howlers because he'd been an idiot.

His phone, which he'd left on his nightstand, had been ringing ever since he'd pushed through the revolving door that led back into his room. He ignored it and stretched out on the floor beside his bed. Shifting back to human form would not be pleasant, but he knew that doing so would help speed the healing.

Gritting his teeth, he shut out the sound of the phone and concentrated on his shift. His leg throbbed, and as the shift moved relentlessly through his body, he felt as if he were being stabbed with hundreds of sharp knives.

After an eternity in which he almost wished Neil had finished him off, he lay naked and trembling on a carpet that was fine, but not the same grade as he'd enjoyed in Kate's suite. His leg still hurt, but not as much as before he'd shifted. Carefully moving it back and forth, he decided it wasn't broken.

His phone had stopped ringing, but a second later it started again. Gripping the side of the mattress to steady himself, he rose to his knees, wincing as his battered body protested. He glanced over at the phone.

The light blinked rapidly, indicating messages left. The phone stopped ringing again and beeped as another message was placed on it. Reaching over, he pressed a button to turn the damned thing off. The human in him protested that he needed to respond to those messages, but the wolf in him was stronger, and the wolf wanted to retreat and lick his wounds.

Neil would be doing that, too. Being bested in a fight was one thing. Having an entire group of Weres turn against him was worse. A Were needed community, a pack, an identity. Rarely one thrived as a true lone wolf.

In other words, Duncan's impulsive challenge had probably created more of a problem than it had solved for the Stillman pack. No wonder Kate had said she'd never forgive him for this. He might have transformed an annoying Were into a dangerous one.

Of course, he also could have killed Neil. But he wasn't a killer. He couldn't say the same for Neil, though. That Were would have crippled him or worse if he'd been able to, and his fury would only grow as time went by. Duncan vowed to stay alert during the twelve hours or so he would remain in Colorado.

Rising carefully to his feet, he tested his leg again. Thank God for the healing power of Weres. If he stayed off it as much as possible for a day or so, he should be fine. No more challenging Weres.

He'd brought a pair of sweatpants along and he took those out of his suitcase and put them on, along with his University of Edinburgh sweatshirt. Better. He was beginning to feel more human again. He smiled at his own little joke.

Checking the time, he thought about the event tonight, the gala ball that was supposed to be the conference's grand finale. He'd rather miss it, but that would be bloody rude, especially after all the support he'd received from the delegates during that fight. He wouldn't relish the attention he'd inevitably get, though. He didn't want to be hailed as a hero when in fact he'd caused the Stillman pack more difficulties in the long run.

Angela Sapworthy would be lying in wait for him, too. She'd be bound to ask that typical question about whether he wore anything under his kilt. As he contemplated that unpleasant thought, a rap sounded at his door.

He hoped he hadn't somehow conjured her up by thinking about her. Fortunately he had a peephole in his door and could check to see who was out there. Maybe it was Kate.

His heart beat a rapid tattoo at the thought it might be her. If so, he'd fling wide the door, pull her close, and beg her to forgive him for making everything worse with his out-of-control ego. If he could hold her, maybe she would find it in her heart to go easy on him.

He didn't expect he'd ever be allowed to make love to her again. That would be asking too much. But he would very much like to hold her in his arms one more time before he got on that plane.

To his great disappointment, Kate was not outside his door, but to his great relief, neither was Angela Sapworthy. Instead, he saw Elizabeth, her image distorted by the rounded lens of the peephole. Even distorted, she managed to look regal.

She'd lifted her hand to rap again when he opened the door, startling her. "Oh! You *are* here." She gave him a swift, thorough glance. "And on your feet. That's an encouraging sign. May I come in?"

"Of course." He stepped back and she walked into the small room, which contained only a bed, one easy chair, two nightstands, and a dresser on which stood his smallish flat-screen. He gestured toward the easy chair. "Please have a seat."

"Thank you." She looked a little less pulled together than usual. Her blond hair was windblown, her lipstick was gone, and her pale green, wide-legged pants were stained and damp all around the hems. She settled into the chair and surveyed the room. "We should have found you a better one than this."

"It's perfectly fine." He sat on the edge of the bed and faced her. Mentioning that he hadn't actually spent a night in this room would be indelicate, so he didn't point that out.

"Howard's left several messages on your phone. Others have, too."

"I turned it off. I needed—"

"To hide in a cave for a little while. My mate used to need that, too, after a trying experience of some sort or another, often because of me." She gazed into the distance with a faint smile. "I remembered that and almost didn't come. But I had to."

"Why is that?"

"I wanted to apologize," she said, "and to make certain that you're not badly injured."

"I'm not, as you can see. A little soreness in one leg. I'll be fine."

"I'm glad."

"But I'm the one who should be apologizing to you and Kate, and everyone in the Stillman pack. I shouldn't have challenged him. It was an arrogant and rash decision, and I regret it."

"You were defending your honor! And Kate's!"

"That sounds wonderfully noble, doesn't it? But after what happened out there, you will have a nasty problem on your hands."

"We'll deal with my great-nephew." A hard glint flashed in her eyes. "That's assuming he dares to come back."

"I'm afraid he will come back. He's not going to give up what he had here so easily. He's liable to be a thorn in your side for a long time, and I regret that more than I can say. I hope someday you'll be able to forgive me."

Her beautifully arched eyebrows lifted. "You're asking for *my* forgiveness? After my interference almost got you killed?"

"Your interference didn't really change anything. I was prepared to let him go and walk away. The outcome would have been the same, with or without your well-meaning gesture. I was never going to kill him."

"But you had him by the throat." Her manicured hand went to her own neck. "I thought . . ."

"I only wanted him to yield. I thought he had. That would have been enough to satisfy me. He put up a terrible blog that dishonored the Were that I . . . that dishonored Kate. That deserves some type of punishment, but certainly not the death penalty. At least not in this century it doesn't." And he'd almost let something slip, something he'd barely acknowledged to himself. He hoped she wouldn't notice.

Of course she did. "Dishonored the Were that you . . . what, Duncan? What did you start to say?"

He looked away from those blue eyes that were eerily

like Kate's. Elizabeth saw too much, guessed too much. And why wouldn't she? She'd been there for his primitive demonstration of how a male Were, especially a Scots Were, defends the honor of his chosen female.

Except that Kate was not his chosen female. Or more precisely, he was not her chosen male. In addition to disagreeing with all he stood for, she'd quite rightly forbidden him to fight Neil. He'd done it anyway, and she'd said she'd never forgive him for that.

True, she'd started toward him after the fight as if to make certain he was all right, but he was sure that had been pure reflex on her part, the action of a naturally compassionate Were. If she'd had time to consider, she wouldn't have done it.

"I know you care for her," Elizabeth said gently.

"Of course I do." He met her understanding gaze. "She's wonderful, but I don't have to tell you, do I? You've known her all her life, and I've known her for a weekend." He paused and shook his head. "It feels like so much longer."

Elizabeth smiled. "It usually does when you fall in love."

That sentence floated in the air between them as he tried to decide how he should respond. He should deny that he was in love with Kate, but Elizabeth wouldn't believe him if he did. So in the end, after a long pause, he let out a breath. "Yes, I suppose so."

She looked triumphant. "What are you going to do about it?"

"Not much to do, is there? We don't see eye to eye on much of anything. And then I go and complicate her life by fighting her cousin. I'm sure she can hardly wait to get rid of me. Oh, and that's another thing. I'll hire a cab to go back to the airport in the morning, in case you had any idea of asking her to be the chauffeur again."

Elizabeth sighed and leaned back in the chair. "Are you seriously planning to leave the country without telling her how you feel?"

He looked her straight in the eye. "Yes, Elizabeth, that's exactly my plan. And I would greatly appreciate it if you would keep this entire conversation to yourself."

She didn't like that answer. Her mouth flattened into a thin line.

"Do we have an understanding on that?"

"Oh, I suppose." She gave him a frustrated glare. "But it was all going so well at first. Obviously I couldn't control the weather, so that snowstorm was a bonus I hadn't counted on. But then you were forced to work together on the mission statement. I had such hopes."

"Hopes?" He stared at her. He'd never guessed she'd had matchmaking in mind. "What sort of hopes?"

"The minute that online rivalry developed between you two, I saw the way she perked up. She hasn't been that involved with a male Were in her entire adult life."

"Is that so?" He enjoyed hearing that, but he was still digesting the information that Elizabeth had intended to promote a romance between Kate and him.

Elizabeth leaned forward, into her subject now. "You see, I adore her, but she can be a bit . . . rigid."

"Really? I hadn't noticed."

She laughed. "That's exactly what I mean. You don't let her take herself too seriously. And you don't agree with her at every turn. You force her to consider the other side of the question once in a while. She needs that desperately, especially if she's going to lead this pack one day."

"Elizabeth, thank you for saying those things, but have you thought about how a relationship with me would affect her standing with the Howlers? They'd accuse her of fraternizing with the enemy."

"They might have before the fight, but you won a lot of hearts out there. You might be surprised how her followers are reacting. Besides, she can always say she's acting as a check and balance on your actions, just as I believe you'd be on hers. It would keep each of you from going to extremes."

"You really think I could have that kind of effect on her?"

She nodded. "I do."

"You must think I have great powers of persuasion."

"In a way. Your persuasive powers are what I might call supercharged."

That made him grin. "Supercharged powers of persuasion. Can I quote you on that?"

"Of course not. I only say it because she's in love with you, too."

His chest tightened. "I think you're wrong."

"No, I'm not. I've seen the way she is with some of the Weres she's dated. Watching them together has been as exciting as watching paint dry. But with you two—sparks are flying everywhere!"

"Because half the time she hates my guts!"

"No, she doesn't. Can't you tell that she loves matching wits with you?"

He wanted to believe what Elizabeth was saying, but she hadn't considered all the facts. "Maybe she used to, but less than an hour ago she said if I fought Neil, she'd never forgive me. And I fought him. So there you have it."

"Oh, for heaven's sake! She would have said anything

to stop you from getting hurt, because she *loves you*. You can't take that comment seriously."

"I don't know. She sounded bloody serious to me."

Elizabeth blew out an impatient breath and stood. "All right, let me put it this way."

Duncan stood, too.

"If you don't tell her how you feel before you leave the country, then *I'll* never forgive you. And unlike Kate, I mean that sincerely." She gave him a penetrating look before turning toward the door. "See you at the ball. I hope you're wearing your kilt."

"Aye. I will be wearing it."

"Good." She opened the door and glanced over at him. "That will help your cause. Not many females can resist a handsome Were in a kilt." Then she left, closing the door behind her.

Duncan stood quite still after she left, but his brain was spinning. She'd known Kate for a hell of a lot longer than he had, so he couldn't simply dismiss what she'd said. But if Kate loved him, wouldn't he know it? What if Elizabeth was wrong, and he laid his heart at Kate's feet, and she stomped all over it?

But what if Elizabeth was right, and he left for Scotland tomorrow without telling Kate that he loved her? That seemed like the greater risk. The first would be humiliating and he'd go home with his heart torn to bits, but at least he would have tried. With the second, he could live the rest of his life regretting what he hadn't done.

That left the issue of when and how to talk to her. They'd have no privacy at the ball, and besides, she might snub him at first. After all, he'd warned her off when she'd tried to comfort him on the field of battle. He'd done it for her own good, but she might not have realized that.

And perhaps he wasn't the best judge of what was right for her. He should simply tell her how he felt, and let her decide if she would allow that to affect her life, including her fight for the cause she believed in. The idea that they'd balance each other out appealed to him. Maybe, just maybe, it would appeal to her.

Walking to his closet, he took out his kilt and laid it on the bed. If Elizabeth was also right about the lure of a kilt, he'd use that lure. He needed all the help he could get. He only had to decide whether to wear it with or without.

Kate circled the ballroom making sure that the buffet tables were properly placed near the setup for the bar. The musicians tuned up on the dais, and round tables had been brought in, covered with white linen, and arranged in a semicircle to create a dance floor.

Kate had chosen the centerpieces herself. Each table held a small globe in a brass stand set into a wreath of pine sprigs and small pinecones. White votives tucked into the wreath would add atmosphere once the lights were dimmed and the candles were lit.

She'd had such high hopes for this final party. She'd imagined it as a joyous finale to a successful conference. But if she was honest with herself, she'd also painted a rosy picture of delegates adopting her agenda as they realized that Weres should band together instead of mingling freely with humans.

Duncan's views hadn't figured into her vision of the conference at all. In hindsight, that had been naive of her, but maybe she'd hung out with Howlers for so long that she thought the delegates would immediately see the sense in the Howler creed. They wouldn't want to risk eventual annihilation by supporting the Woofers' reckless plan.

Instead, the Woofers remained strong and might have gathered more recruits after Duncan's heroic battle in the snow. Meanwhile, she'd heard rumors that Jake Hunter had started a new group and was coaxing Howlers to abandon HOWL and join him in campaigning against Were-human mating. When she'd texted Howard, he'd confirmed that Jake had resigned from the council.

They'd need a replacement, and she wanted it to be another Howler. She'd suggested Heidi, but the rest of the council would have to vote on any nominee. At least Howard had assured her he wouldn't put either Aidan's or Roarke's name in the hat. He understood that would smack of nepotism, and Kate shuddered to think how the council would govern with a member who was already mated with a human.

Gazing at all the globes resting in their brass holders, she remembered the thrill of walking into this room on Saturday morning and hearing all the different accents. She'd reveled in the excitement generated by delegates who'd traveled halfway around the world to attend this historic event.

It was still historic, she reminded herself. Without this conference Weres would be forced to make difficult choices without hearing all sides. If nothing else, all sides had been heard this weekend. She still believed in her vision of the future, but hers wasn't the only one out there.

Penny's voice was out there, too, and she couldn't ignore what her sister had said during the debate. Neil had asked Penny to speak so she'd sabotage Kate, but in the end, Kate was glad she'd made that speech. Ever since hearing it, Kate had been reevaluating her thoughts about love and destiny.

History was riddled with stories of lovers who claimed they were meant for each other, even when everything seemed against their love. Maybe love wasn't always neat and tidy. Maybe love sometimes created challenges to test those who were drawn to each other.

Of course these thoughts brought her to Duncan MacDowell. He might be Were, but he was almost as wrong for her as Tom was for Penny. They disagreed on the most basic issues. They lived an ocean apart. And perhaps most important of all, Duncan had stated, loudly and publicly several times this summer, that he intended to mate with a human someday.

So, given all that, why did she yearn for him in a way that she'd never yearned for any other Were? Why did making love to Duncan feel as if she'd found the other half of her soul? And why had she died a million deaths watching him out on the field of combat this afternoon? Why had his refusal to let her comfort him cut so deep?

Now that she'd had time to think about that, she realized that he could have warned her off because he'd been thinking of her reputation. Although the Howlers had supported him in this uneven fight, they might not be crazy about their leader openly embracing the King of the Woofers.

She'd been concerned about that very thing herself two days ago when she hadn't wanted her followers to know what went on in the cabin. But she no longer cared what they knew. Associating with Duncan was not going to taint her in some way. If the Howlers thought so, then that was a rigid stance she couldn't tolerate anymore and she'd step down from her leadership position.

Penny would say her thinking had changed because she'd found her one true love. Kate could almost see her lapsing into big-sister mode as she smiled indulgently at Kate and welcomed her into a secret club that she'd finally become eligible to join.

Had she, though? She still resisted the concept because it implied that she was Duncan's one true love, his destiny, his fate. But he didn't want to mate with a Were, which left her out entirely. In his own way, he was as dedicated to mating for political reasons as she was.

And yet he'd said he believed in love and destiny. She remembered that quite clearly. They'd been discussing it right before they shifted to go out and play in the snow and do . . . other things in the snow. Things that made her hot every time she remembered them.

But good sex didn't necessarily mean he was her one true love or she was his, did it? All this love and destiny nonsense made her head ache.

"Penny," she muttered, "it's quite possible that you're full of crap."

With one last glance at the ballroom, she went upstairs to put on her sparkly clothes.

Chapter 20

Before heading to the ballroom, Duncan answered all the messages on his phone except for one. Neil had shifted to human form, at least long enough to locate his phone and send a cheesy threat—*Watch your back, Woofer.* It could be an empty threat, too. Neil wouldn't have the nerve to show up when a party was in full swing.

Neil had counted on his brawn to give him the victory. Because that hadn't worked out, he'd look for some other way to catch Duncan at a disadvantage. Confronting him in a crowd made no sense.

Duncan left his room and was immediately hailed by other Weres coming out of their first-floor rooms. He'd thought he might be the only one wearing the costume of his native country, but he grinned happily at the sight of the Mexican delegate in a black sombrero and a Zorro-like outfit while his mate wore a tiered skirt, a peasant blouse, and a flower in her hair. The Austrian delegate coming from the other direction was dressed in lederhosen and a hat with a feather in the brim.

All three asked how he was feeling. Although he still had a shooting pain whenever he put pressure on his injured leg, he assured them he was in fine shape. He'd get enough unwanted attention as it was.

They joined the other Weres streaming into the lobby and down the wide hallway to the open doors of the ballroom. Duncan recognized the sound of live music and wondered if the evening would include dancing. He could manage something slow without too much pain, and if he could lure Kate onto the dance floor, he could use the time to ask for a moment to talk privately.

The ballroom had been transformed. The former businesslike decor of folding chairs and lecterns had been replaced with soft lights, flickering candles, fine linens, and joyful music. He glimpsed colorful costumes from every land, from Russian pantaloons to Japanese kimonos.

Best of all, the delegates had left their logo T-shirts and slogan buttons in their rooms. Duncan noticed the small globes in the center of each table and wondered if they had been Kate's idea. The spirit in this room tonight illustrated what they'd tried to convey in the mission statement.

He knew from a quick phone discussion with Howard that the mission statement had passed, but he also knew a vocal minority was unhappy about that. Yet as concerned Weres came over to inquire about his health, not a single one mentioned the controversy. It seemed that the delegates had checked their politics at the door so they could enjoy the evening.

Still, he braced himself as Angela Sapworthy approached. Her long black dress was sprinkled with what seemed like a million rhinestones. Her spiked hair was also covered with rhinestones. She would have blinded him in full light, but candles helped mute the effect. Still, she made his eyes hurt.

"Duncan MacDowell! May I have a word?"

"Which word did you have in mind? I know several."

She tittered. "You're so droll. How about the word *underwear*? Do you know that word?"

"I'm familiar with it."

"Is it a word that goes with *kilt*? Or not?" She batted her glitter-covered eyelashes.

He should have a good answer for this question after all these years, but he didn't, so he decided to stall. "Depends on the occasion."

"What about *this* occasion?"

"MacDowell!" The Russian delegate who'd promised to buy him all the vodka he could drink approached with a glass in each hand. He acted as if he had no idea he'd interrupted Angela's attempt at an interview. "I decided Scotch would be your preference." He handed him one glass and kept the other.

"Aye, 'tis." Duncan took the glass. "Thank you. You know, I still can't pronounce your name."

"Doesn't matter. Call me Nick."

"Then thank you kindly, Nick."

"You're most welcome. To WereCon2012!" Nick tapped his glass against Duncan's.

"Hear, hear!" Duncan took a sip.

"To the Worldwide Organization of Werewolves!" Another tap.

"Aye! To WOW!"

"To . . ." Nick looked over at Angela. "I'm sorry. You don't have a drink. You can't toast with us if you don't have a drink." He put his arm around her. "Let's go get you one."

Duncan grinned as he watched them leave. That little save had been worth twenty drinks. He'd find Nick later and tell him so. And he'd eventually figure out how to pronounce his whole name.

He'd seen no sign of Kate. He'd been searching the room ever since he'd walked in, but no luck so far. He continued to watch for her as he talked to delegates about everything except their political views. He heard funny stories of shifting mishaps, and Were jokes cropped up everywhere. He even heard one that started out, "Three werewolves walked into a bar." He wanted to tell Kate about that. Where the devil was she?

He desperately wanted to see her, but even beyond that, he needed to tell her something that was becoming more obvious the longer he stayed in this room. No matter what the future held, Weres would always require a gathering place that belonged to them alone. Their experience as Weres set them apart from humans, and they understood one another. Nonshifters, or the "shifting disabled," as one Woofer had suggested calling them, just wouldn't get it.

He wasn't giving up his dream of a day when Weres and humans interacted with full knowledge that they weren't the same species. That secret was causing too many rifts among families where interspecies mating had already taken place. But this special gift of Were solidarity had to be protected. He wanted to tell her that.

So far, however, she hadn't made an appearance. Surely she wouldn't hide in her room. She had more intestinal fortitude than that. He hadn't seen Elizabeth, either, and when he did, he planned to ask her where Kate was. He was growing impatient.

The band ended their latest song. And that was another thing. He'd heard several that would have been perfect for dancing. Other couples had taken the floor, and he'd been asked to dance more than once and declined. He was waiting for Kate.

The band broke into a jazzy little riff, and suddenly, there she was, climbing the steps of the dais behind her grandmother. A spotlight followed them to the microphone, in case anyone might miss their entrance. Considering the glittering picture they made, that wasn't likely. Pride swelled in his chest as he watched Elizabeth and Kate take center stage.

Elizabeth wore a flowing, floor-length gown made of an iridescent material that shimmered in ever-changing colors as she moved. She wore an extravagant necklace of amethysts and diamonds, and those same gems dangled from her earlobes. Duncan appreciated the grace and style of her outfit, but he spent very little time looking at it.

He spent quite a lot more time staring at Kate's red, formfitting dress covered in sequins. Elizabeth's outfit was lovely, but Kate's ... The plunging neckline had surely drawn the attention of every male in the room. As if that weren't enough to send their libidos into overdrive, the skirt had a slit up the side that ended dangerously halfway up her creamy thigh.

A ruby pendant dipped tantalizingly close to her cleavage, and she'd worn her hair piled on top of her head to show off ruby earrings that brushed her shoul-

ders. Duncan was so entranced that he took an unconscious step forward, as if he needed to reach her before
any other Were got the jump on him.

Fortunately he snapped out of his daze before he
made a complete ass of himself. He'd made a semi-ass
out of himself, though, because those on either side of
him gave him a knowing glance, and the Russian delegate winked. They knew. His besotted state was obvious
for all to see.

Therefore he might as well confess his feelings to her
soon and get it over with. Besides, if he didn't act quickly,
she was liable to have six more offers before the night
was out. He couldn't imagine that any single Were in the
place wasn't thinking of Kate in very lustful ways. Woofer
or Howler, they were all normal male werewolves with
typical reactions.

He hoped that Jake Hunter wasn't here, but the minute he had the thought, he spotted Jake from the corner
of his eye. Jake seemed as transfixed by Kate as Duncan
was. And to top it off, the bastard was wearing a tuxedo.
Duncan hoped that Elizabeth was right about the lure of
kilts, because Hunter had bloody well dressed to impress.

Elizabeth took the microphone first while Kate
stepped back. "Welcome to our party!" She lifted her
arms and the crowd cheered.

Duncan listened for woofs and howls, but didn't hear
any. Good. He hoped the evening would remain apoliti-
cal, for everyone's sake, especially his. This atmosphere
could aid his cause by helping focus on the positives in
their relationship instead of the negatives.

"I'm pleased to see that you're all having such a great
time," Elizabeth said. "Thank you all for coming to
WereCon2012. Stillman Lodge is honored to have

hosted all of you this weekend and we would love to see you all back here for WereCon2013!"

More cheers greeted that suggestion. Duncan wondered what his life would look like a year from now. He was beginning to hope it might be very different, but uncertainty still gripped him. So much depended on Kate's reaction to what he had to say, and he couldn't predict what it would be.

"I only need one more minute of your time," Elizabeth said. "Before you return to a much-deserved celebration, please give a round of applause to the person who worked very hard to make this conference happen, my granddaughter Kate Stillman!" Stepping back, she motioned Kate toward the mike.

The applause was deafening. Instead of howls or woofs, the air was pierced by loud whistles and cries of *"Kate, Kate, Kate!"* Duncan was positive he'd made an ass of himself, because he was surely the loudest of them all.

"Thank you all." She swallowed and swiped her fingers quickly under her eyes. "Thank you," she said again, her voice husky. "This weekend has surpassed my wildest dreams. And it couldn't have happened without my grandmother." Turning, she started another round of applause for Elizabeth, who came back to the microphone and slipped an arm around Kate.

Elizabeth leaned toward the mike. "Now go enjoy yourselves!" As the band played another catchy sequence, both women started down the steps.

Duncan had already begun to move. He probably shouldered a few male Weres out of the way as he headed for the base of the steps. Too bad. When they reached the bottom, he planned to be there, and he would beat Hunter to the spot, too.

He made it just ahead of the Alaskan. Glancing back at him in triumph, Duncan turned toward the steps and offered his hand to Elizabeth. "You look beautiful tonight," he said.

"Thank you." She eyed his kilt. "You don't look so bad yourself." With a smile she squeezed his hand and released it before stepping toward Jake. "Mr. Hunter! I've heard so much about you this weekend, but we haven't had a chance to talk. How would you like to get me a drink?"

Duncan made a quick mental note to thank her for that later. But right now, he had to concentrate on Kate. He held out his hand to help her down the steps. He wasn't even sure she'd take it.

But she did, her gaze locked with his as she descended the steps. "Nice kilt, Woofer."

His pulse leaped at the warm glow in her blue eyes. "Nice dress, Howler." The band was playing a waltz. He would have preferred something a little less taxing, but he'd take it. "Can you dance in it without causing a riot?"

"Can you dance in your kilt without causing one?"

"I couldn't say, lass. The sway of a kilt does tend to cause some excitement."

"As does the flash of a naked thigh."

"Then let's put on a show, milady." His idea of a quiet interlude was disappearing fast, but he couldn't resist the challenge in her eyes. If she wanted to display their connection for all to see, he was done with protesting. She knew what she was doing.

He'd been taught to waltz at a young age, and while it was very romantic, he wouldn't be allowed to mold her body to his as he'd hoped. Placing his palm in the small of her back and cupping her hand in his, he looked into her eyes. "I love you." Ah, he hadn't meant to say *that*.

Her lips parted as her breath caught. "Way to throw off a girl's concentration, Woofer."

"Sorry. Let's dance." He began to twirl her around the floor as he cursed his loose tongue. What a blunder that was. He'd meant to lead up to it, find a quiet time, a secluded spot . . . and that plan was in ashes.

"Is that it?" She danced as beautifully as she did everything else. They moved together as if they'd been doing this for years. "You blurt out that you love me and then we just waltz?"

"I dinna mean to say it." Turned out his bad leg was good for only a couple of times around the floor. Now he winced every time he put his weight on it.

"Because you *don't* love me? Is it because I'm not a human? Is that it?"

"Nay, I do love you, and I love that you're Were, too. That's the best part, which is ironic considering how I've been sounding off on the subject. But this wasn't how I . . . bloody hell. I've made a mess of this." He sucked in a breath as pain sliced through his leg.

"Duncan, what's wrong with you? Are you hurting?"

"It's nothing."

"It's not nothing. Your jaw is clenched and sweat is popping out on your forehead. Unless you really hate dancing with me, and after saying you love me I doubt that, you have a problem."

"Just keep dancing. I don't want anyone to . . . Just keep going."

"But you're in pain. I can tell."

"I don't want them to know I'm injured. The fight caused too much commotion as it is."

"All right. Then I'll have to come up with a different reason why we've stopped dancing."

"I can't imagine what that would be."

"I can. Get ready because I'm about to stop. On three. One, two, three."

Before he knew what she was about, she'd come to a halt and thrown her arms around his neck. Then she pressed her mouth against his. At first he simply stood there in shock, unable to believe that she'd truly kissed him in front of the entire roomful of delegates, including Howlers and Woofers.

"Kiss me back," she murmured as she continued to press her mouth to his, "or I'll look like a fool."

Of course he didn't want that, so he wrapped her in his arms and got serious about this unexpected event. At first he was aware of the other dancers who had slowly stopped moving to stare at them. But as the heat of passion rose in him, he lost touch with his surroundings.

The world disappeared and there was only Kate, the love of his life, here in his arms as if she meant to stay there for a very long time. His arms tightened and he kissed her with all the tenderness in his heart, which turned out to be quite a bit. Once he started kissing her, he couldn't seem to stop.

Eventually he became aware of someone tapping him on the shoulder. How annoying. He glanced up to tell the intruder to bugger off. The intruder turned out to be Elizabeth Stillman.

"I think you've made your point," she said with a smile. "We all get it."

Slowly he remembered where he was, but he didn't let go of Kate. Keeping one arm firmly around her waist, he turned to the group of curious onlookers. "I suppose you're all wondering what this means."

Knox Trevelyan was one of the bystanders, and he chuckled. "We're all adults here, MacDowell. We have a pretty good idea what it means."

Beside him, Kate stood up straighter and took a deep breath. "It seems I've fallen in love with the King of the Woofers."

Duncan stared at her. "You have? That's wonderful news, lass!"

She flashed him a smile. "Yeah." Then she continued to address the crowd. "If my followers want to kick me out, then I understand, but personally, I don't think it would be such a bad thing if we had greater cooperation between the two groups. We could keep an eye on each other that way."

Heidi stepped forward. "I can't speak for all the Howlers, but I don't see how anyone with a heart could help falling for Duncan MacDowell. I'm half in love with him myself."

Kate laughed. "Hey."

"Just kidding. Sort of. But most of us suspected you two had a thing for each other. I'm glad it's out in the open. I, for one, don't see a problem. Like you said, you'll keep an eye on each other. Worthy opponents."

Duncan glanced around at the group and was gratified to see heads nodding in agreement. "Those of you who know Kate won't be worried that I'm going to convert her to my way of thinking. She has strong opinions and that won't change." He couldn't believe that she'd made his argument for him. "But I can keep an eye on her. And she can do the same with me."

"Fine speeches," Elizabeth said. "Well done, both of you." She handed Kate a small evening bag. "Here's your purse, dear. Now get out of here. I'm sure you have better things to do than hang around this ballroom."

That brought another laugh, but Duncan thought it was a fine idea. "We do, at that."

As they left the ballroom with their arms around each other, Kate lowered her voice. "Lean on me if you need to."

"Nay, lass. I can make it under my own power." He gritted his teeth. "But it'll be good to stretch out."

"We'll take the hotel elevator to the third floor."

"Don't want to be seen leaving like a cripple."

"No, you'll be seen leaving like a Were eager to be alone with his lover. An elevator is faster than stairs."

He was in no mood to argue, so he walked with her into the spacious elevator. She punched a button for the third floor.

Holding her close by his side, he gazed into her upturned face. "Did you mean what you said back there?"

"Did you?"

He was willing to go first. "Aye. It must have been bubbling up in me, waiting to get out. I couldn't stuff it down another second, and out it popped. I love you, Kate. I think I loved you before I met you, but once I glimpsed you in the airport with that furry hat and your blond hair peeking out . . . I was a goner."

As the elevator creaked upward, she smiled at him. "I think I loved you before I met you, too, Woofer. You and your torch, and the ability with a tire iron, and your . . . ability with all that you're hiding under your kilt."

He laughed. "You're wondering, aren't you?"

"I am. It's part of the mystery of a kilt. On this side of

the ocean, we're told that a true Scotsman wears nothing underneath. Are you a true Scotsman?"

"You'll find out soon enough, won't you?"

"I could find out now." She eyed the drape of his plaid.

"Not yet. I want to preserve the mystery a little longer. Your grandmother said that a kilt made a powerful lure, so I want to make sure I have you well and truly caught before I reveal my secrets."

As they walked down the hallway toward her suite, their arms still wrapped around each other, he couldn't imagine a moment when he'd been happier, or more filled with anticipation for the future.

At the door to her suite, Kate paused to dig the card key out of her tiny purse.

Duncan tried not to be impatient. The night was still young, and they had it all to themselves.

She found the key and opened the door. "Did you get anything to eat while you were down there? Do you want something from the kitchen?"

He guided her inside and turned to lock the door behind them. "All I want is right here." He drew her into his arms.

"Now, that's so touching," said a voice that Duncan knew only too well. Kate gasped and stiffened in his arms. Dread sent a cold chill up his spine. He pushed Kate behind him as he turned to confront Neil leaning in the archway that led to the living room. His neck was bandaged, but otherwise he looked strong. And he held an ugly gun in his hand.

"Come on in," Neil said. "I wasn't sure whether Kate would come back alone or with you, but having both of you here is terrific. You're earlier than I expected, which is good. We've run out of things to talk about and could use some company."

Behind Duncan, Kate quivered, either from fear or rage. "We?"

"Penny and I. We have a little proposition for you."

Chapter 21

Cold fury settled in Kate's stomach. She should probably have sense enough to be afraid, especially because Neil had a weapon. Instead she wanted to launch herself at him and scratch his eyes out. But before she took any action, foolish or brave, she had to find out what Penny was doing here.

Neil pushed himself away from the arched opening and backed into the living room, keeping the gun trained on Kate and Duncan. "Kate, you can join your sister on the sofa. MacDowell, you stand behind the sofa. That way I have a clear shot at all three of you." He positioned himself with his back to the fire he'd obviously made while he waited.

Penny looked very pale and un-Penny-like with her hands clenched in her lap. "I'm sorry, Kate. I'll bet when you kept my ID on the elevator code for old times' sake, you didn't expect something like this."

"Not exactly." Kate had meant the elevator to be an escape route if Penny had ever needed to hide. Her grandmother had agreed they should leave the code in place. They both worried about Penny's vulnerability living in the human world. Instead, the threat to Penny had come from the Were world in the form of Neil.

Kate eased down onto the sofa next to her sister as Duncan positioned himself behind them both. Kate felt his solid presence there and took comfort from it. They would figure this out . . . together.

She covered Penny's cold hands with her own. "What's going on?"

Penny took a shaky breath. "Neil's been blackmailing me for years. It wasn't much, because I couldn't afford much."

"You bastard." Kate regarded him with loathing. Yet she couldn't say she was surprised. Furious, yes, but not surprised. She'd always known that Neil was capable of treachery. The switched blog was child's play compared to this, however.

"It was gas money," Neil said with a shrug. "Elizabeth always was stingy with me, so I needed a supplement. But now . . . thanks to your main squeeze there, Kate, I need more because it looks as if I won't be the pack alpha, after all. I'll need to keep on the move, and I'll need funds. I figure you and Woofer-boy can ante up now, too."

"Dream on, you creep." Kate glared at him. "We won't do it."

Neil rocked back on his heels. "That's not a very good attitude, cousin. You see, what with the cell phone craze, all the members of Penny's human family have 'em.

They're on one of those family plans. And I have Tom and both of their kids on speed dial."

"You really are a first-class heap of dung, aren't you?" Duncan said in a conversational tone. But his anger blazed hot enough for Kate to imagine she could feel it.

"You have the *first-class* part right, Woofer, and that's how I plan to travel from now on, with your help, of course."

"You won't get away with it," Kate said. "First chance I get, I'll turn you in. We'll hunt you down."

"You wouldn't want to do that. Any hint that you've become a tattletale, and those three people will receive my text messages."

"They won't believe you," Duncan said. "They'll think you're a lunatic."

"Maybe, maybe not. They'll have questions. Penny might crack under the pressure of all those questions, because the fact is, she's never been a particularly good liar. The texts won't be identical. Taking all three together, there'll be enough detail for them to search out the truth."

Penny's hazel gaze was filled with agony as she looked at Kate. "I worry so much about losing my kids. I've tried to tell myself that nobody would believe something like that, but I'm not sure. Tom's had questions over the years. I know he has. I think a word from Neil, and Tom would begin to put it all together."

"And that's not only bad for Penny," Neil said. "It's bad for the entire Stillman pack. Much as MacDowell yearns to usher in a new age between werewolves and humans, it ain't here, yet. The pack might take me out, but in the process all of you could find yourselves facing a mob with pitchforks, so to speak."

Kate glared at him. "That's nothing compared to what's going to happen to you if the pack ever catches on to what you've been doing."

"They won't unless one of you tells them, and if that happens—I'll be able to send those texts before they bring me down. My life won't be worth much at that point, but neither will any of yours. So let's all play nice, shall we? We can negotiate this. I'll throw out some figures, and then you throw out some figures. I'm reasonable. I'm willing to haggle."

As Kate tried to think her way out of the situation, she discovered that looking at Neil just made her see red instead of helping her concentrate. She searched for something else to focus on. She studied the books on her bookshelf, as if they might have some words of wisdom for her.

Wait. Did the bookcase just move? It couldn't have. Probably wishful thinking on her part. No one else had the code except her grandma, and she'd have no reason to come up here.

Neil trained the gun specifically on her. "So here's what I was thinking, Kate. You should chip in a little more, because Penny's your sister, but the Woofer can probably afford a fair bit, too, because he's like royalty or something over in Scotland. You said he lives in a castle, so that has to make him worth something, right?"

"I don't have a lot of money," Duncan said, "but you might be interested to know that I can use a broadsword."

"Oh, I'm so scared. A *broadsword*. Whew."

Kate glanced at the barrel of the gun, but couldn't

keep looking at it, so she settled her gaze on the book-case again. Then she blinked. She hadn't imagined movement there! The bookcase was opening ever so slowly and carefully, as if whoever was behind it didn't want to make a sound and give away that anyone was there.

Her heart beat faster. Someone was there, but who? She hoped to God it wasn't her seventy-five-year-old grandmother hoping to get the jump on Neil. Surely not. But whoever had come up in the glass elevator understood how it operated and had kept the light off. If it was her grandmother, did she realize Neil had a gun?

"Okay, Neil," Kate said. "I don't appreciate being held at gunpoint. Could you put that thing away so we can talk like civilized beings?"

"I rather like this gun, Kate. I've never seen you quite so nervous before, and it does my heart good. You and Penny always thought that you were better than me, but I'm the one in control now, not you."

Beside Kate, Penny tensed. She must have seen the bookcase moving, too. Duncan's breathing had changed slightly. He must also be aware that someone was back there.

"What's the bottom line, Stillman?" Duncan asked. "How much do you want for this blackmail scheme, and how are we supposed to get it to you?"

"Well, well. It appears that your sweetheart is a sensible Were, Kate. He's figured out there's no way around the problem, and besides, it's only money, right? The safety of family is way more important than a little cash."

Kate prayed her grandmother wasn't about to leap out from behind that bookcase with a baseball bat. Neil would turn and shoot her. Grandma Elizabeth had many wonderful skills, but dodging bullets wasn't something she'd ever had to learn.

"Come to think of it," Duncan said, "Kate has her purse right here. She might be able to give you something immediately, to tide you over until we can arrange for more."

Kate had nothing in her purse but her room key and a tube of lipstick, but she guessed Duncan might be looking for a way to distract Neil. "Actually, I do have a fair bit in here," she said. "I was planning to give the staff a bonus in cash tonight, rather than make them wait until payday. They've done a fabulous job this weekend."

Neil's eyes glittered. "Then I'll just take that little purse as a down payment."

"Here." She threw it straight at his head, grabbed Penny, and jerked her to the floor. She got a quick glimpse of two large bodies hurtling through the open bookcase wall. Neil's yell was followed by the thud of fists against flesh. The gun went off. Her stomach pitched at the thought of someone being shot. *Please not Duncan.* She lifted her head to look.

"Stay down!" Duncan's shout was music to her ears.

More thudding sounds followed, punctuated by crashes, grunts, groans, and curses, some in what sounded like Gaelic. Finally, it was quiet except for the sound of heavy breathing.

A hand touched her shoulder. "It's okay, lass." Duncan gulped air. "You can get up now."

Kate scrambled to her feet and Penny got up more slowly. The room was in chaos, with lamps smashed, books scattered, and a curtain ripped. Neil lay facedown and very still on the hearth. Duncan stood on one side of the fireplace guarding Neil's prone body while Aidan and Roarke Wallace stood on the other side. All three struggled for breath. Their fists were raw and bleeding.

"Is it over?" Grandma Elizabeth peeked out through the open bookcase wall.

"Grandma!" Kate started to rush over, but a sharp warning from Duncan made her pause.

"There's glass everywhere," Duncan said. "Best stay right there for now."

At least Kate knew how Aidan and Roarke had accessed the elevator. "Is Neil . . ." She couldn't bring herself to say the word. Much as she hated him, she hoped they hadn't killed him, especially in front of Elizabeth.

"He's alive," Duncan said. "Just out cold."

The knot of tension in Kate's chest eased, and when she glanced at her grandmother, Elizabeth briefly closed her eyes in obvious relief. Then Kate studied Duncan, Aidan, and Roarke. They were battered but didn't appear to be shot. "The gun went off," she said. "I heard it hit something soft."

"I'm afraid he put a bullet in your lovely sofa, milady."

"Who cares?" She let out a breath. The bullet hadn't gone into living flesh.

"Well, somebody needs to organize things, so I guess it will be me." Elizabeth picked her way around the debris as she walked into the room. After one glance at Neil, she averted her gaze. "Shameful. Just shameful." Then she raised her voice. "Howard! You all can come in now."

Kate turned toward the entryway and her eyes widened as Howard walked through the door followed by Emma, Abby, and . . . Angela Sapworthy? She turned to Duncan, who only shrugged. He seemed as bewildered as she was.

Although both her table lamps had been destroyed in the battle, Kate's overhead kitchen lights were on, and Angela's rhinestones created a strobe effect when she moved. She walked around the suite inspecting everything and everyone. "Amazing," she said. "This will make *such* a great story."

"Excuse me." Kate faced her grandmother. "But why is Angela here? I realize that eventually we'd have to make a statement of some kind, but it seems as if you actually invited her in."

Elizabeth's expression was sheepish. "We really had no choice. She's the one who tipped us off about Neil."

"That's right." Angela continued to take careful inventory of her surroundings. "I saved the day."

"How?"

Angela walked over to her. "I was so fascinated by this romance between you and that hunk of a Scotsman that I followed you up here. This lodge is old, you know, and the doors don't fit very tight. I thought maybe if I listened at your door, I'd hear some interesting sweet talk."

Kate gasped. "That's a terrible invasion of privacy!"

"It may be," Elizabeth said, "and I don't condone her methods, but in this case they came in very handy. She heard Neil's voice, heard him mention Penny, and knew you had big trouble."

"So I hotfooted it down to the ballroom, alerted Howard and Elizabeth, and voilà." Her rhinestones flashed as she twirled around, causing everyone to squint.

"We had some help from Duncan and Kate," Roarke said. "I knew Kate had seen the bookcase move when she started talking about the gun. Factoring in the gun meant we needed a distraction so we could rush him, and

Duncan suggested that Kate hand her purse to Neil. But she threw it, which was even better."

"And you had sense enough to duck." Duncan bestowed a warm smile in her direction.

"She was much more resourceful than I was," Penny said. "She's become quite a leader. All I could do was sit there and shake."

Those words of praise about her leadership ability meant more to Kate than Penny would ever know. She put an arm around her sister and gave her a squeeze. "Of course you were terrified. You had the most to lose."

Emma stepped forward. "Penny, I don't think we've met. I'm Emma Wallace, Aidan's mate." Stepping carefully, she rounded the sofa and held out her hand.

Penny shook it warmly. "I know all about you. I've read your books, although I'm careful not to let my family know. I don't want to introduce the subject of werewolves, even in a work of fiction."

"I understand. And please don't think I'm trying to interfere in your business, but . . . I have an idea for you to consider."

Penny looked wary. "What's that?"

"I haven't checked it out with Aidan, either." Emma's gaze sought her mate's. "But I think he'll agree with me. I can imagine how much you long to share your secret with your mate, and the distress it's causing you not to, even without Neil making your life miserable."

Penny sighed. "I admit the pressure becomes greater every day. And then I think about my human kids. They know they're adopted, but not the real reason I didn't have children of my own. Tom doesn't know, either, of course. Maybe they should, but I can't imagine just throwing it out there."

"I can't, either." Emma glanced over at Aidan again. "So here's my idea. Plan a family vacation to New York. Stay with us at the Wallace family compound. You can say we're old friends of your folks, whatever excuse you want. But let Tom and your kids see how normally we live. Then, when we're all around, including Abby and me, who are human like Tom and your kids, break the news."

Aidan smiled. "Brilliant, Emma."

"I agree," Howard said. "Well done, Emma. It could work."

"Or it could backfire," Kate said. "It's still very risky."

"It is, but not as risky as me telling them when I'm surrounded by humans." Penny studied Emma carefully. "And living the way I do now is torture and not fair to them, either. They don't really know me."

Emma gave her a quick hug. "Think about it. And let me know. I hate to see you suffering."

"Yes, but I put myself in this position, didn't I?"

Not long ago, Kate would have said the same about her sister. But she saw the situation differently now. "You put yourself in this position because you found your one true love." She looked over at Duncan and took a long, slow breath. "I finally understand that." She absorbed the warmth of Duncan's answering smile before turning back to her sister.

The tension in Penny's expression eased. "You do?"

Kate nodded. "Uh-huh. Found him."

"Oh, Kate! Congratulations!" Penny hugged her tight. "That's so wonderful." Then she stepped back and turned her attention to Duncan. "You'd better treat my baby sister like the treasure that she is."

"Aye. I plan to."

"And on that note," Elizabeth said, "it's time to put things to rights around here. Aidan and Roarke, if you wouldn't mind loading Neil onto the elevator, I'll ride down with you. I'd rather not haul him out through the lobby." She pulled a cell phone out of a small evening bag. "I'll arrange for members of our pack to meet us at ground level."

Roarke nodded. "We can do that. Come on, Aidan. Let's dispose of this unwanted garbage." He walked over to Neil, who had begun to stir. "He won't be happy when he comes to, so we need him out of here before then." He leaned down and grabbed Neil's feet.

Aidan moved into position and took hold of his wrists. "Should we put a blanket over him? It's cold out there."

Roarke looked at his brother. "No."

"Right."

Elizabeth sighed. "Taking him out the back way may be silly. I realize it'll be all over Sniffer soon, but I'd rather not supply a visual to go along with it. You notice I didn't allow Angela to bring her camera crew up here."

Upon hearing her name, Angela paused in her cataloging of the details of the scene. "And what will happen to him, pray tell?"

"I have an idea about that," Howard said. "Now that WOW exists, I propose that we use the council to determine the fate of our rogues. But he's from the Stillman pack, and we'll be setting a precedent. Elizabeth, you should weigh in. What do you think?"

"I think that makes perfect sense. Chances are he'd get a much harsher sentence from his pack once they discover he was blackmailing one of us and threatening to expose all of us."

"I guarantee the council won't go easy on him, either,"

Howard said. "Can you detain him for us temporarily, until we set up our procedures?"

"I most certainly can."

"If you'd like to transport him to Scotland, I can provide a dungeon." Duncan seemed quite taken with that idea.

"It's tempting to turn him over to you, Duncan," Elizabeth said, "but I can create something very dungeonlike right here."

"Good." Howard nodded in satisfaction. "Then we'll be in touch, and I'll work something out as soon as possible."

"I'll await your instructions." Elizabeth's glance fell on Penny. "I'll arrange for a car to take you home, sweetie."

"That would be great."

"Abby and I will walk with you downstairs," Emma said. "On the way we'll help you come up with a good cover story to tell Tom. I'm an expert at that kind of thing after keeping my mother in the dark for all this time."

Penny smiled. "I have a feeling I'm going to be very glad I met you, Emma Wallace."

Elizabeth surveyed the room with obvious satisfaction. "Then we're all set." She started toward the elevator and paused to glance at Kate. "I'll send a cleaning crew up here right away. They'll bring replacement lamps for you, as well."

Kate exchanged a quick glance with Duncan and was fairly sure she knew what he was thinking. "Could you hold off on that until morning?"

Elizabeth frowned. "I can't imagine why you'd want to put up with this mess until morning."

Angela looked over at her. "Oh, I can, Elizabeth. There's nothing wrong with the bedroom." She batted her glitter-covered eyelashes. "If you get my drift."

"Oh." Elizabeth cleared her throat. "Yes, well, I suppose you're right. Then I'll be off. I'll meet the rest of you at the party when this matter is handled."

"Wait." Kate stepped cautiously around scattered books and broken lamp parts to give her grandmother a tight hug. "Thank you, Grandma."

Elizabeth hugged her back just as fiercely. "You were very brave," she said in a low voice. "You're going to make a fine alpha."

"Thank you." Her throat tightened in a rush of unexpected emotion. She hadn't realized how much she'd longed to hear those words.

"And we're outta here," Emma said. "Penny, I've already thought of several excellent excuses to give your mate."

"Wonderful." Penny made her way over to Kate and hugged her. "Be happy."

"I already am."

Howard cupped his hand under Angela's elbow. "Time to go, Ms. Sapworthy." He propelled her toward the front door. "And I want it understood that there will be no more listening at the door tonight."

Angela looked offended. "I wouldn't dream of it." Then she giggled. "I have so many juicy tidbits, I won't have to listen outside doors for at least another week."

Kate followed them to the entryway and called out a few more good-byes before closing the door and twisting the dead bolt. Then she turned, walked back into the living room and straight into Duncan's arms. "Now, where were we?"

"On our way to your bed, milady." Guiding her gently through the bedroom door, he nudged it closed with his foot, shutting out all the ugliness and closing in all the beauty.

Duncan learned that a dress that fit like a glove and sparkled like a galaxy of stars was extremely complex and difficult to remove from the female wearing it. But he also suspected that this particular dress cost the moon and stars, too, so he finally stopped his search for a way into it. Reluctantly ending a most satisfactory kiss, he drew back.

"You'll have to get yourself out of that contraption, lass. I canna do it. Or I could, but I'd ruin it for sure. It's too lovely to ruin."

Flushed with the effects of his kisses, she smiled, reached under her arm, and pulled down a side zipper.

"Ah, so that's the trick."

"That's the trick. Once the zipper's undone, it slides off like a peel from a banana." She demonstrated by pushing it down to the floor and stepping out of it.

His breath caught. She wore nothing but her ruby jewelry, skimpy lace panties, and red high heels. "I'm glad I let you do it. I have to stand back a bit to appreciate the view." He'd thought his need for her couldn't get any more desperate. He'd been wrong.

"Do you want me to leave any of this on?"

He shook his head. "It's a fantasy, I suppose, but . . . to tell the truth, all I want is you." He took a deep breath to rein in the wolf in him, a wild creature yearning to take her in a surge of passion that left no room for tenderness. "Just you, Kate."

Her eyes grew misty. "And I feel the same about you." She took off the earrings and laid them on the dresser beside her. Then she removed the necklace and put it there, too. Last she kicked off her shoes and removed her lingerie. "Do you . . . do you have to leave in the morning?"

"I do." He would hate leaving. He would hate it so much that he didn't know how to put it into words.

"Oh."

"Just to settle some things. It might take a week. Is that too long? Perhaps I can do everything in less, but I'm not sure that I can."

Her expression was endearingly hopeful. "You mean, after this week of settling things, you'll come back . . . to stay?"

"Aye. If you'll have me."

"Of course I'll have you!" She rushed into his arms, nearly knocking him over. "I thought you'd have to stay in Scotland. You'd really be willing to live here, with me?"

"You're to be the pack alpha one day, so that seems like the right choice for us. I can do my writing and my work with the Woofers anywhere. We can visit Glenbarra whenever you're ready, but for the most part, I think—" He was prevented from further explanation when she began kissing him as if she would never stop.

But finally she did pull back a little, her voice breathless. "But you're still dressed."

"So I am." He regarded her with amusement. "Perceptive of you to notice."

"I'm no better at taking off a kilt than you are with a side-zipper dress. And I almost forgot. I still don't know what you have on under it."

"The usual."

"That sounds like what you'd say to Angela Sapworthy. It tells me nothing." Slipping out of his embrace, she stood with her arms crossed. "Proceed, Woofer."

He undressed for her, and mindful of what Elizabeth had said, he left the kilt on until the very end.

She moistened her lips. "I'll say this for you. You know how to build the suspense."

"No point in wearing a kilt if I don't plan to make the most of it." And then he took it off.

Her eyes widened and her hand went to her mouth as she gasped. Then she met his gaze and smiled. "So tell me, how does it feel to waltz like that?"

"Waltzing is no problem." He moved toward her. "There's enough room between us in case this starts to happen." He gestured toward his erect penis. "The tango could be a different story. But I've lost all interest in dancing."

"Good. So have I."

"We have something else we need to do." He quivered as he thought of what was to happen between them. It was perhaps the most important event of his life. Yet he had no doubt that she was his destiny, his one true love.

"I know."

He searched her expression. "Are you willing, then, to be bound to me?"

Her gaze didn't waver as she placed her hand in his. "Yes. You are my soul mate, Duncan MacDowell."

"And you are mine, Kate Stillman." His heart pounded. "We'll plan a proper mating ceremony when I return, but ..."

"It's the binding that counts." She took a shaky breath. "I know, Duncan."

He held her hand firmly in his, wanting to make sure there were no doubts. "For life."

She didn't hesitate. "For life."

"Come, then."

They walked hand in hand to the bed. And there on that firm mattress, as she braced herself on hands and knees, he took her in the traditional way, the position in which Weres had mated since the beginning of time. He took her with murmured promises, with great tenderness, and with love filling his heart. Her body shuddered against his and his climax answered.

It was done. His body hummed with quiet jubilation. Against all odds they'd found each other. Despite their differences, they'd defied logic to create this perfectly imperfect union. And he knew without a doubt they would love as a mated pair was meant to love . . . forever.

Epilogue

WERECON2012:
MACDOWELL/STILLMAN NEW POWER COUPLE!

**Exclusive report for *Wereworld Celebrity Watch*
by Angela Sapworthy**

DENVER—As conference delegates take planes, trains, and automobiles home to their respective packs, the buzz is all about the match of the century between Woofer leader Duncan MacDowell and Howler leader Kate Stillman! Who would have guessed three days ago that this warring pair, who stand on opposite sides of all the major problems facing Weres today, would fall in love?

But such are the vagaries of the Were heart, dear readers. Newly elected president of WOW Howard Wallace was more than willing to comment. "By combining forces, Kate and Duncan will help unify the various elements of our fledgling organization without sacrificing its diversity. I couldn't be happier about their announcement."

This reporter was privileged to speak with Kate Stillman as she returned, teary-eyed, from taking her one true love to the Denver airport. "I love him desperately," she said. "We don't agree on anything else, but we agree that we can't live without each other."

And there you have it, my friends. No one can predict where Destiny will lead us. When asked what she thought about Jake Hunter's new organization, Weres Against Random Mating (WARM), she said, "He has to do what he feels is right. We have a big-tent philosophy in WOW, and I would prefer that he align himself with our organization, but he chooses not to."

This reporter caught up with Jake as he was loading his duffel bag into a cab. When asked about his future plans, he expressed great faith in his new project. "I'll work on my presence in cyberspace," he said, "because WARM needs that visibility, but I'll also take my message directly to each Were's doorstep."

And how will he do that? one might ask. "I'll start my campaign in Alaska, where all North American packs originated. I'll be using a snowmobile to reach the backwoods areas of my home state. There's strong support for our cause there, and I intend to mobilize that support."

With a spokesWere who looks like Jake Hunter, finding WARM recruits should be no trouble at all!

In other news, Neil Stillman has been placed

under house arrest by the Stillman pack while awaiting his trial before the newly formed WOW council. The bullet that was extracted from Kate Stillman's red leather sofa (a sofa and bullet viewed personally by this reporter, who no doubt will be called to testify due to her personal involvement in the case) has been entered into evidence.

Rumor has it that Aidan and Roarke Wallace also will be asked to testify, along with Duncan MacDowell. That hunky lineup should pack the courtroom with adoring female Weres! For details, follow me on Sniffer @newshound or #riveting trial because this reporter plans to be there, once again, to serve as your eyes, ears, and nose!

Read on for a look at the next
Wild About You novel
by Vicki Lewis Thompson,

WEREWOLF IN ALASKA

On sale in July 2013 from Signet Eclipse

July 15, 2010
Polecat, Alaska

Lurking in the grocery aisle of the Polecat General Store, Rachel Miller pretended to shop while she eavesdropped on the conversation between the store's owner, Ted Haggerty, and the broad-shouldered customer he'd called Jake. She'd recognized the guy the minute he walked in, despite the fact that he was fully clothed.

Although they'd never met, she knew three things about Jake. He lived across the lake from her grandfather's cabin, he liked to skinny-dip, and he was built for pleasure. Among other things, Grandpa Ike had left her his high-powered binoculars.

After opening the screen door of the general store, her neighbor had glanced in her direction but hadn't seemed to recognize her. Apparently he hadn't been keeping tabs on her the way she had on him. That was disappointing.

Then again, she only spent a couple of weeks in Polecat every summer and she wasn't the type to plunge naked into an alpine lake. Still, she would have taken this opportunity to introduce herself if he hadn't paused in front of the small display of her wood carvings.

She'd immediately turned away, grabbed a can of salmon and studied the label with fierce intensity. If she ever intended to move from hobbyist to professional, she'd have to get over being self-conscious about displaying her work for sale, but she was brand-new at it. Asking Ted last week if he'd like to carry her art in his store had required tremendous courage.

Today when she'd come in and noticed that nothing had sold, she'd been tempted to cart it all back to the cabin. Ted had talked her out of giving up and now her gorgeous neighbor was discussing the carvings with him. She hoped to hell Ted wouldn't mention that the artist was right there in the grocery aisle. Then the guy might feel obligated to buy something, and how embarrassing would that be?

"So who's this Rachel Miller?" Jake had a deep voice, which matched his lumberjack physique. His name fit him, too.

Rachel held her breath. Now would be the logical time for Ted to call her over and introduce her. She prayed that he wouldn't.

Ted hesitated, as if debating whether to reveal her presence. "She's local."

Rachel exhaled slowly. She might not be a skinny dipper, but there were many ways to be naked, and this, she discovered, was one of them. She could leave and spare herself the agony of listening to whatever Jake might say about her work, but then she'd be tormented by curiosity for days.

Besides, she'd already put several food items in the basket she carried over one arm. Leaving the basket and bolting from the store would make her more conspicuous, not less.

"I like her stuff."

Clapping a hand to her mouth, Rachel closed her eyes and savored the words. He liked it!

"Especially the wolf."

"That's my personal favorite," Ted said.

Validation sent a rush of adrenaline through her system. It was her favorite, too. The other carvings were forest animal figurines, none any bigger than eight inches tall. Her friends back in Fairbanks raved about them, but friends were biased. Their opinions were cherished, but not always believed.

She'd broken new ground with the wolf, though. After finding a ragged chunk of driftwood about two feet long, she'd left the basic shape intact while carving the wolf in bas-relief on the smoothest side. Powerful and majestic, the wolf appeared to be emerging from the piece of wood.

Ted had praised the carving, but Ted had a natural tendency to encourage people. His comments didn't pack the same punch as those from someone who didn't know her and had no reason to protect her feelings. Now her excitement made her giddy.

A moment of silence followed. She wondered if Jake had wandered away from the display to begin his grocery shopping, but she didn't dare look to make sure. If he'd finished admiring her work, that was fine. He'd given her a gift simply by commenting favorably.

"I want to buy it."

Her chest tightened. *A sale.*

"All righty, then!" Ted sounded pleased.

Rachel was in shock. A complete stranger was willing to pay money for something she'd created! She stifled the urge to rush over and shower him with thanks. On the heels of that urge came another—to snatch the piece and announce it wasn't for sale, after all.

Once Jake bought that carving, she'd never see it again. She hadn't expected to be upset by that. Apparently the wolf meant far more to her than she'd realized.

Jake might like what she'd done, but he couldn't fully appreciate it unless he'd also caught a glimpse of the magnificent black wolf that had inspired her. She'd only seen it once, poised in a clearing. Grandpa Ike had taught her how to get good pictures of wild creatures—stay downwind and seek cover. She'd been in luck that day, perfectly positioned for an awesome shot.

The photo was still tacked to a bulletin board in the cabin so she could use it to carve another likeness. Yet she couldn't guarantee the next attempt would capture the wolf's essence in quite the same way. She'd known this piece was special the moment it was completed.

Finishing it had given her the confidence to approach Ted in the first place. Not surprisingly, it had become her first sale. If people bought her work, maybe she could give up her veterinarian internship and carve full-time.

She'd thought she would love being a vet, but the surgery and death that were inevitable parts of the job drained her. Wood carving gave her nothing but joy. Still, it might not bring in enough to support her. One sale was hardly a guarantee that she could make a living as an artist.

It was a positive sign, though, and thanks to what she'd inherited from Grandpa Ike, she had a place to live and a little money to tide her over if she decided to switch gears. The prospect was scary, but exciting, too. She had Jake the skinny-dipper to thank for jump-starting her dreams.

From the corner of her eye she could see him rounding the aisle where she stood, a basket over his arm. Walking in the opposite direction, she ducked down a parallel aisle and carried her basket to the counter, where Ted was wrapping her carving.

He glanced up and smiled. "Do you want to tell—"

"No." She kept her voice down. "Thanks for not saying anything."

Ted spoke softly, obviously sensing her nervousness. "Decided that was up to you." He finished taping the end of the parcel and set it aside. "Congratulations, though. He lives across the lake from you."

"Thought I recognized him. What's his name, again?"

"Jake Hunter. He's a wilderness guide. Earns good money doing it. Quite well-off."

"I see." Judging people's financial status was tough in a place like Polecat, where everyone kept a low profile, dressed casually, and drove dusty trucks and SUVs. She was flattered that a successful wilderness guide found value in her work.

Ted rang up her groceries and bagged them in the canvas tote she'd given him. She hadn't bought much because she'd been so distracted, so Ted finished quickly. Fine with her. She would have prefered to be out the door before Jake returned to the counter.

She almost made it. She was tucking her change back into her purse when he walked up, his basket stuffed with everything from canned goods to paper products. He must have been a fast shopper.

Not wanting to appear antisocial, she met his gaze while keeping her expression friendly but neutral. "Hi."

"Hello." He glanced at her with the same carefully neutral expression. But then a spark of interest lit his green eyes.

Her breath caught. She'd never looked into those eyes before. Grandpa Ike's binoculars were good, but not that good. Yet she felt as if she'd met his gaze before, and seeing it again brought back a half-remembered thrill. Crazy.

Even crazier, she flashed on the image of the black wolf in the clearing—a green-eyed wolf with dark, luxurious fur the same color as Jake's collar-length hair. Clearly his purchase of the carving was messing with her mind.

The interest reflected in Jake's eyes slowly changed to speculation. Maybe something in her expression had given her away, or maybe he'd picked up enough of her quiet conversation with Ted to figure out who she was. In any case, she needed to vamoose before he started asking questions.

Quickly breaking eye contact, she grabbed her canvas bag from the counter. Her smile probably looked more like a grimace, but it was the best she could do. "You two have a nice day!" She headed for the screen door.

As exits go, it wasn't her best. Heart pounding, she climbed into the old truck Grandpa Ike had willed to her, started the ancient engine, and pulled out onto the two-lane road that skirted the lake. She'd escaped, but the adrenaline rush of making her first sale stayed with her.

Logic, the tool that her lawyer father embraced, told her that Jake buying the wolf carving wasn't reason enough to change her life. Intuition, the tool that her photographer mother preferred, whispered that she'd reached a major turning point and shouldn't ignore it. Grandpa Ike, who had been more intuitive than anyone else on her mother's side of the family, would have told her to listen to her instincts.

Rachel wondered what Jake Hunter would have said if she'd had the courage to admit she'd carved that wolf. Or maybe, judging from the quiet assessment in those green eyes, he already knew.

Also available from

Vicki Lewis Thompson

Werewolf in Seattle
A Wild About You Novel

The last thing Colin MacDowell wants is to inherit his Aunt Geraldine's mansion in the San Juan islands off the coast of Washington. As the pack leader of the Trevelyans in Scotland, he has little time to travel halfway around the world to take care of his inheritance.

But the trip takes a pleasant turn when he meets Luna Reynaud, the young secretary his aunt hired shortly before she died. He isn't sure which surprises him more—Luna's clever plan for turning the mansion into a resort or the fact that she's drop-dead gorgeous. Both intrigue him— until he learns that Luna is only a half-breed. There's no way a pack leader can mate with a woman who's partly human…or is there?

"Another keeper. This is not just another werewolf romance."
—The Romance Dish

Available wherever books are sold or at
penguin.com

facebook.com/ProjectParanormalBooks